PENGUIN BOOKS

PREM PURANA

Usha Narayanan had a successful career in advertising, radio and corporate communications before becoming a full-time author. She has written several books, including the suspense thriller *The Madras Mangler* and the fun office romance *Love, Lies and Layoffs*. Her books *Pradyumna: Son of Krishna* and *The Secret of God's Son* have been praised as 'Indian mythology at its fiercest and finest'.

When she is not travelling, writing or editing, Usha reads everything from thrillers to the Puranas. To know more about her, visit www.ushanarayanan.com or email her at author@ushanarayanan.com. Find her also at www.facebook.com/writerusha or tweet @writerusha.

BY THE SAME AUTHOR

Pradyumna: Son of Krishna
The Secret of God's Son

Prem Purana

MYTHOLOGICAL LOVE STORIES

USHA NARAYANAN

PENGUIN BOOKS

An imprint of Penguin Random House

PENGUIN BOOKS

USA | Canada | UK | Ireland | Australia
New Zealand | India | South Africa | China

Penguin Books is part of the Penguin Random House group of companies whose
addresses can be found at global.penguinrandomhouse.com

Published by Penguin Random House India Pvt. Ltd
7th Floor, Infinity Tower C, DLF Cyber City, Gurgaon 122 002, Haryana, India

Penguin
Random House
India

First published in Penguin Books by Penguin Random House India 2017

ISBN 9780143440086

Typeset in Adobe Jenson Pro by Manipal Digital Systems, Manipal
Printed at Replika Press Pvt. Ltd, India

www.penguin.co.in

For my brother-in-law, K. Sampath,
a gracious and magnanimous soul

Contents

III. Damayanti's Riddle

GANESHA'S BRIDES

1

The Parijata Forest

A happy Ganesha was riding on his mouse through a forest of parijata trees. The fragrance of the orange and white blossoms pervaded the air, making him feel as if he was in heaven even though he was on earth. The moon shone brilliantly in the skies—a silvery, unblemished orb. The world was celebrating Ganesha Chathurthi, in honour of the elephant-headed son of Lord Shiva and Goddess Parvati. It was the season of music and dance, of feasting and rejoicing, for Ganesha, worshipped by 108 different names, was beloved in all the realms. His devotees on earth loved the merry young god who was easy to please. They brought him fruit and his favourite modakas, dumplings stuffed with dry fruits, grated jaggery and coconut. In the heavens, the devas worshipped him with red hibiscus and white conch flowers.

Parvati's young son was happy, his stomach full with all the modakas he had eaten, his heart filled with joy as he went along merrily on his path. But just then, a snake slithered across his path, and the startled mouse dropped the young god in its haste to escape. Ganesha, heavy with all the food he had eaten, was unable to get up for a moment. He muttered angrily, snatched up the bothersome snake and bound it tightly around his stomach as if to ensure that the modakas within would not spill out. As he did so, he heard a laugh from above. Soma, the moon, had watched him fall and had dared to laugh at him.

Ganesha's big ears flapped in agitation and he hurriedly rose to his feet. He broke off a piece of his tusk and hurled it at the full moon. 'You will suffer for your insolence, Soma!' he said. 'Your light will fade gradually and you will become dark in fifteen days.' The tusk shattered the moon's surface and created a crater, and Soma scudded in fear to hide behind some clouds.

Still angry, Parvati's son pulled out a plantain tree by its roots and flung it on the ground. 'Everyone laughs at my big belly and elephant head!' he muttered. 'If only I were as handsome as my brother Karthikeya . . .' His eyes fell on the uprooted plantain tree. 'Oh my Kola Bou, my banana wife! Forgive me!' he exclaimed as he stroked its lush green leaves.

Then he heard the laugh again. Ganesha's ears turned towards the sound. Had Soma returned even after he had been cursed? There was a flash of red and Ganesha dashed forward to capture the culprit. As his hands grasped hold of an arm, he closed his eyes in ecstasy, his nostrils filling with an ambrosial scent. His hands stroked the silky soft arms that were now straining against his grip.

'Let me go!' whispered a girl's voice as she struggled to free herself.

'Soma, come back and show me your light!' he shouted, holding her tighter. By the light of the broken moon, he saw a charming maiden clad in red, looking up at him with a mixture of fear and excitement.

'Who are you?' he asked her, his anger turning into fascination as he saw her enchanting eyes and her sylphlike form.

'I am Riddhi. You must have heard of Brahma's beautiful daughter!' she said proudly. 'I study at Sage Kapila's ashram nearby.'

'Yes, of course I have,' he said, wanting to please her and keep the conversation going. He gazed at her, spellbound, unwilling to let her go. She stared back at him for a moment and then pulled free.

'I know who you are too!' she exclaimed. 'Everyone knows about Parvati's golden son, Gajamukha, with the head of an elephant. Now tell me, why did you call the plantain tree your bride?'

Watching the expressions chasing one another across her vivacious face, Ganesha took a moment to answer. Riddhi's eyes danced with pleasure as she noted the effect that she had on him.

'One day, I saw my mother Durga eating her food with all ten hands!' Ganesha said. 'When I asked her why, she told me that when I married, my bride would not allow her to eat in peace. So she would eat to her heart's content before that happened.' Riddhi's eyes widened as she imagined the sight. 'In order to reassure her, I promised her that I would marry only a plantain tree since it would not be able to harass her!'

'You are such a loving son, though you appear to be a little crazy!' laughed Riddhi. 'And what a wonderful idea—to marry a tree! I have an idea too, so please wait here for just a moment.'

She darted away, with not a doubt in her mind that he would be there when she returned. There was hardly a man or god who would not wait for her, entranced by her beauty. She returned soon, laden with various objects in her hands. First, she washed the stem and leaves of the plantain tree with some water she had brought from the river Ganga that flowed nearby, and smeared vermilion on its leaves. Then she draped the tree in a white sari with a red border, bringing one end of the sari over its top to make it look like a veiled bride.

Riddhi then clapped her hands in delight. Before her was the tree that now looked like a shy newlywed, with its drooping leaves moving gently in the breeze. She disappeared again and returned to place a decorated pedestal on the ground and arranged some flowers and incense sticks before it. Then she conducted a bemused Ganesha to the seat and placed the plantain tree on his right. The god's eyes twinkled as he conjured up garlands for himself and his bride.

He looked at Riddhi's happy face and then shook his head with a smile. 'My Kola Bou is beautiful, no doubt,' he said. 'But I do not wish to be married and be caught in a web of troubles!' He gestured with his hand and at once the plantain tree was restored to its original state with its roots in the ground.

'Really?' asked Riddhi, tossing her hair. 'Why do you say that?'

'Do you know what my father Shiva said to my uncle Vishnu?' he asked in return. 'He said that love destroys your peace of mind like a Brahmastra in the hands of Kama. And that a woman's beauty is the cause of all delusion, tempting you with nectar that conceals the poison beneath!'

'Do you really believe that?' retorted Riddhi, her eyes blazing fire. 'Why would Shiva say such a thing when he himself is married and has two sons besides?'

'Maybe that's why!' he chuckled. 'Just imagine his plight. The serpent Vasuki that he wears around his neck looks hungrily at my mouse. My brother Karthikeya's peacock waits for a chance to kill the snake. Durga's lion glares at me because an elephant is his arch-enemy. And Durga herself frowns jealously at Ganga who adorns my father's head. No wonder then that Shiva drank the halahala poison that emerged from the cosmic ocean when it was churned!'

Looks like he will never stop talking! thought Riddhi. 'I think I should go now,' she said out loud. Yet she lingered, shifting restlessly from foot to foot.

'No, no! I did not mean to offend you,' said Ganesha. 'Please do not go.'

She looked at his anxious face and decided to forgive him. He was interesting, with all his strange ideas. 'So tell me,' she said. 'Why did you choose a mouse as your vehicle instead of a lion or a bull like your parents?'

'Do you think I look funny—a giant mounted on a little mouse?' he asked, looking woeful.

'No, of course not,' she replied, not wishing to hurt his feelings.

'Come, let us eat some modakas and I will tell you the story,' he said, sitting on the rich carpet of flowers under a parijata tree and patting the ground by his side in invitation. She smiled as she sat down gracefully, her golden anklets tinkling.

'I love all animals,' said Ganesha, his face lighting up. 'Indeed, I could have chosen a bull like my father or even an eagle like my uncle.'

'Your uncle?' asked Riddhi, nibbling at a delicious modaka. His mouse appeared silently by his side, drawn by the sweet smell, though he was afraid that Ganesha would curse him for toppling him to the ground. However, his master smiled at him and gave him a piece of modaka to eat.

'Yes, Vishnu is my mother's brother, as both of them are Devaki's children,' he explained. 'When he was born as Krishna, my mother Durga took his place as Devaki's child, in order to safeguard him from his uncle Kamsa. As for my mouse here, he was originally a gandharva named Krauncha. When roaming the skies, he saw the beautiful wife of Sage Sabari and was overpowered by desire. He entered the hermitage and grabbed her by the hand. She screamed, arousing the sage from his meditation, and he cursed Krauncha to become a mooshika, a mouse. Shaken by the curse, Krauncha begged for forgiveness and Sabari told him that he would be redeemed when he received my blessing. Krauncha was huge and powerful and he ravaged everything in his path as he roamed the earth looking for me. Finally, he arrived at the ashram where I was studying and attacked the rishis there. Irked by his behaviour, I hurled my danda at him. My staff thundered forth, spewing flames like the fire at the end of the world. Krauncha's body was scorched and he tried to escape by burrowing down to patala but the danda followed him there as well. He flew through the nether regions of nagas and yakshas, danavas and daityas, and finally surfaced on earth.'

Riddhi had stopped eating and was listening to him wide-eyed. Ganesha could not help wishing that she would stay there forever. 'Krauncha led my danda on a merry chase,' he continued. 'He fled to remote corners of the earth, trying to hide in snowy caves and desert lands. Many years passed in this fashion until one day he fell gasping to the ground, unable to run anymore. My danda pinioned him with coils of fire and dragged him to me. Krauncha fell at my feet and pleaded for his life. "Allow me to become your vaahana and to serve you for eternity," he said. Poor Krauncha had already paid for his sins over a long period of time. So I granted him his boon, making my body light so that he could carry me easily!'

Riddhi smiled as she looked at the amiable pair, sitting together and eating modakas. Gajamukha was fun to be with. She rose to her feet reluctantly. 'I must go back to the ashram,' she said. 'My guru will be looking for me.'

Ganesha did not want her to go but knew that he could not say anything, considering that he had met her only that day. She smiled as if she could read his thoughts and then turned to walk away towards the ashram that was just a short distance away.

Ganesha was forlorn as he watched her disappear from view. He would happily brave his mother's wrath if he could have a chance to court this lovely damsel. Maybe Riddhi would come back again the next day. Perhaps she would even look for him. He would linger in this fragrant forest, praying that she would return.

2

A Delightful Surprise

Fortunately for Ganesha, Brahma's daughter returned the next day. Rather, he came upon her during one of his restless rambles through the forest. She was seated under the tree where they had been talking the previous day and he smiled, thinking that she had come there to meet him. He stopped some distance away, admiring the lovely picture she made, looking like a parijata blossom in a beautiful white sari with an orange border, her eyes fixed on the flowers she was stringing.

'Greetings, fair maiden!' he called out as he rushed forward. She sprang to her feet, startled, toppling the silver basket holding the blossoms.

'Forgive me!' he murmured as he bent down to gather the flowers and place them back in the basket. 'I was so happy to see you that . . .'

He saw then that she was gradually backing away from him, her eyes wide with fear. Her expression was a total contrast to her liveliness the previous day. What had happened? Had her guru warned her to stay away from him? But he had always shown the deepest respect to Sage Kapila who was venerated on earth and heaven for his learning . . .

'Is something the matter?' he asked her as she stood before him, twisting her hands anxiously together. Her luminous eyes drew him into their depths and made it difficult for him to speak cogently. 'Parvati's son . . . we met yesterday . . . we were speaking . . .' he stuttered.

'Buddhi! Where did you disappear?' The clear voice broke the silence between them as they stood staring at each other with wary eyes.

Ganesha turned and saw another girl burst into the clearing. She greeted the young god with a warm smile and said, 'Oh, you seem to have met my sister!'

This was definitely Riddhi, so the maiden he had greeted earlier must be Buddhi! Parvati's son saw that the two girls looked identical, except for their demeanour. While Riddhi had started chattering to her sister, telling her about meeting Ganesha the previous day, Buddhi stood calmly listening, her eyes darting between him and her voluble sister.

'Poor Soma!' exclaimed Riddhi, remembering his curse. 'What happened to him?'

'He came to me as a pale crescent, distraught and repentant,' said Ganesha. 'I took pity on him and told him that he would lose his light for fifteen days and regain it during the next fifteen.'

'That was kind of you,' said Riddhi, nodding her approval. 'Now, tell me, what were you saying to my sister?'

'Nothing, really,' he said. 'I guess I frightened her. I think she was preparing to flee!'

'Not she!' laughed Riddhi. 'All the animals of the forest adore her and will tear you to bits if you should try to harm her. Did you mistake her for me? We look alike, no doubt, but you can see that I am far more beautiful.'

Buddhi smiled at this and Ganesha gasped as he noticed the two perfect dimples that appeared in her cheeks. Suddenly, he heard the sound of galloping hooves and saw a girl riding towards them, her face flushed and her eyes fiery. He looked at her and then at the other two with him, and Riddhi laughed at the shock on his face.

'Another sister!' Ganesha exclaimed. 'How many more do you have?'

'There are only three of us!' laughed Riddhi.

The newcomer jumped lithely off her horse when she was close to them, and he saw that she was eyeing him suspiciously.

'You are here just in time, Siddhi!' said Riddhi, putting an arm around her sister's waist. 'Tell our new friend, Parvati's son Gajamukha, what you think of marriage. He is very interested in your answer!'

Ganesha was puzzled. He and Riddhi had talked about marriage, of course, but that had been the previous day. He looked curiously at Riddhi, wondering why she was bringing up the topic now.

'Marriage? Who cares about marriage?' snapped Siddhi, casting a scathing glance at him. 'And why would I discuss it with a stranger?'

Aha! So Siddhi has strong views on this topic and her sister wants to provoke her, thought Ganesha, seeing Riddhi's eyes glinting mischievously.

'Perhaps he is another foolish suitor for me to dispose of,' continued Siddhi, glaring at him. 'Listen to me, Parvati's son! I am not interested in marrying you or anyone else. Let me warn you that I wish to emulate the virgin goddess Kanyakumari who destroyed the mighty Banasura.'

Ganesha nodded, his eyes twinkling, noting the bow and the quiver that Siddhi carried on her shoulder. At least he had not been caught eating modakas. That would have created quite a bad impression on the warlike goddess!

'See what we have to contend with,' said Riddhi to him. 'Siddhi is the firstborn and we cannot marry unless she does. But she is happy roaming about, looking for an asura to kill!'

'Talking about marriage, I have a riddle for you,' said Ganesha. 'See if you can guess who I am talking about.'

All three nodded.

Ganesh began,

A 1000-headed snake is his bed on the sea
While an eagle hovers overhead, waiting to kill.
His one wife can't stop talking
The other can't stay still.
The playful Manmatha, his son,
Inflames the world with passion
What can the poor husband do now
But lie inert in the ocean?

He stopped then and looked expectantly at them, hoping that his banter would camouflage his growing fascination for the threesome.

'Oh, so this is your great riddle?' scoffed Siddhi. 'I knew that the answer was Vishnu as soon as you started speaking. Anyway, I have no time to waste talking. I came here to take my sisters back to the ashram. There is news that fearsome Prince Gana is coming towards us, travelling along the course of the Ganga, killing and plundering. Our father warned us that he is the lustful Kamasura reborn, made invincible by Shiva's boons. But I am not afraid. I rather hope that he comes to our ashram so that I can fight him and kill him!'

'The asura is coming?' Ganesha exclaimed, his big ears flapping and his trunk swinging from side to side.

But Siddhi was no longer there to answer him. She had heard a rustle among the trees and vaulted onto her horse's back to find out if danger lurked near. Her sisters hurried away too, though Riddhi turned back once to smile at him. Ganesha realized then that he had not heard Buddhi speak a single word all this time. *What really goes on in her mind?* he wondered. It would be fascinating to find out. And he would love to make her smile, just to see those charming dimples again!

During the days that followed, Ganesha saw the three sisters often and was gradually able to distinguish one from the other, more by their manner than by any physical differences. Riddhi was the friendliest and often came looking for him. She was vibrant and quite talkative. Red seemed to be her favourite colour and she always wore glittering necklaces and belts that drew attention to her shapely neck and tiny waist.

Siddhi was often just a flash of gold or orange as she sped by on her horse. She kept her distance from him, though he sometimes caught her watching him suspiciously. Whenever he came upon the girls studying, or gathering jasmine flowers, Siddhi would walk away, refusing to acknowledge his greeting. Ganesha wondered why she was so hostile. Was it because of his unusual appearance? Or had he said something inadvertently to offend her?

Riddhi was equally puzzled by Siddhi's behaviour. 'She has always been volatile,' she said. 'But even so, her hostility towards you is quite extreme and difficult to understand. Did you meet her earlier in the forest or cross her in any way?'

Ganesha shook his head in answer.

'Perhaps it is just her anxiety about Prince Gana,' Riddhi speculated. 'She is afraid that she will be caught unawares when he appears in our forest. All three of us are expert in the astras, but it is only Siddhi who wishes to use her skills in battle. Now her sole purpose is to confront the asura and defeat him. She has no time for thoughts of marriage or friendship even.'

'What about you? What do you look for in a husband?' asked Ganesha, studying her face intently.

'We have countless suitors to choose from,' she replied, jutting out her chin proudly. 'Powerful kings and devas like Surya and Agni. After all, we are Brahma's daughters and so beautiful besides. I have decided that I will marry someone who is supremely handsome like Vishnu and will sweep me off my feet.'

Ganesha nodded ponderously, running his hands over his elephant face, wondering for the hundredth time why he was not dashing like his brother Karthikeya. Riddhi saw his crestfallen expression and inwardly chided herself for having spoken thoughtlessly.

There was silence then and Ganesha turned his gaze towards Buddhi who was seated in a padmasana some distance from them. Perhaps she would not place so much value on a perfect face.

'Buddhi is interested only in those who are learned and intelligent,' said Riddhi, following his gaze. 'She is truly Saraswati's daughter.'

'The three of you are so different,' remarked Ganesha, watching Siddhi gallop past, her long hair flowing behind her. 'As for Siddhi, her name means enlightenment, and we all know that it is not easy to attain!'

Ganesha spent long periods of time in dhyana and Buddhi came upon him one day, meditating on the banks of the Ganga. She saw that his trunk was turned towards his right, indicating that he was praying to the gods and was not to be disturbed. If it was turned to his left instead, it would indicate that he was open to this world and its experiences.

As she stood watching, she saw a beautiful girl approach him. She recognized her as Princess Tulasi, who often came to worship Vishnu in a temple nearby. Tulasi gazed raptly at the magnificent young god, admiring his radiant face and the aura around him. She then drew closer and tapped him with the stem of the lotus bud she was holding in her hand.

Gajamukha emerged from his meditation and looked enquiringly at her. 'I am Tulasi, the daughter of King Dharmadvaja,' she said to him. 'Take me as your wife, Bright One, for your divine form and face have captured my heart!'

He was taken aback by her request and her forthright manner, but seeing that she was youthful and innocent, he replied gently, 'Greetings, princess! I am honoured to receive a proposal from someone so young and beautiful. However, I must confess that I am unable to accept. My destiny compels me to follow a different path in order to complete a task given to me by the gods. I wish you well though, and pray that you find a suitor who will reciprocate your feelings.'

Buddhi listened and wondered about the path he had mentioned. Did his words mean that he had decided to remain celibate? But his manner towards the three sisters was often that of a suitor for their affections. What were his true intentions then?

She saw that Tulasi was shocked by his refusal, but the princess persisted, captivated by his grace and charm. Ganesha turned her down again and she at once became angry and resentful. 'You are foolish to reject a beautiful princess like me and will soon regret your decision!' she retorted. 'One day soon, you too will yearn for someone and will then understand how I feel!'

Ganesha's face turned red with anger. He had been polite in speaking to her, but she was brash and threatening. 'You are too arrogant, Tulasi, and you will pay the price for it,' he retorted. 'You will marry a rakshasa and end your life as a shrub!'

Brought to her senses by his fierce curse, Tulasi began to weep loudly. She fell at his feet and begged his forgiveness. Ganesha was now calm again and was touched by her grief. 'The great Vishnu will release you from your life with the rakshasa and transform you into a tulasi plant,' he said. 'Devotees will offer your leaves to him in order to be redeemed from sin. However, I myself will never accept the tulasi in worship.'

As the princess moved sadly away, Buddhi began her own meditation in a sylvan spot under a parijata tree. The fragrant blossoms with vibrant orange stalks fell softly around her as she focused her mind on Lord Krishna.

Riddhi came to greet Ganesha, and he could see that she was bubbling over with happiness.

'What makes you so buoyant today, Riddhi?' he asked her, confident that he could speak freely to her.

She blushed, bit her lip in hesitation and then opened up. 'I think I have found the right man to marry—someone who will cherish me forever!' she declared.

Ganesha froze, and gazed at her in shock. 'True love—and so suddenly!' he exclaimed.

'I met a poet in these very woods when he came looking for inspiration,' she replied. 'Needless to say, he found it in my beauty! He is everything I desire, for he is as handsome as Kama and loves me beyond reason. He makes me garlands of conch flowers that are more precious to me than pearls. His face is sublime and his eyes so enchanting that I can see the skies, the birds and all heaven in them! His body is powerful and flawless like the vaidurya gem that captivates the eye with its glitter.'

'You seem to have settled quickly for a mortal when you could choose any of the gods in heaven,' said Ganesha, frowning.

'Great Shiva is married and so is Vishnu. Indra and Surya have beautiful wives and many apsaras to captivate them. I hear that your brother Karthikeya, though single, is always angry! Who else is left, tell me?'

What about me? Ganesha wanted to ask, but restrained himself. What if she said something brash and hurtful in reply?

'Judging by your description, it appears that your poet is more enchanting than Lord Krishna,' he said morosely.

'Undoubtedly!' she replied. 'Even if Krishna were to appear in front of me now, I would still choose my poet. Did Damayanti not choose to marry King Nala even though all the devas courted her?'

'But this man is not a king! He is just an impoverished poet!' Ganesha protested.

'Why do you insist that I marry a god, Ganesha? Are you jealous by any chance?' she asked, her eyes dancing merrily when Ganesha flushed red. He shook his head in denial but was not willing to give up.

'If you were in some danger, how will he protect you? With the feather he writes with? And when he himself is dependent on the largesse of kings, how will he support you in the life of luxury that you are used to?'

'I have enough riches for both of us, for I am blessed by the divine Lakshmi,' she retorted. 'And I find that immortality pales when compared to the magic of eternal love. My poet swears that he will love me even when I am old and wrinkled. He says that though we may age, fall sick and die, our life together will be blissful as long as it lasts. Ultimately, is this not what matters? Therefore, I have decided to remain on earth as a goddess in his eyes rather than reign in heaven.'

It seemed as if the flighty girl he had met had grown wise overnight. She now considered love to be essential to happiness, not good looks or wealth.

But was Ganesha ready to give her up so easily?

3

A Duel for Love

'I fear your poet is too good to be true, Riddhi,' said Ganesha finally, unable to think of any further arguments against her choice. 'Perhaps he is a trickster looking for a wealthy bride. Bring him to me so I may find out if he really loves you.'

Riddhi agreed and skipped away lightly to look for her poet, leaving behind a glum suitor.

Ganesha turned his attention to the serene Buddhi, a vision of loveliness, seated on a carpet of flowers. Near her hovered a fawn, while a brilliant blue bird perched on her shoulder and ate the fruit she offered. She seemed tranquil and happy and smiled at Ganesha. He took that as an invitation and hurried to her side.

'I call my bird Neela,' she said. 'Not very imaginative, I admit, but she is so brilliantly blue!'

'The truth, though, is that Neela is a male bird, not a female,' chuckled Ganesha. She looked startled and then smiled back. She was at least talking to him now, and he was delighted to hear her soft, musical voice. Finally, she had broken her silence.

'I presume Riddhi told you about her poet,' Buddhi continued. 'I hope he is everything my sister wishes, though I dread being separated from her when she marries him. Sometimes I even wish that the three of us could marry the same groom, so that we may never be parted.'

I wish that too, as long as it is me that you three wed, thought Ganesha. But it seemed unlikely that even one of them would say yes to him.

Buddhi stared thoughtfully at Ganesha. 'May I ask you something?' she asked finally. 'I am not sure if I should and you need not answer unless you want to.'

He looked into her calm, clear eyes and wondered if she was interested in him or was merely curious. Whatever it was, he would take this as an opportunity to get closer to her.

'You may ask me anything!' he smiled, and waited courteously for her to speak.

'I saw you turn away Tulasi and wondered why you are so opposed to marriage,' she said.

'I must tell you the truth now,' he said, smiling mischievously. 'Two beautiful maidens, Kamala and Vimala, had been praying to Shiva, seeking to marry him. He could not accept them for he was married already and so—'

'So you married them and pretended that you were unmarried!' said Buddhi, her face turning red.

'But I am not married—not in this life!' Ganesha said. 'It happened in another age. You may be aware that the gods are born in different yugas in different forms to carry out their purpose, though the lessons they teach are the same. This is sometimes difficult to understand unless you realize that the gods existed before Time began. It is only through our sages that we come to know about their earlier lives. Why, in the future, the great poet Tulsidas will even say that Shiva and Parvati worshipped me, their son, before their marriage! Now, that is a paradox to tease your mind!'

He saw her thoughtful face as she tried to unravel all this and said, 'Let me invoke a crow who will tell you more about this.'

'A crow?' whispered Buddhi.

'Yes. Your love for earth's creatures must have revealed to you that they are more intelligent and loving than anyone can imagine.'

She nodded, knowing that he too shared her affection for all life forms. His mouse was indolent and extremely pampered. She had seen Ganesha whispering comfort to a wounded deer, and sporting in the waters of the Ganga with playful dolphins.

'A cow sheds tears for you when you are in pain,' he continued. 'And crows intercede for you in the world of our ancestors. In fact, I once took the form of a crow myself in order to make the river Kaveri flow in the south.'

He saw the eager look in her eyes and took it as encouragement to tell her the story. 'Long ago, Shiva requested Sage Agastya to go to the south of Bharata Varsha, carrying the water of the Ganga, in order to create a river there to relieve the drought. The sage travelled south but became so absorbed in his prayers that he forgot to release the water he was carrying in his kamandal. I took the form of a crow and pushed down the pot so that the water could flow, pure and perennial, making the earth verdant. The sage opened his eyes wrathfully and I turned into a young lad so that I could explain the reason for my action. However, he began to chase me, angry that I had disturbed his prayers. Did he manage to catch hold of me and punish me? Well, that is a tale for another day!' Ganesha chuckled.

'Now, all that talking has made me hungry,' he said as he brought out some modakas to share with her. 'Do you know that your father, Brahma, has promised me a wife?'

'Well, none of us has said yes!' teased Buddhi.

'Why does it have to be one of you sisters?' he mocked her in reply. 'Aren't all the girls in the universe Brahma's creations?'

Before she could come up with a suitable answer, a crow with glossy black feathers alighted on a low branch before them.

'Salutations, Sage Bhushunda!' said Ganesha. Buddhi looked at him suspiciously, wondering if he was playing a trick on her.

'I bow to you, Mangalamurti!' said the crow, startling Buddhi by speaking in a deep, resonant voice. 'I worship the great god whom Shiva worshipped before killing Tripurasura, and Parvati before slaying Mahishasura!'

It was strange to hear that Ganesha's parents would worship him, but Buddhi chose to remain silent for now.

'Bhushunda lives in heaven on the kalpavriksha, the wish-fulfilling tree, in the form of a crow, and prays to Vishnu,' explained Ganesha to her. 'He is the chronicler of antiquity, the seer of the past, present and future.'

'I will speak now of the mysteries of the yugas as per your bidding,' said Bhushunda. 'I have survived countless cycles of creation and dissolution. I have seen the earth sink five times and lifted up as many times by Vishnu in the form of a tortoise. Twelve times have I witnessed the great battle of gods and asuras, and the uprooting of the Mandara mountain to churn the nectar from the ocean. I have watched Vishnu come down six times as Parasurama, and seen Shiva destroy Tripura thirty times.'

Ganesha smiled at Buddhi's startled expression and interrupted the sage with a question. 'How is it that you have lived through so many yugas, O sage?' he asked.

'The power of dhyana has kept me alive through the ages,' said Bhushunda. 'It has freed me from sorrow, desire and disease that drain us of our life force.'

'You mentioned Shiva and Vishnu, but have you not seen Ganesha in previous yugas, great sage?' asked Buddhi, eager to seek some answers herself.

'I have witnessed the young Gajamukha fight Bhandasura in the service of Devi Lalita,' replied Bhushunda. 'The valour he displayed was extraordinary and his devotion to the Devi was truly exceptional. However, you must understand that these avataras are merely fleeting illusions, like a drop of water on a lotus leaf. The ultimate reality is the divinity you discover within yourself through meditation.'

They bowed to the great soul as he fluttered away. 'What is this fight with Bhandasura that he spoke of?' asked Buddhi.

'The story begins when I was just a child looking for a playmate,' Ganesha replied. 'I moulded a figure out of the ashes of Manmatha, the god of love, who had been burned by Shiva's anger. The figure came to life and sang the praises of Shiva. The lord blessed him with unrivalled powers. Using these boons, Bhandasura, as he was now called, began to terrorize the worlds. The Trimurti themselves were helpless as their astras were powerless against Shiva's boons. The devas performed intense tapasya and surrendered themselves to Shakti who manifested as Lalita Tripurasundari. She recreated the world that had been rendered barren and devoid of love by the asura. When I prayed to her to allow me to make amends for creating the demon, she smiled and nodded her consent.'

'What did you do then?' asked Buddhi, her eyes gleaming with excitement.

'From Lalita's smile were born six Vinayakas who led crores of Herambas, each with ten arms and five elephant heads. They annihilated the asuras in a trice while I myself killed Gajasura, the dire commander of the asura army. It was then that I understood that not even Shiva or Vishnu can attain anything without the

Devi. My task on earth too can be completed only when Shakti smiles upon me.'

Buddhi was silent as she contemplated all that she had seen and heard. The two sat together companionably until Riddhi appeared before them, hand in hand with her poet. Behind them came Siddhi, looking as suspicious of this suitor as Ganesha had been when he had first heard of him.

Buddhi stepped forward to greet Riddhi's chosen one, unaffected by Siddhi's resentment.

'He is perfect in face and form—perhaps too perfect,' muttered Ganesha to Siddhi as they gazed at the lovelorn pair. 'But has he ever fought an enemy? Does he even know how to use a weapon?'

Siddhi curled her lip at the stranger. In her view, a man who could not prove his mettle in battle was no man at all. 'Look at the flowers he wears on his head like a crown,' she scoffed. 'He looks as if he spends his days perfuming his body and smoothing his curls. He even carries a flute, pretending to be Krishna!'

Ganesha beamed at her, happy that they were in agreement for once. 'I will unmask the pretender before your eyes,' he said and stepped forward to bar the poet's path.

'Who are you? What is your name and lineage?' he shot at him, disregarding Riddhi's cry of protest at his rudeness.

'I am Sumukha, and my father is an ascetic,' the poet replied, his face calm and unperturbed.

'Sumukha!' mocked Ganesha. 'You seem to be aptly named, as your face is your only fortune.'

'Why do I need riches when my Riddhi is as lustrous as gold and as brilliant as a diamond?' the man replied, smiling at his beloved.

Riddhi clapped her hands in delight, but Ganesha frowned. 'So you propose to dawdle all day singing songs to the arch of her eyebrow and the curve of her hips?' he jeered.

'I forgive you, Gajamukha, for I can see that your hostility springs from jealousy,' said Sumukha. 'How can someone like you hope to compete with my good looks and charm?'

Ganesha stomped his foot angrily, but the poet continued, unfazed. 'In times gone by, the demons yearned for the beauteous Lakshmi, but she had eyes only for Vishnu,' he said. 'And now, a misshapen god yearns for Riddhi, but she has chosen me!'

Ganesha raised his staff threateningly at the insult. 'You have shown us that you can talk, but can you fight, dapper poet?' he challenged.

'May I ask you if you can write poetry, my friend?' Sumukha retorted. 'Can you love her like I do? Moreover, where is the need for me to fight when I have won her already?' A smug smile lit up his face.

Ganesha took a step forward, his ears flapping furiously. 'You are an annoying gnat and I will take great pleasure in destroying you!' he swore.

'No! You cannot fight him, Ganesha!' shouted Riddhi, trying to come between them. 'He is a poet, not a warrior. You said that you would talk to him, not kill him.'

'The foolhardy mortal mocks me and I must avenge the insult,' declared Ganesha. 'Let us see how he fares against Gajamukha.'

'Calm yourself, dear friend,' Buddhi intervened, her eyes pleading with him. 'It is not fair for you to fight someone so unskilled in weapons.'

'Yes,' mocked Siddhi. 'The man carries a flute, after all.'

Ganesha halted his headlong advance but his words were not too encouraging. 'I will make one concession,' he said. 'I promise not to attack him unless he manages to wound me.' Ganesha's expression made it clear that he did not think the poet capable of doing this.

Riddhi looked at his implacable face and turned to appeal to her suitor instead.

'Do not fight him, Sumukha!' she said. 'If you do not draw blood, he cannot kill you. Just tell him that you do not carry a weapon.'

Siddhi rolled her eyes at her sister's cowardly suggestion and moved forward to offer Sumukha her own bow and arrows. He looked at the challenging expression on her face and then gingerly took the weapons from her. Riddhi clutched his arm in panic. But the poet's pride had been aroused and he freed his arm from her hold.

'I will do this for you, though I may die in the process, my sweet Riddhi!' he declared.

Riddhi stomped her foot in anger, but neither of the opponents was willing to listen to her.

Ganesha smirked as he saw Sumukha struggling to hold the bow upright and position the arrow. Then he stood, legs apart and his arms crossed over his chest, mocking the poet with his own relaxed air.

Sumukha's first arrows wobbled forth and fell just a few feet from where he stood. Siddhi scowled at him. The poet's face grew red with exertion and embarrassment, but he persevered. Finally, one of his arrows managed to reach Ganesha, though it was not forceful enough to wound him. Ganesha snorted in amusement. The poet seemed heartened by his success and let loose more arrows, getting better with each one.

Riddhi grew more anxious and held out a hand in a silent plea, only to be ignored. Sumukha's next arrow was true to its mark. It struck Ganesha's forehead and drew blood.

'At last!' exclaimed the young god, his eyes gleaming. 'Now I will kill you!' He fitted an arrow to his bow.

'Have mercy, he is human!' shouted Riddhi, trying again to step between the rivals. But her sisters held her back. She wept with grief and guilt. Why had she brought Sumukha to meet Ganesha when there was no need to seek his approval? Parvati's son was evidently jealous that the poet had succeeded where he could not. Now it was too late to stop the tragedy. Her sobs grew louder.

Ganesha released his first arrow. Riddhi screamed and shut her eyes, unwilling to see her swain fall. But Ganesha had angled his bow upward at the last moment and the arrow blazed through the skies and disappeared from sight. Riddhi opened her eyes in dread and saw that her poet was still standing and aiming arrows at his foe. She turned desperate eyes to her elephant-headed friend. Had he granted his rival a reprieve? But no, he was drawing the bowstring again. Was he playing with Sumukha like a cat teasing a mouse? Could he be so cruel?

The birds chirping in the trees fell silent and the air grew still as the second arrow flew forth, aimed directly at Sumukha. This was the end. Riddhi screamed and Buddhi began praying to the gods. But what use were her prayers when the attacker was the first among the celestials? Even Siddhi felt her stomach churn as she regretted the role she had played in provoking the contest. It was not valorous to kill a foe who was so much weaker.

The arrow roared forward, erupting crimson flames, straight towards Sumukha's chest. The girls looked on, petrified. They knew that an astra shot by Shiva's son could not fail. The arrow would cleave open the magnificent body . . . Sumukha's beautiful face would be distorted in the agony of death . . . His eyes would cling to his beloved in his last moments . . . What a tragedy, and a needless one at that! Riddhi moaned in anguish.

Then they saw that the poet was laughing, with his head thrown back and his hands on his hips. Had he been crazed by fear? Had the astra failed in some mysterious way? For if he had been struck, blood would be pouring down in torrents by now. Riddhi rushed to him, filled with a desperate hope. Sumukha reached out for her and she saw that instead of a wound, his chest was now adorned with a garland of red hibiscus. One more arrow flashed towards him and this one turned into a garland of durva grass and dropped gently around his neck.

Riddhi turned her confused gaze on Ganesha and saw that he too was laughing. Instead of his elephant head and rotund body, he now had the face and physique of her Sumukha. In fact, he looked exactly like the poet and was wearing two garlands himself. Had the jealous god taken Sumukha's form in order to taunt her? Or had her senses been disordered by the threat to her beloved?

4

Nara Mukha

'Do you not know me?' asked her Sumukha, embracing her warmly. As her body touched his, she sensed that her handsome poet was not dead. She began to cry again, this time in relief.

Ganesha spoke then, still in his dazzling human form. 'Sumukha and I are one and the same, Riddhi!' he said. 'To kill him, I would have to kill myself. Forgive me for sporting with you, my love. But it was merely to show the world that every man can become divine when he realizes the Supreme within himself.'

Sumukha took Riddhi's hand in his own and reiterated his love. 'My goddess, my Shakti!' he said. 'You have shown the world that love is the true remover of obstacles. You were ready to give up everything, even your immortality, for the sake of the man you loved. We are now part of each other, together until the end of time.'

A delighted Riddhi smiled at him and pulled him away to their usual retreat in a fragrant garden on the banks of the Ganga. Here Sumukha made sweet amends for making her suffer pangs of anxiety.

Siddhi gazed long and hard at Ganesha who still stood in his human form and a shadow crossed her face. She clenched her fists and walked away without a word.

Is she jealous of Riddhi and her happiness with Sumukha? wondered Buddhi. She herself was entranced by Ganesha's beautiful form that reminded her of the old tale of his creation.

'My guru once told me that when you were first created, you had a human face, and that you were beheaded by your own father. How could this happen? The very idea keeps me awake at night,' she said.

Touched by her tender heart, Ganesha revealed to her in a vision all that had happened:

Devi Parvati had placed Nandi on guard outside her mansion when she was taking a bath, and ordered him not to allow anyone inside. However, being Shiva's devotee, he had been unable to stop the three-eyed god from entering. The angry Parvati decided that she must have someone who would obey her orders alone, and created a heroic son for herself from the turmeric paste that anointed her body. She named him Vinayaka, the unparalleled leader, and smiled at his glorious face and form that shone like a thousand suns. She clothed him in silks, adorned him with jewels and gave him a mystic staff imbued with her powers. 'Guard our home and allow no one to enter,' she commanded.

Buddhi watched as Parvati's indomitable son stopped the great Shiva from entering his wife's abode. She clutched at Ganesha's arm in fear.

'Who are you, fool, that you dare to stop me?' roared Shiva.

'I am Vinayaka, Parvati's son!' the young lad replied proudly.

'I am her husband and I command you to step aside!' said the angry god, striding forward. However, Vinayaka raised his staff and crimson flames erupted from it to bar Shiva's way.

'Nandi!' shouted Shiva. 'Make this boy understand the danger of challenging the god of gods.'

Nandi and the ganas attempted at first to cajole the boy into stepping aside. Then they threatened him and raised their fists.

But Vinayaka was unmoved and raised his voice in defiance. 'Leave now or die!' he said to Nandi, fixing him with a fierce glare. The mighty bull felt strangely uneasy and stepped away.

But just then, he heard his master's command. 'Kill the intruder! Toss him down the mountain. Show him who you are!'

Nandi could not ignore Shiva's direct order. He pawed the ground, tossed his head and charged forward, his fierce ganas at his heels. Buddhi closed her eyes in fear. How would the young lad survive this horrific attack?

However, the radiant Vinayaka was unfazed. He laughed in Nandi's face and scorched him with his flaming staff, forcing him to retreat with a bellow of pain. The youth attacked like a whirlwind, his movements too swift to be seen. His laugh rang out, shrill and clear, while his staff spun through the air with an eerie howl, breaking backs and smashing skulls.

Seeing his attendants scatter like straw, Shiva rushed into the fray with his bow raised. The lustrous staff flew from Vinayaka's hand, knocked the bow from Shiva's grasp and returned to the boy's hand. The devas gasped in fear and fled the scene. Vishnu alone rushed forward, mace in hand. But Vinayaka rebuffed him with one powerful blow of his staff.

'Kill him from behind while I engage him in front,' said Vishnu to Shiva. He mounted Garuda and flew at the young warrior. His incandescent chakra blazed forth to behead the youth.

Buddhi moaned in fright. Ganesha smiled at her and whispered that all would be well.

Vinayaka's danda rose in the air and shattered the fiery chakra. Then it struck the lord of Vaikunta and pushed him off Garuda's back. Undaunted, Vishnu began to grapple with the boy, trying to crush him with his four powerful arms. While Vinayaka was pinioned by Vishnu, Shiva advanced on him from behind, with his trident raised. How could Parvati's son escape this twin attack?

'No, no! He is a mere boy. Look at his divine face. Do not kill him this way,' whispered Buddhi, watching the drama unfold in Kailasa. Ganesha took her hand gently in his and held it tight.

The next moment, Shiva's trident took off the head of the valiant Vinayaka. The headless body continued to wrestle with Vishnu for a few moments, obedient still to his mother's command. The devas, the ganas and the Trimurti stood ashamed, regretting the death of the indomitable lad by deceit.

Parvati came out then and wailed in anguish on seeing her son so cruelly cut down. Her wrath leapt forth like a fierce fire and dried up the seven oceans. Then the flood of tears from her eyes filled up the oceans again so that the waters became salty. She transformed herself into dire Bhadrakali and from her sprang thousands of Shaktis—fanged, four-armed, ferocious. They crushed the devas, ripped the ganas apart, trampled the gandharvas under giant feet, smashed the yakshas and swallowed the rakshasas. Shiva and Vishnu stood trembling, unable to appease the furious goddess. The sages sang hymns of praise, fell at her feet and pleaded for mercy. Bhadrakali stopped her attack, though her eyes still rolled angrily.

'I do not wish to see any more,' said Buddhi, her limbs shaking at the violence that she had witnessed. 'How could Shiva kill you when you were merely obeying your mother's orders? How did the gods have the heart to destroy a child so luminous and brave? Look how your mother grieves. Shiva's act has resulted in so much violence and death. And I am distressed that you had to face all this as soon as you were born!'

Ganesha basked happily in her attention and her sympathy. But being Buddhi, she was interested in finding out the reason behind all that had happened. 'You were so powerful, imbued with your mother's divinity. Could you not sense the imminent attack, though it came from behind you?' she asked.

'I could indeed. But I forced myself to submit, because it is my mother's shakti that presides over the trishul. After all, I owe my very existence to her.'

She nodded slowly. He was truly a lofty soul to have chosen respect for his mother over his own survival. 'It is puzzling that the Vighnaharta himself had to face so many obstacles. Why did all this have to happen?'

'In an earlier age, Shiva struck Surya on the chest for attacking two of his devotees,' Ganesha replied. 'An angry Sage Kashyapa, Surya's father, cursed the three-eyed god saying that his own son's head would fall off one day. Even the gods have to pay for their actions, you see.'

'But I ache for the young lad who was sacrificed for no fault of his!' Buddhi exclaimed.

'You must see what happened later . . . how my mother was appeased,' Ganesha said. They returned to the scene of the angry Bhadrakali who demanded that her son be restored to life.

Shiva ordered his ganas to travel north and fetch him the head of the first creature they encountered. They returned with the head of Airavata, Indra's elephant. The lord of Kailasa attached the head to Vinayaka's body and brought him back to life. 'Henceforth, he will be Shiva-suta and Parvati-nandana, the son of both Shiva and Parvati,' he said.

The vision faded and Buddhi stood alone in the forest again with Ganesha. What she said now startled him and made him laugh.

'Poor Airavata! Why did he have to lose his head for you?' she asked.

'There was a reason for that too,' Ganesha replied. 'Once, Vishnu gave Sage Durvasa a divine flower, and the sage in turn gave it to the king of the heavens. Indra carelessly placed it on Airavata's head, and the proud elephant shook it off and trampled it underfoot. Durvasa was furious, and cursed Indra and the devas that they would lose their powers and Airavata his head. Indra prayed desperately for relief and Vishnu, the protector of the universe, promised him that their powers would be restored when they drank the amrit that emerged from the cosmic ocean. His elephant too would rise from the kshira saagar in his original form.'

Buddhi nodded, storing all this knowledge in her mind. 'I can see the original Vinayaka in your present form,' she said. 'Why do you not retain your human face as a tribute to your mother's love?' She paused for a moment and quickly added: 'Not that I think you do not look majestic as Gajamukha!'

She is so careful not to hurt anyone with her words, thought Ganesha. *She is afraid that I will think that she is mocking my elephant face.*

'I could easily take up the form of Adi Vinayaka,' he said. 'But I choose to retain my elephant head as my devotees find it endearing. They look at me and smile. They come to me freely, for no one can fear a god who looks like I do and chooses a small mouse to carry him! They regard me as their child, born in their family to make their lives better. Through me, they can approach my father, the fierce Rudra, and my mother, Parvati, who holds me as a child on her lap. I will do anything to make my devotees happy, even sipping a little milk from their cups when they offer it to me! You see, the impossible becomes possible when you are unusual like I am.' He looked at her gentle face and added,

'Today, in honour of your loving heart, I promise that I will appear with a human head whenever I am alone with you and your sisters.'

Buddhi gazed raptly at his flawless body and his handsome face that was as splendid as Manmatha's. 'I will appear as Nara Mukha to my devotees too in a few rare temples,' he said. 'Those who pray to me there will be blessed with happiness in all their relationships.'

He paused and looked into her eyes and asked her teasingly, 'So, have you fallen in love with anyone yet, my adorable Buddhi?'

She lowered her eyes in confusion but then raised them again to proffer a quick reply. 'Maybe. Maybe not! You will have to find out for yourself,' she said, with dimples dancing in her cheeks.

But Ganesha was not looking at her any longer. His eyes seemed to be gazing at something that was not visible to her.

'Is anything the matter?' she asked anxiously.

Ganesha transformed before her eyes into Gajamukha and in his hand pulsed the mystic danda. 'I see a powerful warrior near my father's cave and am waiting to see what his intentions are,' he said. 'I hope he will not attempt to enter forcibly and disturb Shiva.'

'Shall I leave then?' asked Buddhi. 'Siddhi will probably come looking for me, for she is more protective than my mother who is often immersed in her learning!'

'No,' he replied, unwilling to let her go. 'Please stay awhile. Nandi has stopped the intruder and I may not be needed.'

As if Buddhi's thoughts had conjured her up, Siddhi came down the forest path, looking agitated. Riddhi came with her, prattling about the charms of her Sumukha. She looked shyly at Ganesha as if to say, *I know that you and my Sumukha are one and the same, but somehow I love him more!*

Ganesha replied with a smile that lit up his face.

'What is it?' Buddhi asked Siddhi, sensitive as she always was to the moods of others.

'There is word that Kamasura is camped within a few days' ride of this forest,' said Siddhi. 'His army ravages all the ashrams on the riverbanks, and our guru is anxious for our safety.'

Riddhi gave a little cry of fear, her beautiful face clouding over. Ganesha's eyes glittered and his fists clenched but he stayed silent, listening. Buddhi placed a gentle hand on Siddhi's shoulder to calm her down, and turned to Ganesha. 'You must be careful, my friend,' she said. 'Kapila says that the asura cannot be killed by Shiva or Vishnu, by yaksha or gandharva, by man or beast. Even Indra has fled the heavens and hides in patala, his lustre dimmed and his grace destroyed. Having subdued devaloka, Kamasura has descended to earth to bring all the kingdoms under his sceptre. Many evil kings have sold their souls to him in exchange for occult powers and weapons with which they torment the righteous.'

Ganesha nodded. 'Earth is in turmoil, except for small regions such as ours that are protected by the tapasya of great sages,' he said. 'Virtue declines and only the wicked prosper. The rains fail and people starve and prey on their neighbours. Men's hearts are overcome with greed and depravity. Families are torn apart by envy and pride. Lust reigns supreme and anarchy claims the world.'

Shiva's son had been born on earth only to kill Kamasura and re-establish peace. But he did not wish to say so, as it would seem boastful to make such a claim.

'I have resolved to kill this monster Kamasura even if it means sacrificing my life!' declared Siddhi, her face set in grim resolve.

38   Prem Purana

'Though the thought of war and bloodshed revolts me, I realize that sometimes there is no option except to fight,' said Buddhi softly. 'Maybe Ganesha can help in your battle.'

'I will protect you all!' Ganesha exclaimed, unable to remain quiet any longer.

'We do not need your protection!' Siddhi shot back, her eyes spewing fire.

He nodded, knowing that he could have expected nothing else. 'Nevertheless, you can call on me if you should need me,' he said. 'At this moment though, I am needed at Kailasa to stop the intruder who is too powerful for Nandi.'

'A battle?' asked Siddhi, her eyes lighting up. 'Who is this intruder?'

'It is Parasurama, Vishnu's avatara and an ardent devotee of my father,' he replied. 'He is armed with my father's parasu which makes him invincible.'

'I have heard tales of this mighty warrior and would like to see him, even if it is only from a distance,' Siddhi said, looking expectantly at Ganesha.

'You could come with me and witness our encounter,' he offered, eager to use any opportunity to spend time with her.

'I would like that. Maybe I will learn something from him when he overpowers you!' Siddhi laughed.

'Or maybe I will surprise you with my skills!' Ganesha chuckled. 'Let us leave for Kailasa then.'

Buddhi frowned. Why was he encouraging her sister who showed him no respect? If he had wanted someone to come with him, he could have chosen Buddhi. Did they not share a special relationship already? She paused for a moment to collect her thoughts. Why was she reacting so violently? Anyone watching them would think that she was jealous that Siddhi was getting closer to Ganesha. *Nothing can be further from the truth*, Buddhi told herself firmly.

Ganesha stood with Siddhi on the sacred soil of Kailasa, offering worship to the linga that Parvati had installed. He glanced at his companion's proud face, knowing that he had embarked on a rough path in attempting to win her over. For now, however, he had to focus on his confrontation with Parasurama whom Shiva had blessed with his great axe.

Siddhi watched from a safe distance as Ganesha bowed to the warrior and requested him to wait until Shiva granted him permission to enter. But Parasurama angrily pushed him aside and strode towards the cave. Ganesha intercepted him, causing the angry warrior to raise his axe to threaten him.

Finding that his antagonist would not listen to mere words, Shiva's son extended his trunk by many lengths and wound it around Parasurama 100 times. He then raised the warrior into the skies so that he could see the seven mountains, the seven oceans and the seven islands of the earth below him. Then he whirled him around and showed him all the lokas including Vaikunta, where Lord Vishnu presided on his lotus throne with Devi Lakshmi. With his yogic power, Shiva's son granted Parasurama a vision of Goloka, the purest of realms, where blue-hued Krishna resided with Radha and his gopis.

After showing Parasurama how insignificant he was when compared to the primordial universe spanning endless time and space, Gajamukha dropped him gently on the ground outside Shiva's cave. He smiled at Siddhi who stood dazed, clinging to a tree for support, as she too had been granted the supernal vision by Ganesha's grace. She realized now that her cheerful friend was called Vakratunda not because of his crooked trunk, but because he was the one who straightened out the crooked.

Parasurama recovered from his stupor and saw that he was lying on the ground at Ganesha's feet. Incensed by this humiliation, he sprang to his feet and took up his mighty axe. The parasu hurtled towards Ganesha with a deafening roar. Siddhi trembled, certain that her friend would not survive the dire power of his father's weapon.

5

Fiery Durga

Strangely enough, Gajamukha made no attempt to counter Parasurama's axe. Instead, he joined his hands in worship to the parasu and stood calmly as if reconciled to his death.

Siddhi heard a horrific crack as the parasu struck one of Ganesha's tusks and severed it completely. It fell to the ground with a crash, smeared in blood, looking like a crystal mountain covered in red chalk. Shiva rushed out of the cave, followed by Parvati, who turned into fiery Durga when she saw that her son had been wounded. She discerned what had happened and raged at the warrior who stood before her with the axe that had returned to his hand.

'O Parasurama!' she said. 'You may be learned and wise and the son of a great sage, yet you have allowed wrath to overcome you. You received your parasu from your guru, Shiva, but abused your gift by using it to wound his son. Ganesha, on the other hand, allowed the axe to sever his tusk due to his respect for his father's weapon. What next will you do, Parasurama? Will you assail mighty Shiva himself? Presumptuous warrior! I curse you this day that though you are an avatara of my beloved Vishnu, no one on earth or heaven will ever worship you!'

Parasurama cowered before the angry goddess whose fury grew by the moment. 'It is only due to Ganesha's forbearance that you are still alive, for he can kill a hundred thousand Parasuramas in the blink of an eye,' she said. 'But I am unwilling to be so tolerant and will end your life today!'

Durga rushed towards him, with her trident aimed at his head. Parasurama stood unarmed and unresisting. He closed his eyes, joined his hands together and surrendered to Krishna.

'Om Namo Bhagavate Vasudevaya!' Parasurama chanted, invoking his god with his last breath.

At once, Krishna appeared before him, lustrous and omnipotent, granting him protection with one raised hand. Durga stopped mid-stride and gazed at Krishna. Her wrath vanished, dissolving like mist in the light of the sun. A beatific smile adorned her face. She offered him a reverential welcome along with Shiva.

Krishna addressed them gently, a calm smile on his face. 'I have come here to rescue my devotee,' he said. 'Though Parasurama has committed a grievous sin, I request you to forgive him, Parvati. He is your son too, for you are the divine mother, the refuge of all creation. As for you, Parasurama, you have to undertake a severe tapasya to attain forgiveness. Worship the Devi who animates the three realms in the form of the gentle Gauri and the fierce Durga. Seek the blessings of Ganesha who is now Ekadanta, the lord with one tusk.'

Having offered his counsel, the lord returned to Goloka. Parasurama prostrated himself before the gods and laid his axe at Ganesha's feet in tribute. He then retreated to a distant mountain to begin his worship. Parvati took her son into her mansion, to coddle him after his fierce encounter.

Siddhi resolved to return to Kapila's ashram, only to find that her sisters had followed her to Kailasa, anxious about Ganesha's encounter with Parasurama. She assured them that all was well and that they should return to earth. But before they could leave, they were confronted by an irate Durga.

'You must be Brahma's daughters with whom my son spends all his time!' she exclaimed, casting a jealous eye on the three of them. They bowed to her and looked at her warily.

'Do you not realize that it is unlikely that my son will ever marry? He has promised me that he will only consider marriage with someone as beautiful and virtuous as his mother,' said Durga. 'But who in the universe can equal me?' Her eyes glittered in challenge.

'I have no desire to marry your son or anyone else!' retorted Siddhi, unable to stop herself. 'I regard marriage as a bond that traps a person in a world of meaningless pleasures.'

'Hush!' said Buddhi to her sister before turning to the Devi. 'She means no insult,' she said to her. 'It is just that she wishes to remain unmarried like Goddess Kanyakumari.'

This appeared to amuse Durga and she began to laugh, her mood changing abruptly. 'Come with me now,' she said. 'I will show you how my son is revered by men and gods alike. You are fortunate to be able to witness this.'

Night had fallen, and a brilliant moon shone down on Kailasa. Ganesha's mansion seemed to float in the air like an opal, taking on the colours of myriad gems. One moment, it appeared to be spun from pure white marble, for Parvati's son embodied the light of the divine. The next, it gleamed like a giant ruby, symbolizing the muladhara chakra over which he presided. Around the mansion there were scented gardens with iridescent flowers unseen on heaven or earth. Inside, his vast court dazzled with its silver columns and turquoise floors. The walls and ceilings bore exquisite paintings, for the young god was the patron of art, music and dance. Buddhi gasped as she studied the paintings of Krishna preaching the Gita, his son Pradyumna confronting Yama in order to save mankind and Parvati holding the young Gajamukha on her lap.

Ganesha sat on a throne set on a crystal dais within the Prabhavali, an arch of flames that represented creation, preservation and dissolution. On top of the arch resided Mahakala, the god of time, offering worship to the young god who was radiant in yellow silk. A white mouse wearing a golden necklace saluted Ganesha by joining its tiny feet together.

'Krauncha seems to have taken a snow-white avatara here,' whispered Buddhi, nodding to Ganesha who welcomed them with a beaming smile.

'He is more than just a small mouse worshipping a huge god,' said one of the rishis attending on the young god. 'Krauncha represents our ego and animal instincts that we must subdue with the help of Gajamukha. Parvati's son enlarges our spirit, opens up our hearts and shows us the way to bliss. Look down on earth and you will see how his grace falls upon his devotees like gentle rain on scorched land.'

They saw below an aged woman offering prayers to the tusked god in mellifluous Tamil verses. 'This woman, Avvaiyar, sought a boon from Ganesha to be rid of her youth so that she could devote herself to his worship,' said the rishi.

'My big ears help me hear not just her prayer, but her every thought!' chuckled Ganesha. 'She is anxious now because two other devotees have started their journey to Kailasa already and will reach me before she does. One is Sage Sundara who rides on a celestial elephant, and the other is King Cheraman whose horse moves swiftly, imbued with the power of the mantra Om Namah Shivaya.'

'I yearn to travel with them to meet my lord, but how can I do so when I am merely a poor old woman?' Avvaiyar cried out aloud.

The next instant, Avvaiyar heard Ganesha's voice in her ear. 'Complete your prayer in peace, mother,' he said. 'I will take you to Kailasa myself.' Her face broke into a delighted smile and she finished her worship calmly. Then Ganesha appeared before her, lifted her up gently with his trunk and conveyed her to Kailasa. The king and the sage gasped when they reached their destination and saw her there before them, adoring the young god with blissful song.

The girls gazed with awe at their whimsical friend from the forest who was now seated on a throne, holding a string of prayer beads, an axe and a goad in three hands, while granting boons with his fourth hand. 'Bless us, Vighnaharta!' prayed his devotees, worshipping Ganesha in his many forms.

'Sumukha!' whispered Riddhi with a smile.

'Adi Vinayaka!' said Buddhi.

If I ever felt any fondness for him, I would call him Ekadanta, thought Siddhi, recalling his encounter with Parasurama. *He proved his valour that day, showing me that he knows a trick or two. Perhaps he is not only interested in eating modakas and flirting with girls!*

The three maidens watched as Indra came to Ganesha seeking his blessings before embarking on a battle. Kama sought his help in composing a new verse extolling the beauty of his wife, Rati. On earth, students prayed for his help in their studies, and travellers invoked him before setting out on their journey. They performed aartis and offered him laddoos and fruits. Some devotees broke coconuts before his image, signifying the breaking of the ego's hold on their mind. Others adorned him with garlands of durva grass.

'I have seen that Sumukha too likes offerings of durva more than gold necklaces or gems. But why is that?' asked Riddhi.

'The rich bring me diadems of gold,' Ganesha replied. 'But I prefer durva grass as it is often the only offering that the poor can afford. You may wonder why they offer this grass and none other. To explain this, we must go back to a time when a wicked asura was born from Yama's uncontrollable desire for the apsara Tilottama. This asura became known as Analasura because he emitted fire from his eyes, burning everyone he encountered. Not even the devas could destroy him as the fierce heat made it impossible for them to stand before him.

'The asura prowled undeterred, his raucous laughter echoing between earth and heaven. The devas ran to Shiva. "Ganesha is the only one with a belly large enough to contain the asura!" Shiva laughed. When Indra sought my help, I took the form of a young boy and confronted the demon.'

Ganesha paused to quench his thirst and then continued. 'Considering me easy prey, Analasura assailed me with huge fireballs. When I continued to advance, he decided to devour me whole. I showed myself to him as Gajamukha and expanded myself to enormous proportions. While he stood dumbstruck by my giant form, I opened my mouth wide and swallowed him. The devas rejoiced on seeing this and Indra came to shower me with rare gems in thanksgiving. But alas, their fight for survival had not ended.'

'Why? What other threat did they face now?' asked Riddhi.

'The gods soon realized that though the asura no longer lived, his heat remained unquenched. It rose in waves from my belly and burned all the lokas. The ganas anointed me with sandalwood and showered me with huge pots of milk and a hundred thousand lotus flowers. Indra placed the crescent moon on my forehead hoping that his silvery rays would douse the heat.

Shiva removed the cobra from around his neck and tied it to my hip. Varuna submerged me in his cooling torrents. But all their efforts were in vain. Analasura's heat remained unabated.'

Brahma's daughters listened wide-eyed, wondering how the tale would end. 'Then, 88,000 sages came to me, each carrying a bunch of durva grass,' Ganesha continued. 'They placed the grass on my head and body and chanted potent slokas to quell the heat. Miraculously, the burning subsided and the realms were finally at peace. I declared then that anyone who offered me durva garlands with true devotion would receive my blessings. Since then, the durva grass remains close to my heart!'

Seeing that his pretty friends were overwhelmed by all that they had seen and heard that day in Kailasa, Ganesha attempted to lighten the mood. 'Now that you have seen my world, maybe you wish to join me here,' he joked. 'I promise that I will consent to marrying the three of you, provided you can show me that you can make delicious modakas like my mother!'

Buddhi smiled politely but the other two remained silent. 'I will try to ignore the fact that none of you is really perfect,' he continued, trying to provoke them. 'You are too quiet, Buddhi. Siddhi is difficult to please. I do love Riddhi, but I find that she is too fond of rich clothes and ornaments!'

This caught their attention and they gazed angrily at him. But before they could retaliate, the goddesses Lakshmi and Saraswati appeared before them. Lakshmi wore a resplendent red silk while Saraswati was clad in a white sari woven with sparkling stars.

'Blessings, my children!' said a smiling Lakshmi, as they bowed to them in worship. 'I heard what you said, Ganesha. But I would advise you not to disparage Riddhi who unites my shakti with yours!' she laughed. 'It is natural that each of us should have our own likes and dislikes. Why, my lord Vishnu himself is an alankarapriya like Riddhi and delights in adornments. As for Shiva, he is an abhishekapriya who is happy when devotees shower him with milk and honey.'

'What is Ganesha fond of?' asked Riddhi, tossing him a mischievous glance.

'He is a bhojanapriya, of course!' said Lakshmi. 'He enjoys feasts and will travel to the ends of the earth if you offer him laddoos or modakas, sugarcane or pomegranates.'

'It is not that I seek them, Devi,' Ganesha interrupted hurriedly. 'You know that devotees offer us what they themselves desire, out of their love for us.'

'That is true,' agreed Lakshmi. 'I must also tell you girls of a time when Shiva used Ganesha's fondness for eating to humble Kubera, who wished to show off his opulence at a grand feast. Ganesha went to Kubera's mansion in the place of his father and ate up all the food there and then began to devour the walls themselves. A desperate Kubera asked him to stop, but Ganesha threatened to eat him too if he did not satisfy his hunger. The lord of treasures was helpless and went to/Shiva who advised him to offer his son a handful of puffed rice with true devotion. Kubera did so and Ganesha calmed down, having taught the god a much-needed lesson!'

'Let me offer you something refreshing to drink,' said Ganesha, hoping to distract the goddess from talking about him. But Devi Lakshmi had already embarked on a fresh tale.

'Ganesha's adventures are almost too many to tell,' Lakshmi continued. 'Once, Vibhishana, the king of Lanka, was on his way back from Ayodhya. Rama had given him a Ranganatha vigraha in gratitude for his help during his war with Ravana, and told him not to place it on the ground before reaching his destination. But Vibhishana had to stop on the way to offer prayers and entrusted the idol to a young cowherd while he went to the river to make his ablutions. The boy promptly set the vigraha down and ran away, not willing to allow the beautiful image to leave this sacred land. When Vibhishana returned, he tried to lift the idol up in his arms but could not, however much he tried. He gave furious chase to the boy who was none other than Ganesha, and cornered him on top of a hill. Vibhishana gave him a few knocks on top of his head before leaving to return to his own country. Well, you can still see the marks on Ganesha's image installed there on top of the hill!'

Lakshmi paused then, and murmured that she could sense that her lord was waiting for her. She took her leave, but not before gifting them with fine silks and jewels.

'I too brought an emerald necklace for you, Riddhi, though I am unable to find it,' said Saraswati Devi. 'I rejoice at your choosing Ganesha as your husband.'

'Bless me, mother,' said Riddhi, touching her feet. Buddhi helped her mother remove the necklace that she had worn around her own neck and forgotten about, so that she could present it to Riddhi.

Saraswati smiled at Buddhi and touched her head fondly in blessing. 'You too will find your groom soon,' she said and turned to her firstborn. 'Siddhi, I know that you dream of defeating asuras and riding into battle on a lion. Perhaps you can achieve all this and be married too,' she advised.

Why did everyone provoke Siddhi by talking of marriage?

Buddhi looked anxiously at her sister. Hopefully, Siddhi would not respond rudely to their gentle mother.

6

A Son Like Krishna

Though her eyes flashed angrily for a moment, Siddhi stayed silent, not wishing to offend her mother. Buddhi breathed a sigh of relief. Saraswati turned to Ganesha. 'I remember why I came looking for you!' she exclaimed. 'You must go to Vyasa, my son, for he has a task for you. Take Buddhi along, for it will help you attain your goal.' Saying that, she returned to her world.

Ganesha transported himself with Buddhi to Vyasa's hermitage. The sage, renowned as Veda Vyasa due to his success in classifying the Vedas into four parts, welcomed them warmly.

'Omkareshwara!' Vyasa said in worship to the one who embodied the pranava mantra. 'I seek your help in transcribing an epic of immense proportions. I wish to tell the story of the great war between the Pandavas and the Kurus, during which Lord Krishna blessed the world with the Bhagavad Gita.'

'I am honoured and happy that I will be the first to hear your divine verses,' said Ganesha. 'And Brahma's daughter Buddhi will hear them with me, for she has a great thirst for learning. But before we start, I would like to enliven our task by making it an intellectual challenge.'

When Vyasa nodded his consent, the young god said, 'I will inscribe what you recite only as long as you recite the verses without pausing.'

'I agree, and challenge you in return,' said the sage. 'You can write down what I recite only after you have understood the verses.' Ganesha smiled, realizing that Vyasa had bought himself some time to think by placing this condition. He agreed happily, for he loved nothing more than a battle of wits.

The sage took his place under an enormous banyan tree, and Parvati's son sat before him like a humble student. Vyasa began his narration, and Ganesha found it easy to keep pace. But then, the sage began to intersperse his couplets with difficult verses that were more like poetic riddles. Buddhi looked quickly from sage to student, unable to decipher the verses, but hoping that Ganesha would be able to unravel them.

The epic tale that Vyasa named Jaya was in itself pregnant with meaning and had much substance to provoke thought and debate. It was a shastra, a textbook that taught one about life and how to live it. But it was also a mystic sutra, a philosophical treatise on the mysteries of the universe. Ganesha thought deeply when faced with a conundrum, chuckled loudly when he deciphered it and continued writing. The sage smiled at him and carried on. Buddhi watched the drama unfold as one great mind was pitted against another. Would her friend be able to complete the saga without stopping? The flow of thought and plot was so rapid that she could barely keep up. Several questions rose in her mind and she resolved to clarify them later with Ganesha's help.

And then, an obstacle sprang up in the path of the Vighnaharta himself. The quill with which he was writing snapped. He would have to seek time to replace it. Would that not be construed as defeat? Should she rush to Vyasa's ashram to fetch him another quill? She looked anxiously at Ganesha and wondered for a moment why she was so eager that he should win. But by then Parvati's son had already come up with a solution, that too an unexpected one. He conjured up the tusk that had been broken by Parasurama's axe and began to write using it in the place of his quill. She laughed at herself for fearing that a broken feather could stop Shiva-suta.

'But why do you use your tusk instead of another quill?' she asked him when he paused for a moment.

'A feather could break again, could it not?' he replied. 'But the real reason I chose to use my tusk is that Vyasa's epic deserves to be written with a nobler instrument than a mere feather!'

Many days later, Vyasa completed his narrative of 8800 splendid verses and the scribe finished his writing. The two bowed their heads in respect to each other. 'This is just the beginning,' Ganesha said to him. 'Your Jaya will be enlarged by your student Vaisampayana and become known as Bharata. The story will capture the imagination of future generations who will add to its glory with thousands of verses. Finally, this saga of more than a hundred thousand verses will be renowned as the Mahabharata. And learned men will exclaim in awe that "what is here is elsewhere, but what is not here is nowhere else!"'

When Ganesha had returned with Buddhi to the forest, he asked her teasingly, 'Did my writing prove to you that my big head contains some amount of intelligence?'

She smiled at him but remained silent. He wanted to woo her with passionate words, telling her that she embodied the purity of the white lotus, the splendour of the snow-covered mountain and the brilliance of tapasya. But he knew that she valued depth more than declamation and wisdom more than words.

'Accept my love, Buddhi,' he said simply, yet earnestly. 'Be the music in my flute and the truth in my understanding.'

Buddhi blushed. 'Did Sumukha write some verses for you to recite?' she asked. 'I must first unravel all the secrets you are hiding, especially about your marriage to Kamala and Vimala!'

'Not just these two. I was married to Pushti when I was born due to Krishna's boon,' he said. 'Together, we granted our devotees good fortune and prosperity.'

'Yet another wife!' exclaimed Riddhi, who had come there looking for her Sumukha.

'Yes,' he said. 'And Pushti was sweet and delightful, never fighting with me or mocking me.' He cast a sidelong glance at the two girls to see if they were jealous. 'She always said that she adored my handsome face, my lively mind, my virile charm . . .'

'Stop, stop!' said Buddhi, raising a hand in protest. 'Did she ever say that you boast too much? Also tell me, why was it necessary to marry so many times? Was it because you were born through Krishna's blessings?' She turned and walked away in a huff, leaving Riddhi behind with him.

'O Krishna! How did you placate all the women you wooed? Was it with your music or your smile?' he murmured, looking up playfully towards the heavens.

As if in answer to his words, the forest filled with the melody of Krishna's flute and the sound whirled them back through the ages to a time when Parvati was performing a vrata in order to have a child.

Riddhi and Ganesh stood invisible, watching events unfold in Kailasa.

'The Punyaka vrata is like the Satya among yugas, the purana among poems, Narada among sages and Rama among kings,' said Shiva to his wife. 'Perform this vow with devotion and Krishna himself will be born as your son.'

Parvati gathered together offerings of parijata, champaka and kadamba. She worshipped Vishnu with diamond lamps and golden parasols and adorned his image with pearls and coral. She bathed him in milk and honey and lived an ascetic life for one long year. The sages came to bless the vrata and with them came the gandharvas, apsaras and yakshas. Parvati's father Himavan came with gifts of radiant gems, wild elephants and horses. Priests and bards gathered there as did the poor to receive the generous alms that would be distributed. Indra presided over the offerings and Kubera over the treasury. Surya advised them on the rituals to be performed and Varuna supervised the feasts. Lakshmi made an ambrosial pudding with her own hands, and through her grace, the sacrificial ground flowed with rivers of honey and milk, ghee and butter.

The radiant Sanat Kumara, son of Brahma, officiated over Parvati's vrata. She was delighted when she finally came to the last day of the vow. Her desire would be fulfilled and Kailasa would echo with the laughter of a divine child. 'Allow me to complete my vrata by giving you gold and jewels as offerings,' she said to Sanat Kumara.

'What can a priest do with gold, noble Parvati?' he said in reply. 'I desire something else.'

Parvati smiled and nodded, not realizing what she was agreeing to. 'Hand over Shiva to me, goddess, as my fee!' he said. Parvati looked at him in shock and then tried to coax him into accepting some other gift. But the priest was adamant, and she began to weep helplessly. Shiva comforted her with his gentle touch and said, 'Give him the fee he seeks so that your sacrifice may be completed, Devi.'

'But how can I give you away and then hope for a child? How is it possible to build a palace in the air?' she protested.

The devas and the sages were dumbfounded and the ganas wept for their goddess. Then the turmoil was silenced by the sound of Vishnu's divine conch, Panchajanya, signalling the appearance of the Supreme Protector. From a loka far away arrived a luminous chariot with diamond wheels, a golden body and a dome studded with gems and inlaid with pearls. The ratha was accompanied by majestic, four-armed beings wearing garlands of wild flowers. As the chariot floated near the earth, the blue-hued Narayana descended from within, a beatific smile on his face and a hand lifted in blessing. All those present in Kailasa fell prostrate before the lord of Vaikunta.

'Let us exalt the goddess who has performed this vow in order to enlighten all beings,' said Narayana. 'The wise know that Parvati needs no boon to attain what she desires, for she embodies primordial energy without which there is no life.'

He turned to the goddess then and said, 'Divine One, offer Shiva to Sanat Kumara without any fear. Then you may take your lord back in exchange for a cow, which represents the divinity of the gods.' Having offered his counsel, he returned to his ratha and disappeared into the skies.

Trembling in anxiety, Parvati gave her precious husband to the head priest as his fee. She then sought to reclaim him by making an offering of not one but a hundred thousand cows. But to her horror, Sanat Kumara refused to make the exchange.

'What will a priest do with so many cows?' he asked her. 'Am I a fool to give away the omnipotent Maheshwara who grants moksha and eternal joy?'

The goddess was dumbstruck at the turn of events. How could the blessings of Narayana go awry? Her vrata had not yielded the boon she sought, and worse still, she had lost her lord as well.

A sudden light illumined the skies with a blinding radiance. A fierce heat burned up the slopes of Kailasa. Then the heat changed into the silvery coolness of the moon's rays and a divine fragrance permeated the air. The devas shielded their eyes with their hands and trembled as they beheld the dazzling form standing before them. Divine Krishna had descended from Goloka, clad in golden silk, and wearing his Vaijayanthi garland.

With his arrival, the delusion that had held the world captive was lifted. Sanat Kumara bowed to Krishna and released Shiva to the Devi. She bowed in adoration to Krishna and prayed for a son in his likeness. Krishna granted her the boon and vanished. The joyful Parvati distributed gifts to the poor, and the festive celebrations in Kailasa began.

When the guests had finally departed, the Devi celebrated her love with Shiva in the beautiful gardens surrounding their mansion, where cuckoos sang sweetly and parrots warbled of love.

But their bliss was not to continue for long. An emaciated Brahmin appeared at the doorway of their home and called out to them. Parvati hurried out to welcome him, as the scriptures mandated that a guest be treated like a god. 'I am hungry and thirsty, divine mistress,' said the visitor. 'I heard that you hosted a great feast to celebrate your vrata seeking a child. Treat me as your child, goddess. Honour me with choice foods flavoured with almonds and saffron, and sweetened with sugar and honey. Bring me rice and vegetables cooked in ghee, ripe fruits and sugarcane. Offer me pure water and betel leaves infused with camphor. Then worship sublime Krishna who will come to you as your child.'

Parvati hurried to gather the foods that would please their guest, but was distressed when she returned and could not find him. She was afraid that she had offended him in some way and sent the ganas to look for him. Then she heard a voice from the skies that proclaimed, 'It was Krishna who came to you in the form of an ascetic. But now, he has transformed himself into a child. Your precious son awaits your embrace, Devi!'

The goddess sped through her home on winged feet. She discovered the lustrous infant lying on her bed, his face like the moon and his body the colour of the champaka flower. She called out to Shiva as she lifted the child into her arms and soon the three-eyed lord came to stand beside her and look with pride upon their son.

Brahma came first to bless the newborn. 'You will fill the world with laughter and will be adored in many forms,' he said.

'Time itself will begin with your creation,' said Yama. 'May you be wise like your father and dispense justice in all the realms.'

Then arrived the ascetic god Shanideva, ruler of the planet Saturn. He bowed in the direction where Parvati was seated, but kept his eyes half-shut, meditating on Krishna.

'Why do you not look upon my son?' asked Parvati, construing it as a slight to herself and her child.

'It is because I do not wish to harm the infant,' he replied. 'My wife cursed me because I disregarded her call when I was lost in dhyana. She said that anyone I looked upon would be destroyed.'

Parvati laughed at his explanation and her attendants joined her in mocking him. 'Stop your foolish prattling and look at my son,' she ordered.

And fate stepped in.

7

A Secret Revealed

Shanideva grew desperate. His throat felt parched. Cornered by Parvati's command, he slowly turned his head and cast a sidelong glance at the child. At once, the child's head fell off his shoulders and vanished to merge with Krishna in Goloka. Parvati wailed in agony as she looked down on her son's headless body. Shani hung his head in fear and dejection. The gods stood stupefied like paintings on a wall.

Vishnu reassured them and then flew into the skies on his Garuda. He found a king elephant sleeping with his head to the north and severed his head. The elephant's mate began to wail at the death of the elephant king, and the merciful god drew out another head from the severed one and used it to bring the dead elephant back to life. He then hastened to Kailasa, fixed the head on the child's neck and revived him.

'Parvati's son will be worshipped henceforth as Ganapati, lord of the ganas, and Varaprada, granter of boons,' he said. 'He will obtain the exalted knowledge of Brahma with my blessings.'

Parvati gazed angrily at Shani and cursed him with lameness. However, Shani's brother Yama and his father Surya chastised

58

her. 'Devi, you were the one who ordered Shani to look at your son even after he told you clearly that it would cause him harm,' they pointed out.

The goddess realized that she was at fault and blessed Shani, saying that though she could not retract her curse, he would be venerated thereafter as the king of the planets and the best of ascetics.

Shiva smiled upon his son and said, 'I grant you the throne of meditation, and the power to redeem the world.'

Surya presented him with incandescent earrings and Varuna a bejewelled parasol. Soma brought Ganapati a wreath of brilliant pearls while the sages worshipped him with sandal, aloe and vermilion. Saraswati ordained that he would be the god of memory and magic, of wit and creative genius.

'I bless you with valour, my son,' said Parvati. 'You will embody the light of wisdom that guides devotees to moksha.'

Goddess Lakshmi said, 'At the opportune time, you will marry a girl who will be as lovely and loving as me. Her name will be Pushti and she will help you ensure the well-being of the universe.'

Suddenly, Ganesha and Riddhi were back in the forest amidst the chatter of birds. They could hear the turbulence of the Ganga that was swollen with the melting of the snow in the mountains. Buddhi came to join them, with Neela perched on her shoulder, trilling as she fed him some grapes.

'You have not told us anything about Pushti,' said Riddhi, 'though I am sure that I am much prettier than she could have ever been!' She lifted up her chin in challenge. 'What was so special about her, except that she showered you with extravagant praise?'

'She gave me two sons, Kshema and Labha, who bless my devotees with prosperity and profit,' he replied.

Riddhi stared at him for a moment in silence. There was nothing she could say to this. She walked away, deciding to seek out her Sumukha whose adoration was always pleasing.

Buddhi lingered, her face tense. Ganesha looked silently at her and waited for her to speak.

'Born by Krishna's grace . . .' she murmured. 'And we know that the lord of Dwaraka had 16,000 wives.'

Ganesha looked mournfully at her. He had to win the three sisters over for they were essential to his happiness and the well-being of the world. But it seemed that he took one step forward only to retreat two steps. While Buddhi was deep and brooding, Siddhi was still hostile. How could he ever succeed?

Then he heard a voice in his ear. His face brightened and he nodded vigorously. 'I am truly blessed, divine Krishna!' he said. Who could help him woo these girls better than the god who danced with the gopis? He saw Buddhi staring at him with a question in her eyes. 'I will tell you one day,' he replied. *If I ever succeed in winning your heart,* he added to himself.

In the days that followed, Ganesha spent all the time he could with the three sisters, taking various forms in order to appeal to them. As Sumukha, he courted Riddhi with ardent protestations of love, his eyes stormy and his hair dishevelled and falling in curls to his shoulders.

'When will you be my very own, sweet Riddhi? Do you not hear me call for you through the night like the chakravaka bird separated from its mate?' he asked her as he wove bright jasmine blossoms into her tresses. 'The parrots in the parijata tree will tell you how I toss ceaselessly like the ocean when I am away from you. I waste away like the crescent moon, yearning for you when you leave me each day.'

Riddhi delighted in hearing his extravagant verses and rewarded him with sweet kisses. She made him garlands of wild flowers and showered him with adoration.

'I am jealous of your flute as it tastes your lips by day and night,' she said. 'I envy the sylvan pools that worship your body with their crystal waters. No god can ever equal you in grace or charm, dearest Sumukha.'

As for Buddhi, Ganesha knew that he had to woo her with prose from the puranas and poetry from the Vedas. He taught her the meaning of Om and helped her meditate on the Supreme. He helped her rescue wounded creatures and to transfer fish from a fast-depleting pool to a larger one fed by a babbling brook.

Buddhi called him Adi when they were alone, for to her he would always be the young lad who had defied Vishnu and Shiva for his mother. He was the dauntless Vinayaka with the blissful face and whimsical smile. Taller than most men, with thick dark hair flying in the wind, he was always prepared for a challenge. He would protect them with his might and his wits. He was friendly and generous of heart, blessing his devotees when they brought him a dish of honey, a luscious mango or a blue lily. He would sit with her for hours explaining the laws of karma, or help her understand philosophical texts. Then he would prance blissfully under the trees without a care in the world. His myriad forms and moods intrigued her. Which one was the real Ganesha? Was he everything he appeared to be or was he putting on an act to win her over? She had grown to like him a great deal, but some doubts still lingered in her mind.

Even the quick-tempered Siddhi was impressed by his prowess when he whirled Parasurama into the skies and granted her a vision of the higher lokas. She grudgingly allowed him to teach her how to use her weapons better. However, she swiftly demolished any hopes that Ganesha may have had of getting closer to her with these lessons.

'I seek your help only because I wish to equip myself for my fight with Kamasura,' she said, looking directly into his eyes. 'But that is all. I will give you the respect due to a teacher, but do not misconstrue my actions to mean anything more.'

At least respect is better than hostility, Ganesha consoled himself.

When Siddhi told her sisters and her guru about her progress, Sage Kapila told her that it was essential for her to learn something that was on a higher plane. 'Do not underestimate Lord Ganesha because of his unusual appearance or his impish air,' he said. 'He presides over the muladhara chakra, which is the base chakra and enables you to connect to universal energy.'

'What does that mean to me?' Siddhi asked him.

'It means that he is the only one who can help you unlock your true power, awakening the kundalini shakti residing within you. Shiva's son is the gatekeeper between the material and spiritual realms, and only with his guidance can you control the lower energies such as fear, lust and ego. Hence, you cannot subdue Kamasura without Ganesha's help.'

As Siddhi's sole objective was to defeat the asura, she put aside all other considerations to seek Ganesha's aid in this as well, and he readily obliged. Soon she began to spend all her waking hours with him. They meditated together and performed the mandated rituals to unleash her inner power. Encouraged by their increasingly harmonious relationship, he approached her diffidently one day to ask her something that had been troubling him from the time they had first met.

'We have known each other awhile and I thought I could take the liberty to ask you a question,' he began tentatively.

'Yes?' she encouraged him to go on.

'I would like to find out . . . maybe you can tell me . . . what is the reason for your earlier rancour towards me?' he finished in a rush.

'To understand that, we must return to your avatara as Vikata,' she said. 'You may not remember me, but I remember you—with great anger!'

Vikata. Meaning 'unusually handsome'. Ganesha in this avatara was as splendid and brilliant as Surya. His face was divine; his head was not that of an elephant. His body was exquisitely sculpted and rivalled that of Kama. He was a vision of radiance, his eyes pools of wisdom. His vaahana was a peacock, symbolizing the beauty of the universe with its proudly raised head, its sleek neck and its magnificent feathered fan. The three realms marvelled at Vikata's beauty, while the gods adored him as the embodiment of the cosmic spirit.

Shiva's son sat absorbed in fervent tapasya, wishing to invoke the powers of the Trimurti and the Shaktis. Tales of his scholarship, his prowess in fighting evil and his endearing nature spread far and wide. Devotees flocked to him and stood gazing in wonder as his body glowed with a fierce luminosity. Among them was Siddhi, who too had been enchanted by stories of his myriad feats. Her admiration was transformed to ardour when she saw his lustrous form, and she began to meditate on him, with the desire to be united with him in marriage.

Siddhi watched and admired. She waited and prayed. When Vikata finally opened his eyes, she bashfully approached him and offered herself in marriage. However, he quickly rejected her, not even explaining why he could not marry her. She realized that he had not taken her seriously enough to even glance at her. Her intense prayers to him seemed not to matter either. His stern rebuff in front of hundreds of devotees who had gathered there wounded her pride. He had insulted her, made her feel unworthy. It was as if her piety, her purity and beauty were of no significance. She grew angry and construed his behaviour as a planned insult to her. Why had she demeaned herself by offering her love to someone who did not value it?

Siddhi's heart was broken, her happiness destroyed. Her resentment soon grew into a rage. Vikata was not worthy of her love. She would spurn him one day just as he had spurned her. She finally immolated herself, her heart still burning within her.

Ganesha was distressed to hear the story. His eyes were moist as he attempted to explain that he had meant her no insult. But she was not ready to listen to him. It appeared as if all her anger had returned as she narrated the events.

'I can remember no earlier life except this one, perhaps because I was scarred by your reaction,' she said angrily. 'I recall your arrogance each time I see you, especially when you take a human face that reminds me of Vikata. How do you expect me to love you now when you spurned me so cruelly? No explanation you give can excuse your actions.'

'Nevertheless, I beg you to listen, Siddhi,' he said, looking pleadingly at her. When she did not protest or turn away,

Ganesha was encouraged to continue. He began to tell her everything about his birth and life as Vikata.

Brahma had been performing tapasya with his consort Saraswati, when he grew distracted by her beauty. He knew that this was not the time for such thoughts and plunged himself into the waters of a clear pond. But from his desire and momentary lapse of concentration was born the lustful Kamasura.

Due to his origin in Brahma's energy, the asura was so powerful that one day he captured Soma with his bare hands. Indra and the other devas had to plead with him to let Soma go, as the earth and its creatures suffered immensely without the light of the moon. Kamasura then began an intense tapasya in order to secure a boon from Shiva that would render him immortal. When the heat of his penance tormented devaloka, Shiva was forced to appear before him.

'Bless me with powers that will confound Brahma and Indra,' said Kamasura. Shiva raised his hand in blessing. 'And grant me immortal life,' he added.

'All beings that are born must die,' replied the lord of Kailasa. 'Seek some other boon.'

'Bless me with two lives wherein I will reign unrivalled in the three realms. Let me not be killed by any deva. Grant that I may be defeated only by someone imbued with the energies of the Trinity and their Shaktis, someone with the power to defeat the eight demons—envy, intoxication, delusion, greed, anger, lust, attachment and pride.'

'You seek to make yourself invincible with all these stipulations,' smiled Shiva. 'Nevertheless, I grant you the boon you seek.'

Thus blessed by Shiva, Kamasura invaded heaven and defeated Indra and his retinue and made them pay homage to him. Next he defeated the nagas, the gandharvas, the rakshasas, yakshas and humans.

Seeing Siddhi's rapt face, Ganesha pressed on with his tale. 'Earth was in disarray due to Kamasura's excesses, as were the heavens,' he said. 'I was born then as Vikata for the purpose of destroying him. In order to accomplish this, I embarked upon a severe tapasya to invoke the powers of the Trimurti and the Shaktis. I had to be celibate, abjuring Kama so that I could conquer Kamasura. Hence, I followed the stringent path of brahmacharya—achara or conduct leading to the realization of the Brahman within us. When the great powers awoke in me, I fought a fierce battle with Kamasura and defeated him. But due to Shiva's boon that he would enjoy two lives of unrivalled power, he was able to escape. He has now taken birth as Prince Gana and continues to torment the universe. I hope you can understand why I could not allow love into my life as Vikata. Due to the fierceness of my penance, I could not even look upon your face lest I should be diverted from my purpose. I realize now that I wounded you grievously with my seeming disregard, and beg your forgiveness and understanding.'

He looked at her face with hope, for they were meant to be together. Siddhi saw the love in his eyes, but was not yet ready to give in. She focused instead on setting free the dormant shakti within her without which she could not hope to defeat Kamasura. And to do this, she needed Gajamukha to be her teacher.

'The kundalini rests like a coiled serpent at the base of your spine,' he said. 'To awaken this energy, you need to discard your ego and realize your true self through inner purification. Then you have to raise your awareness to the crown of your head through meditation and devotion.'

He had put it simply, but the path to this awakening was not easy, especially to a girl who was used to having her own way. Siddhi had led a pampered life with a family that indulged her every mood and defended her headstrong temperament. To now control her mind and rein in her impulses was difficult, but Ganesha was with her at every step, always patient, as he explained, guided, pushed and motivated.

'I think it would be easier to defeat a hundred armies than to subdue my mind!' she exclaimed one day, after yet another arduous session during which she failed to attain the mental clarity that she sought. Would she be able to achieve her goal before Kamasura descended on them?

8

The Chintamani

Ganesha was not ready to give up so easily, however. Every time Siddhi glanced at his smiling face, she felt her energy expand once more. She persisted with her efforts, making steady progress, until one day Parvati showered her blessings upon her.

Siddhi was thrilled at the wondrous power that surged through her body and mind like a flood of nectar. She chanted the Devi's thousand names in thanksgiving. And then she bowed gratefully to Ganesha without whom her enlightenment would not have been possible.

Will she accept me now? he wondered. And waited. But there was no time for more.

Buddhi came running to him, carrying something carefully in her cupped palms. He saw that it was Neela, bleeding from a wound on his shoulder. 'Prince Gana—Kamasura is here!' she exclaimed in panic. 'He saw me while I was on my way here and pursued me. I fled down hidden paths in the forest but the monster wounded Neela with an arrow. Adi, you must save him. Can you? Please say that you can. He is in so much pain!' she cried.

Siddhi took up guard with her bow and arrows at the ready, waiting to see if the asura had followed her sister to their arbour. Meanwhile, Ganesha took the bird gently from Buddhi and slowly moved his hand over the bird's bleeding body. A silvery light enveloped the bird and the edges of the wound closed. He moved his palm over the bird again and Neela stirred slowly, giving a feeble cheep. His hand moved a third time and now Neela stood up on Ganesha's palm. Buddhi wept with relief and gave Ganesha a tremulous smile of gratitude. The young god bent to whisper something in the bird's ear and Neela hopped for an instant onto her shoulder and then vanished among the trees.

'What did you say? Why did he fly away?' asked Buddhi.

'It is not safe for him to be near you as long as Kamasura is in pursuit,' replied Ganesha. 'The demon delights in venting his spleen on innocent creatures. Neela will return to you once the coast is clear.'

'Let us go now,' said an anxious Siddhi. 'Kapila and his students will be helpless if Kamasura were to attack them now. We can only hope that he does not reach the ashram looking for Buddhi.'

But her hopes were in vain. It was not difficult for the asura to discover the ashram nestled in the trees near the river. He came with his demon army, tearing down the huts, driving out the ascetics and kicking mud and stones into the sacrificial fires to extinguish them. As he stood laughing at the havoc he had caused, Siddhi emerged with her weapons and shouted at him to stop.

His eyes devoured her beauty and he ordered his men to move back so that he could talk to her. 'So you were the one who fled from me that day,' he said, leering. She stood silent, unwilling to reveal that there were three of them. But, alas! Her sisters had come to stand by her side in a misguided attempt to show their support.

'Three girls, each one a gem!' he exclaimed. 'You three will be the crown jewels in my harem. I thank the gods that I came this way . . . But no! I forget that there are no more gods in heaven. I myself am now Indra, Surya and Brahma. And all that I see is mine!' He roared with arrogant laughter.

He strode forward swiftly, eager to embrace their petal-soft bodies and kiss their sweet lips. Riddhi and Buddhi cowered behind Siddhi as she drew out her sword.

'You will have to kill me before you can lay hands on me and my sisters,' she declared.

He stopped in his tracks, howling in amusement. 'Do you think you can fight a warrior who has defeated Indra?' he scoffed. 'You look so beautiful with your eyes of fire! Tell me your name, sweet one. Whose daughter are you and why do you live here with these dour ascetics?'

'We are Brahma's daughters,' Siddhi replied. 'I hear that you too were born from our father's energy. Hence, we are your sisters, though it is not a relationship that I am proud of. Leave us now, Kamasura, and we will attempt to forget your coarse overtures.'

'I do not obey the rules the gods have laid down,' he retorted. 'And Shiva's boon makes me impervious to your father's powers. Therefore, I see no hurdle to satisfying my desire with the three of you!'

'You are loathsome!' shouted Siddhi. 'Fly from here or I will tear you from limb to limb!'

'I see that you are pretending disinterest so as to inflame my passion, temptress,' he said. 'But your curved body and flashing eyes have already weakened me with desire. Come to me and we will have glorious sons who will rule the universe.'

'Brahma's daughters to become members of your harem? Stop dreaming, asura!'

'So you are jealous of my other queens!' he exclaimed. 'Do not worry, for I will cast them aside, though they may be exquisite princesses and apsaras. I will marry you three and we will reign together until the end of time, like Shiva and Parvati.'

Sage Kapila arrived in haste, aroused from his meditation on the banks of the Ganga by the news that the asura prince had descended on the ashram.

Kapila welcomed the prince with cordial words and escorted him to his own seat under a banyan tree. He had his students bring him the traditional madhuparka, a mix of honey, curd and ghee. He hoped that if he treated Kamasura as an honoured guest, he would be persuaded not to harm his people. The sage saw the asura's lustful glances and wondered if he should send the three girls away to their father's abode. But Brahma was too old to be able to protect them. It would be better that they stayed here under the protection of the valiant Ganesha.

'Let me offer you my humble hospitality,' said Kapila. 'You and your men have travelled from afar and I can provide you with food and drink to refresh yourselves.'

'A beggar offers his prince fruits and berries!' mocked Kamasura before accepting his invitation. Kapila astounded him by conjuring up a huge feast with an unending array of food and wine.

'I have never tasted food so exquisite even in devaloka,' said the asura in astonishment. 'Tell me how an ascetic like you could provide such a rich spread.'

'This is the blessing of the Chintamani gem that Indra gave me, a rare prize given to him by Vishnu,' said the rishi. 'There is nothing that the gem cannot yield, and no boon that is beyond its power.'

Kamasura's eyes widened in greed. 'Such a great jewel should adorn a palace, not a hut!' he exclaimed. 'Moreover, have you not taken a vow to forsake all riches and lead an ascetic life? So give me the gem, Kapila.'

The rishi was taken aback by his demand. 'I offer worship every day to the Chintamani which is dearer to me than life itself,' he replied. 'Ask me for anything else, but not the jewel.'

Kamasura argued with him, but Kapila remained adamant. The asura stayed on in the forest and tormented the sage with his fervid requests to give him the gem. Each time, Siddhi stood guard next to Kapila, resolved to protect him. But the asura refused to take her seriously.

'You must show me your skills in my bed, not in battle,' he told her. 'Your lips are meant to be kissed and your body to be caressed, not pierced by swords and arrows. Come to me, Siddhi, and I will quench your desire. The Chintamani will soon be mine, and with its power added to mine, I will lay the earth at your feet.'

'Who will marry a monster like you?' Siddhi shouted angrily. 'You are vile and abuse the boons given by the great gods. Even if I marry, it will be to someone who is my equal in valour and virtue, not a coward who preys on women and ascetics. Do not delude yourself that I refuse you in order to increase your ardour. My aim is to kill you, foul creature!'

Her harsh words finally struck home. Kamasura screamed abuses like a madman. He cut down the students who guarded the Chintamani and snatched it from its shrine. 'This is my last warning to you,' he roared. 'The gem belongs to me now and so will you. Tonight is the full moon and I leave you now to perform the rituals to invest myself with the powers of the Chintamani. But I will return for you and your sisters. You would be wise not to protest then, or I will kill your guru and his students before your eyes!'

The asura was flanked by his men, monsters all, armed to the teeth with dire weapons and occult powers. Kapila stretched out an arm to stop Siddhi who pushed forward with an oath. He knew that even if she killed Kamasura's men, she could not defeat the asura himself who was armed with mighty boons.

The sage's rage however erupted in a curse. 'I swear now in the name of the god I worship that you will pay for this sacrilege!' he proclaimed. 'Look your fill on this earth, asura, for soon you will burn in the fires of the netherworld.'

As the asura stormed away, Kapila returned to his altar to meditate on Ganesha, saying that only Shiva's son had the power to defeat Kamasura.

However, Siddhi was irate and swore that she would tear the asura prince to pieces and restore the gem to her guru. When she saw Buddhi looking worriedly at her, Siddhi assured her that with her new powers she could easily accomplish the task.

It appears that Siddhi's tussle with her ego will continue every day of her life, thought Buddhi as she hurried to Ganesha to seek his help. She told him what had happened, her hands twisting together in anxiety. 'Once he invests himself with the powers of the Chintamani, Prince Gana will become invincible, and I fear for our safety and that of our guru,' she said. 'I am worried too that Siddhi will attempt something dangerous in the heat of the moment.'

Ganesha nodded in agreement, for he knew well how powerful Kamasura was. He knew also that Siddhi was likely to embark on a hasty mission without thinking it through.

Siddhi frowned when she saw Buddhi enter the ashram with Ganesha. 'It is clear that you do not trust me,' she said to Buddhi. 'But I am determined to fight the asura myself, though I honour and respect Ganesha who has done so much to equip me for this battle.'

'I will honour your wish,' Ganesha replied. 'I will accompany you to the battlefield but remain a spectator unless you call me yourself.' Siddhi gazed at him doubtfully and he offered further assurances. 'I allowed the trishul to behead me and Parasurama's axe to sever my tusk only because I respected my parents. How then will I disregard your wishes when you are so important to me?'

She saw the love in his eyes and lowered her own in confusion. Ganesha stayed silent, waiting for her decision. This was his last chance to win her over. If he failed now, his present avatara on earth would be a failure too.

Siddhi looked up at him, her mind made up. 'Let us hurry to find the asura!' she said. 'The sun hovers on the edge of the horizon, and when the moon rises, Kamasura will begin his rituals. We must defeat him before he joins the power of the Chintamani with his own. He will then be able to multiply his troops and his weapons at will and we will be unable to defeat him.'

Ganesha nodded and they left, silhouetted against the setting sun.

It was not difficult to find the asura's camp as he made no attempt to hide his whereabouts, so confident was he that no one could harm him.

Ganesha and Siddhi mounted two wild horses they had broken in, and approached the clearing where his troops were assembled. Shiva's son stayed back in the shadows while Siddhi blew her war conch in challenge to the asura.

On seeing her galloping towards him alone, Kamasura laughed in scorn. 'Even my young sons will be able to kill you,' he said. 'But I will order them to bind you and bring you to me, so that I may enjoy your beauty in my bed. However, as you so rudely spurned my offer of marriage, I will treat you as a slave and not a queen. And when I have had my fill of your charms, I will cast you out to be used by my soldiers.'

Siddhi roared in anger, and a huge army was born from her newly awakened shakti. From the men's foreheads blazed flames that enveloped the asura's army and sent them shrieking to their death. Kamasura's young sons fought back fiercely with iron clubs, poison-tipped arrows and sorcerous weapons. Their retinue of giants hacked off heads and limbs, while a battalion of misshapen beasts immobilized Siddhi's soldiers with their eerie squeals, and tore them to shreds with their curved tusks, fanged mouths and giant beaks. The field was grisly with blood, and the skies echoed with the screams of the dying.

Brave Siddhi was everywhere, bringing down giants and demons alike, attacking the asura army with her mace and spear, her arrows and trident. Behind her came a phalanx of her men, carrying axes that they used to behead the asuras. Siddhi's foes were so terrified that their mouths continued to clamour for help even as their heads rolled across the battlefield.

Soon, the asura's sons had been captured and the last of their men routed. 'This is *my* last warning to you, Kamasura!' shouted Siddhi, echoing his words to her. 'Return the Chintamani to our guru, seek his forgiveness, and I will let your men leave the field alive. I will spare your life too as long as you give up your wicked ways and choose a righteous path. If you will not do so, I will kill you and drink your blood!'

9

The Mute God

Kamasura felt a frisson of fear. He saw a vision of Yamaloka opening its gates in readiness for him. Siddhi appeared to be fiery Durga herself come to annihilate him. But his ministers would not let him see reason. 'You are invincible, O prince!' they said. 'You defeated Indra who wields the thunderbolt and won boons from Shiva. Your enemy now is but a slender girl riding a wild horse. Why then do you hesitate?'

The asura's arrogance overwhelmed him again. He shook away the dire visions that troubled him, summoned the rest of his fierce troops to accompany him and sallied forth into the battlefield. Siddhi's eyes spewed fire on seeing him and from her energy rose a gigantic, thousand-armed warrior, Laksha. When he twanged the bowstrings of the 100 huge bows he wielded, the sound shattered distant mountaintops and sundered the earth.

Kamasura ordered his generals to fight Laksha while he himself focused on Siddhi, playing with her as if she were a toy. He shot down her horse first and made her tumble to the ground. His next arrows skimmed off the ruby earrings she wore. When she rose to her feet, trembling with rage, he sent a jasmine garland flying on the back of an arrow to fall gently around her neck.

Siddhi conjured up a silver chariot for herself and mounted a blistering attack on the asura with fierce astras that lit up the darkening skies like many suns. But he shot them down, one by one, with astras of his own that flashed towards her with a sinister howl. He trapped her next in a silver cage of glittering arrows, but she broke through them with the might of her axe. Her body was torn and bleeding but her indomitable spirit kept her going.

But for how much longer?

Buddhi and Riddhi ran sobbing to Ganesha who was watching from the periphery of the battlefield.

'How can you watch silently while the asura torments Siddhi?' asked Riddhi. 'Do you not love us enough to help her?'

'We know you promised not to intervene unless she invoked your help,' said Buddhi, her eyes pools of pain. 'But what if she is too foolish to realize that she will be stronger with your help? If she were to die now, could any of us survive the loss?'

Ganesha did not reply but stood frozen like a statue, his eyes alone revealing his anguish at what was happening. Kapila and the other ascetics watched silently, hoping that the elephant-headed god would put an end to the battle and defeat the asura.

Siddhi struck Kamasura with a firestorm of arrows that set his chariot ablaze, but he jumped to the ground before his panicked horses fled into the forest. He created a monstrous chariot for himself, with wheels as high as the tallest trees in the forest. The ratha rolled forward, crushing Siddhi's soldiers like ants in an elephant's path. Siddhi broke the axle of his ratha with her carefully aimed arrows and laughed in her turn when the asura was thrown to the ground. She assailed him with the weapons of Agni and Vayu and he countered them with those of Varuna and Indra. The forest shook, tormented by the force of a hundred hurricanes and tossed by a deluge of a thousand floods. It was a duel of will, a dance of death, where one misstep could result in catastrophe. Siddhi fought long and hard, wounding Kamasura again and again, but Yama could not touch him as long as he was protected by Shiva's boon.

Battered sorely, bleeding from a dozen deep wounds, Kamasura decided to put an end to his foe with the power of his occult weapons. He sent out a sorcerous shaft that separated into a thousand arrows, hiding the single real arrow aimed at her heart. Ganesha stirred in apprehension, torn between his vow to abstain and his fear for his beloved Siddhi. What if the phantom arrows diverted her attention from the actual shaft imbued with the potency of the asura's energy? His hands flew to his own bow but he desisted from arming it with a supreme effort of will and continued to watch, his heart in his mouth.

However, Siddhi's luminous shakti was alive and warned her of the danger speeding towards her. She strung her bow with the Mohini astra that embodied the power of Vishnu to destroy all forms of maya. The astra hurtled into the heart of the firestorm, splitting the asura's potent arrow in two, and making the false arrows disappear. Ganesha laughed joyfully, proud that his Siddhi had mastered the war craft he had imparted and put it to good use.

Alas! Ganesha's movements caught the attention of Kamasura who spotted him standing guard in the shadows. With his instincts honed by tapasya, the asura immediately realized that it was his old foe, Vikata, who had followed him into this life to kill him. He shivered as he felt the dark wings of death brush his body.

Then he forced his mind to shed all fear and called out a challenge. 'Is this the god you invoked to fight me, Kapila? How can this weakling who cowers in the shadows take on the power of my boons?'

'Your arrogance blinds you to the power of the god born to destroy you, asura,' replied Kapila. 'Run away now or pay for your conceit with your life.'

'Watch while I kill your mute god and seize the girls whom Brahma entrusted to your protection!' swore Kamasura, ignoring Siddhi and advancing upon Ganesha. The god's mace, goad and axe sprang into his hands but he stood unmoving, as if cast in stone. Encouraged by his strange stupor, Kamasura directed a fusillade of arrows at him, aiming for the parts left uncovered by his armour. Some struck Ganesha's head and others his arms and feet. 'Look, he bleeds!' laughed the asura. 'Perhaps he is not a statue after all.'

'Ganesha, you must defend yourself, or he will kill you!' shouted Riddhi, her voice shrill with fear.

'I saw you defeat Vishnu and Shiva!' sobbed Buddhi. 'Why do you stay silent now, Adi?'

Siddhi watched as more and more arrows struck Ganesha, causing blood to flow like a flood. Was he ready to meet death rather than forsake his promise to her? Would he sacrifice everything for the sake of his love? She could hear her sisters' wails and the frantic prayers of Kapila and his students. Ganesha's eyes met hers and she heard him whisper in her ear. 'If I do not win your love, I might as well die,' he said.

The triumphant asura approached his foe with his mace upraised, ready to bring it down on Ganesha's head. Riddhi knew that if he died she would lose everything. The three realms would be tormented to eternity by the demon prince. Kapila and his students would be killed and she and her sisters captured. She might as well kill herself now for she could not live without him. What was Ganesha waiting for? Was it for Siddhi to say something? Why was her sister so adamant? Riddhi sobbed as if her heart would break.

Her sisters' sobs and prayers echoed in Siddhi's head. She realized that everything depended on her now. If she remained obstinate, it would cause the death, rather the slaughter, of her benefactor, friend and guru. She knew that despite everything he had taught her, she was still clinging to her ego, the last barrier to self-realization. And the world would pay the price.

Kamasura was just a few strides away from Parvati's son. Siddhi had already shown the world that she could fight the asura. And now she knew that with Gajamukha by her side she could fight all the asuras in the universe. Ganesha would deliver the killing blow at times while she did so at others. The two of them belonged together—as Siddhi Vinayaka. She realized that she loved him and could not let him die.

Siddhi raised her hands and called out to Ganesha for help. But was she too late? The mace had already begun its downward arc. Her scream was echoed by her sisters and by all those who were praying for them. Siddhi closed her eyes to shut out the horror of watching Ganesha's head split open by the monstrous mace. Alas, she was a sinner, doomed to spend her remaining days in torment.

Then she heard Riddhi scream. What was happening? She saw Ganesha's danda consuming the asura's mace with searing tongues of flame. The god was now mounted on a rampant lion that roared so fiercely that the asura's horse retreated in a frenzy of fear. As Kamasura struggled to stay on its back, Shiva's son rode towards Siddhi, a brilliant smile lighting up his face. She sprang up behind the young god so that the two of them could fight the asura together.

A ripple ruffled the treetops as if all the realms were sighing in relief. The devas and sages on high began to chant mantras of worship to Gajamukha. Riddhi and Buddhi prayed to Parvati to watch over her valiant son. Thunder echoed in the skies like

Indra's celebratory drums. Brilliant Soma shone above them, enthralled that he would not be presiding over the asura's victory.

Kamasura managed to rein in his horse and turn it around. He hurled Indra's formidable vajra at his foes. But Ganesha countered with the parasu that Parasurama had given him. The two fierce weapons collided in mid-air and then disappeared in an explosion of light. The asura attacked next with a barrage of arrows, javelins and astras glowing with unearthly power.

Ganesha retaliated with a flurry of golden arrows that blinded the asura with their radiance. When the asura managed to open his eyes, he saw before him countless Ganeshas, astride his many vaahanas—lion, mouse, peacock and even the serpent, Adisesha. One form was blue-hued, another was white. Others had bodies the colour of the blue lotus or the hibiscus. They were clad in robes of regal yellow and brilliant orange. One of them had a single elephant's head, while others had four or five. One form had four arms while others had six or ten. As Vira Ganapati, Ganesha wielded a staff, a bow, a sword and other weapons in his sixteen arms. As Heramba, he glowed like a golden mountain, his cheeks anointed with vermilion and his battle axe proclaiming his victory over the asuras.

Kamasura stood dumbstruck in his chariot, staring at the terrifying forms as they merged into one. He gathered his wits together with great difficulty and charged forward. Siddhi captured him with a luminous noose and Ganesha pierced him with many arrows. She encircled him with fire and Ganesha pounded him with his club as if he were a tabla.

The asura escaped their hold and took up a huge form. He then showered them with a fusillade of weapons. But the lion they rode leapt at him and tore at his flesh while Ganesha pinned him down with his trident. Kamasura knew that he was nearing death but was defiant still.

'Stop!' he shouted. 'By Shiva's boon I can only be killed by someone who has defeated all the eight asuras I enumerated before the three-eyed god. You may have conquered six of them but Abhimanasura is still to be vanquished.'

'You sought a boon that the one who killed you should have the power to defeat the eight asuras, not that he should kill them all before killing you,' Ganesha replied. 'I have slain six, as you just admitted—Matsaryasura, Madasura, Mohasura, Lobhasura, Krodhasura, Mamasura—and you will be next. As for the last one, Abhimanasura, I will vanquish him in Kali Yuga when I am born as Dhumraketu. To convince you of this, allow me take you into the future and show you his death as well. You will then realize that you have truly reached the end of your wretched life.'

Kamasura saw a vision then of Ganesha as Dhumraketu, the god with the smoke-coloured banner, who embodied the destructive rage of Shiva at the end of the world. He had two arms and a human head, and rode across the universe on an ash-coloured horse. He wielded a mighty sword with which he struck off Abhimanasura's head. Then he killed all the sinners who populated the world in dark Kali Yuga, growing angrier by the moment as he saw how evil had spread far and wide.

His rage grew and grew until it heated up all the earth. The mighty Adisesha, who bore the universe on his head, was unable to bear the heat and began to emit poisonous flames from his thousand mouths. The earth was scorched by the dual attack and smoke rose to the skies to form dense clouds. Torrential rains poured for a hundred years and the deluge submerged all creation.

The gods prayed fervently for a thousand years, and finally Adi Vinayaka rose in vishvarupa to remove the darkness and usher in the light of a new kalpa. A new Satya Yuga was born and would be followed in time by Treta, Dwapara and Kali Yuga.

Seeing the mighty god in his primordial form after he had destroyed all the obstacles to enlightenment, Kamasura prostrated himself before him. 'Dauntless Ganesha, I have seen your form as the supreme god with infinite heads, unnumbered eyes and limitless powers,' he said. 'I have watched as you straddled the universe and extended beyond, transcending the past, present and future. The vision has transformed me, destroying the evil within and creating a new gana—your true devotee. Allow me, great god, to atone for my sins by spending the rest of my life at your feet.'

Siddhi looked at Ganesha's face, wondering if he would show mercy. Was it necessary to kill the asura in order to fulfil his mission?

10

A Lost Cause?

Ganesha smiled at Siddhi. Did she even have to ask him what he was going to do? She smiled back. The gracious god would certainly forgive his devotee. Moreover, had Kamasura not been the instrument to bring them together? He raised a hand in blessing over the asura prince.

The survivors from the demon army had long vanished into the forest. Riddhi and Buddhi came running when they saw the asura fall at Ganesha's feet. Kapila and his students followed, raising their voices in praise of their valiant saviour. The chastened asura returned the gem he had stolen from the sage.

'Do me the honour of accepting the Chintamani, Ganesha!' said Kapila. 'I no longer wish for this gem when I see before me the god who is the source of all blessings.'

The rishi installed Ganesha's idol in a sacred spot and offered him worship. Devotees from far and wide flocked to pay obeisance to the lord who soon became known as Kapila Vinayaka.

The devas had been in hiding for long due to their fear of the asura. As they were the embodiments of the panchabhootas, the natural elements too had been in disarray, and chaos had reigned over the universe. But now that Kamasura had been vanquished, the gods resumed their duties and restored balance in nature.

'O Ganapati!' they chanted in unison. 'You are Brahma, Vishnu and Shiva. You are Indra. You are fire and air. You are the sun and the moon. You are Brahman, the supreme soul. You are earth, space and heaven. You are Om!'

The rivers now flowed crystal clear, babbling joyously that evil had been vanquished. Trees grew lush and green and birds trilled happily that life was sweet once more. Bountiful rains revived the parched earth, which blossomed with rich crops, fruits and flowers. Men shed the sickness of spirit that had held them captive and looked to the sages once more for guidance. The Vedas were sung, the gods were worshipped and bliss enveloped the ravaged world.

Kapila smiled at the sisters and told them that they could find no better husband than Ganesha. 'You must seek out and worship the idol of Ganesha made of another gem,' he said. 'The Chandrakanta or moonstone symbolizes the third eye of enlightenment. When Vishnu fought and killed the pious emperor Bali, he broke the asura's body into several pieces that fell to the earth as different jewels. The Chandrakanta is believed to have been created from the gleam of Bali's eyes.'

'Where will we find this temple, guru?' asked Riddhi.

'The Athisaya Vinayaka with a human face sits under a banyan tree in the south of Bharata Varsha. Devotees pray to him seeking true soulmates and virtuous children.' He nodded meaningfully at the sisters.

'I am expected to not only marry, but to also have children,' murmured Siddhi. 'I wonder if there is a goddess who chose not to have children . . .'

' . . . like Kanyakumari chose not to marry?' asked Ganesha cheerfully. She flashed a warm smile at him, wondering how she could have ever thought of living her life without him.

'Thank you, Krishna!' Ganesha whispered to the heavens, only to have the sisters converge on him with questions.

'I already promised Buddhi that I would reveal all,' he smiled. 'I was thanking Krishna for telling me how to win a woman's heart!' He paused, prolonging the suspense, watching the effect of his words on them. Riddhi lifted up a hand playfully as if to strike him, and he capitulated. 'He told me that the secret of courtship is to make each girl feel that she is the only one for you; to make her think that you would die if she did not return your love!'

'So you made each of us believe that we held your heart in our hands!' said Siddhi, glowering at him. He held up his hands in laughing surrender.

Ganesha had to leave them soon, however, in order to inform his parents formally that he had completed his mission on earth. He would have to also seek his mother's consent and her help in arranging his marriage with Brahma's daughters.

When he reached Kailasa, Nandi welcomed him with the news that his father wished to see him and his brother. Karthikeya was already standing before their parents and Ganesha joined him to find out what his father had to say.

'Brahma has come to me with a proposal of marriage,' said Shiva. 'His three daughters do not wish to be parted from one another and he thinks that one of you could make the ideal groom!'

'Brahma's daughters?' Ganesha repeated, his eyes gleaming.

'Yes. Buddhi, Riddhi and Siddhi. As their names signify, they embody jnana, ichchha and kriya. Whoever marries them will have all that he has ever desired.'

'I will marry them, father,' Ganesha said eagerly. 'What greater bliss can there be than to obey your command?'

'No! I will marry them, not you!' asserted Karthikeya, moving forward with his chin thrust out. 'I am the elder son after all, and should be married first.'

'My devotees worship me as Skandapurvaja, elder to Skanda!' Ganesha argued. 'Maybe you have forgotten that your name is Skanda!'

'Let us not fight over this, my sons,' laughed Shiva. 'Parvati and I love you both equally and we will hold a contest beginning at sunrise tomorrow to resolve the matter. Whoever circumambulates the three realms first will marry the maidens.'

Ganesha was anxious when he heard his father's mandate. He might have defeated countless asuras on earth, but here in Kailasa, he had to obey Shiva. He had to win a race with a brother who rode a fleet peacock while his own vehicle was a mouse. 'I will find some way to win!' Ganesha muttered to himself. 'I cannot lose the girls who have captured my heart.'

His task seemed impossible, to say the least. First, he had to win the race. Then he had to placate his mother who would be angry when she found out that her 'little one' wished to marry not one but three girls. And after all that, he would have to cajole the maidens to accept him. Until now, neither Buddhi nor Siddhi had declared openly that they would marry him.

He returned to Kapila's ashram and shared the news of the race with Riddhi, trying not to show that he was anxious. 'I will never marry your brother,' she said candidly. 'He seems to be angry all the time and always ready for battle. Besides, I have already chosen Sumukha as my groom. So you must do something. Ask your Krishna if you need to!'

She tripped away lightly, hand in hand with her Sumukha, to gush and coo over him in their garden where wild flowers bloomed and swans floated in tranquil pools.

Sumukha wove his usual magic with words. 'You are Prakriti, the perfection of nature,' he said in adoration. 'You are Shakti, who spins dreams into reality. You are Maya, the delightful delusion!' Riddhi reciprocated by ushering him through the gates of bliss with her kisses.

Ganesha went looking for Buddhi and told her about his father's command. She looked at him with huge, solemn eyes. 'You must win the race somehow,' she said. 'When you do so, I will be yours—body, mind and soul!'

His face broke into a delighted smile. Surely, no one could be happier than he was at that moment! His mind was already racing to find a solution to his problem.

The new day dawned. Karthikeya shot into the skies on his trusty peacock and was soon lost to sight. The devas came to watch the drama unfold as they had already seen Ganesha courting the girls for many months. The girls were summoned to Kailasa by Parvati who welcomed them with great affection. They looked at her warily, wondering why she was treating them so differently from their last meeting.

Parvati's next words seemed to hold an answer. 'It seems that you three are to wed Karthikeya and not my little Ganesha!' she said in an outburst of joy. Then she added, looking at Siddhi, 'I remember that you do not wish to marry anyone! I will speak to your father and make sure he accepts your decision.' Did she still feel that way? Siddhi felt unsure now that her wish had been accepted.

'Should we start a fire under Ganesha to make him follow his brother?' whispered Buddhi, wondering why he had not yet set off.

'Why are you still here?' Riddhi asked him openly when he appeared before them after a leisurely bath. She saw that he had taken time to adorn himself in silk and gold, completely ignoring the fact that his brother was speeding ahead of him in the race.

'Where is that lazy mouse of yours?' asked Siddhi, looking around angrily.

The young god merely furrowed his brow in thought and refused to answer. Parvati came behind her son and patted his head affectionately. 'It is good that you are not interested in getting married, son,' she said. 'I will bring you some fresh modakas while you wait for your brother to return!'

When she had disappeared, Buddhi came up to him and stared at him with accusing eyes. Ganesha merely sighed and went away to prepare two seats of durva grass.

'What is this for? What is your plan?' scolded Siddhi. He had pretended to court death for the sake of her love and now . . . now he was letting his brother win them in marriage.

The girls watched impatiently as Ganesha seated his parents on the grass mats. Was he going to perform worship before embarking on the race? How did he expect to catch up with Karthikeya after all this while?

The young god joined his hands together in reverence and walked ponderously around his parents, not once or twice but seven times, as Shiva and Parvati watched him indulgently.

'I should have borrowed our mother's swan and circled the world instead of him!' muttered Riddhi.

'Why a swan? We could have used the lion we rode during our battle with Kamasura!' scowled Siddhi. 'I regret now that I did not persist in my quest to become a sanyasin.'

But Buddhi was hopeful still. Her Adi would not betray their trust. She had seen the honesty in his eyes and his determination to win the race, one way or another. She would place her faith in him and in their love.

Ganesha had now come to a stop before his parents. 'I have won the race, great Shiva!' he said, a beaming smile on his face.

'Bless me, father, and preside over my marriage to Brahma's daughters.'

Shiva laughed heartily at his claim while Parvati protested, 'How could you have won when you have not yet begun the race, my son? If you hurry, you may still have a chance.'

'No, mother,' Ganesha replied. 'You saw me circle the realms seven times already, for to me, you and father are my universe. The Vedas too state that we earn the greatest punya by serving at our parents' feet and that to leave them to go on a pilgrimage is a sin equal to murder. Do our scriptures lie? Can we question their wisdom? Further, even the dullest of minds will acknowledge that the great Mahadeva and Jaganmata embody the world. So do not delay in upholding my claim, Divine One. Allow me to marry the maidens at once.'

Shiva laughed again and nodded. Parvati glared at the girls who began to fear that she would end their lives that very moment. The great goddess summoned them closer.

When they stood before her trembling, she gathered them into her embrace one by one and whispered that she had merely been playing with them. Ganesha watched with a relieved smile. His task was done. He had made the impossible possible. The elders would now make arrangements for the wedding.

The youngsters soon returned to their forest, each girl joining her own Ganesha, ready to chastise him in her own way for putting her through such anxiety.

'I presume then that you are willing to marry me,' Ganesha said to Siddhi, concerned that she had still not expressed her consent. It was his turn to wait now as she gave the question serious thought.

'There is a lot to be said for a life of asceticism,' she said finally. 'Earlier, I worried that my sisters would remain unmarried if I took an oath of celibacy. But now that they are marrying you,

I can continue freely on my path without being burdened by marriage.'

'But . . . but . . .' stammered Ganesha, staring at her nonplussed. Had he come so far only to lose her?

11

A Wedding and a Dispute

Siddhi began to laugh, unable to keep up the pretence any more. Ganesha looked into her eyes and saw his love reflected there. He breathed a sigh of relief and reached out to clasp her hand. 'How did you finally agree to marry me?' he asked, eager to hear her say that she loved his majestic form or the way his eyes crinkled when he smiled, or that she had been enchanted by his grace in battle.

But Siddhi was Siddhi and her answer was filled with deeper meaning. 'I value the integrity that made you honour your word to me though your life and mission were put at risk,' she said. 'More than that, I appreciate the respect you gave me by not taking my consent for granted. You have dispelled my doubts and my distrust, dear Ganesha!'

'How could I not respect someone who is so essential to my happiness, my success and my very being?' he replied. 'You are my Siddhi—infinite and eternal.'

He plucked a hibiscus bud from the shrub near them, gorgeous with its glossy red petals and bright green stem, and offered it to her. When she took it from him, the bud turned into a garland and then into a necklace of rubies and emeralds. He fastened it lovingly around her neck.

They heard devotees chant verses to Vinayaka and his Shakti who blessed the world with knowledge, prosperity and bliss.

'He is creation, she its beauty. He is the battle, she its victory. He is the universe, she its energy. He is knowledge, she its liberating power. Together they embody the realms, and beyond them there is nothing!' they sang.

Riddhi and Buddhi came to them and on their necks too were necklaces like the one he had bestowed on their sister.

'Whenever I am born on earth, you three are born with me,' he said to them. 'You take different forms and names; you are worshipped as one or many goddesses, or as part of me. Each devotee sees the gods in the form that he prefers, worshipping Krishna with Radha in Goloka or Vishnu with Sridevi and Bhudevi in Vaikunta. Not even the Trimurti can act without their Shaktis who destroy evil and then redirect their powers to elevate minds and promote good.'

The gods blessed them from above and said, 'May your grace protect the devout from demons and delusions, from poison and perdition. May you keep them safe in forests and deserts, on battlefields and on the high seas.'

Brahma appeared before the blithe god and worshipped him with a verse from the Vedas. 'They call him Indra, Mitra, Varuna, Agni; he is heavenly Garuda, with the beautiful wings. God is one, though the sages speak of him as many. Obeisance to you, the creator, preserver and destroyer of the universe! I return to you the gifts that you bestowed on me,' he said.

Brahma saw that his daughters were mystified and showed them a vision of what had happened when he had begun his task of creation. 'Nothing happened as it should,' he said. 'My efforts went awry as my creations turned out to be the opposite of what

I had conceived. It was then that I realized that I had not sought the blessings of the Prathama, the first among the celestials. I invoked him by chanting "Om Gam Ganapataye Namaha" for twelve continuous years. When he finally appeared before me, I sought the powers of wisdom, action and desire, which he bestowed on me in the form of my three daughters. And with these powers, I created the world.'

The three girls watched awestruck as the sun emerged from Brahma's eyes, the moon from his thoughts, the heavens from his head, the sky from his belly and the earth from his feet. Then they turned adoring eyes to the Adi Vinayaka with whom they were united for evermore.

Ganesha's marriage with Siddhi, Buddhi and Riddhi was performed with great pomp in Brahmaloka. The celestial architect Vishvakarma built a glittering new city with mansions, crystal ponds and lush gardens rich with fruits and flowers. The guardian deities of the eight directions—Indra, Agni, Yama, Nirurti, Varuna, Vayu, Kubera and Isana—arrived to bless the venue. The kinnaras and vidyadharas helped in decorating the hall and in setting up grand thrones studded with gems. The ganas travelled to the fourteen lokas to invite guests. The kalpavriksha and the divine Kamadhenu came to shower them with celestial gifts. The apsaras and gandharvas staged plays depicting Ganesha's exploits. The mountains, the rivers, the stars and the sages arrived to witness the marriage of Brahma's daughters to Shiva's son, for there could be no greater bliss.

The bridegroom bathed in the sacred waters of the Ganga and donned a scarlet silk dhoti. Nandi Deva adorned him with a diamond diadem, garlands and ornaments of rare splendour. Raja Ganapati mounted his lion and began his journey to Brahmaloka, attended by ganas carrying banners and parasols. Shiva and Parvati came seated on Nandi, laden with gifts and followed by the saptarishis, the twelve Adityas and the eleven Rudras.

Krishna welcomed the guests with fragrant flowers and rose water. He regaled the assembly with the story of a day long ago when he had found that his conch was missing. He had traced it by its sound to far-off Kailasa and hurried there, only to find that young Ganesha had swallowed it. He had entertained the boy with some acrobatics—crossing his arms, grasping his ears with his hands and rapidly sitting up and down. The boy had collapsed in laughter and coughed up the conch.

The guests laughed at the story and marvelled that the boy had grown up now to be married to not one but three beautiful girls.

Indrani helped adorn the brides with jewels and rose garlands, and at the auspicious time, beautiful apsaras brought them to the marriage hall. The rishis chanted the sacred mantras while the vidyadharas sang auspicious songs. Saraswati Devi and Brahma performed the rituals to sanctify the marriage. The devas showered rose petals on the happy groom and his brides. There was great cheer and merrymaking.

Then Krishna ushered his sister's son to a swing that hung in the air under a parijata tree, untethered to heaven or earth. 'A reminder of your idyllic retreat on earth!' he laughed. The swing had a jade seat and gold chains studded with emeralds. Parrots and cuckoos sang a sweet chorus from the branches of the parijata.

Ganesha looked at the swing hanging in mid-air and shook his head, a rumbling laugh shaking his belly. 'Sit, my lovely brides!' he said. 'I will transport you to Goloka on this magical swing.'

Krishna whispered in his ear again. 'You are wise to keep standing, Ganesha!' he said. 'How will you sit in the middle when you have three brides?'

Ganesha chuckled and pushed the swing gently forward. Parvati smiled as she stood with Lakshmi and Saraswati, feasting her eyes on her adorable son and his brides.

And then they heard a raucous shriek that split the skies.

Ganesha stilled for a moment and stopped pushing the swing. The devas saw his serious face and halted their revelry. The gandharvas stopped singing. The swing slowed down and finally came to a stop. The brides stepped down and looked around, puzzled. Another shriek echoed in the clouds overhead and they heard giant wings fluttering like a storm in the making.

There was a flash of iridescent blue and green. A huge bird landed in the clear space that had opened up when the devas scuttled backwards from the bridal party. 'Karthikeya is here!' they exclaimed. 'Skanda, the vanquisher of asuras is here!'

From the back of the peacock leapt a glorious warrior with six heads and twelve arms. He bore many dire weapons, foremost of which was a golden lance embodying his mother's powers. His eyes were red, his eyebrows knitted in rage, and his breath came rapidly as he stood gazing at his brother and his brides, still wearing the nuptial garlands.

'What is this?' bellowed the god of war. 'Have you declared the winner of the race before I returned?' There was an ominous silence as no one there wished to answer. 'My brother was still here when I flew into the skies. I saw neither him nor his lowly rodent as I sped over earth, heaven and the netherworld. How then did he claim the prize?'

His scornful eyes gazed at the devas one by one and then settled on Brahma, the father of the brides.

'Ganesha went around your parents seven times, my son,' said the white-haired Creator, his voice a low whisper. 'Then he declared that he had circled the realms, for the Vedas say that one's parents represent the world.'

'So speaks the guardian of the Vedas!' mocked Karthikeya. 'And did the rest of you uphold my brother's claim? It would seem so, for I can see the bridal garlands still fresh around Ganesha's shoulders. But I refuse to accept his dishonest claim and challenge him to a fight. Let him win in single combat with me and prove that he is the better man!'

Karthikeya stood with his head thrown back and his chest thrust out, challenging the fourteen lokas with his might. Would Ganesha take up the challenge? What other recourse did he have?

Siddhi hissed angrily and her bow flew to her hand. Riddhi and Buddhi cast anxious glances at Shiva and Parvati whose eyes were closed in dhyana. Would no one stop this terrible dispute? What if their husband were to be killed before their eyes? After all, Skanda was the god of war, while Ganesha won his battles more with his wit and wisdom.

'Shiva and Vishnu have blessed our union and there is no need for you to justify your actions to your brother,' said Buddhi, ever the arbiter of righteousness.

'Did I not tell you that I dislike your brother?' Riddhi asked. 'He wishes to kill you, no doubt, so that he can marry us. Do not fall into his trap, dear Sumukha!'

Siddhi saw Skanda's lips curl in derision and she hurried to speak up for her new husband. 'Do not fear this braggart, dear sisters,' she said, casting a scornful look at the challenger.

'Ganesha is far superior to him in his martial skills and will send him flying in just a few moments!'

It was great praise coming from the girl who had doubted him for a long time and showed Ganesha that her transformation was complete. His face split wide open in a grin. Then he lifted a pacifying hand towards his wives and moved forward to confront Skanda.

'I agree to your challenge, brother,' he said. 'Let us test our strength against each other.'

The two descended to a barren desert on earth so that no one else would suffer due to their combat. Brahma's daughters watched fearfully from above, along with the devas.

Skanda stood aggressively with his legs apart and gestured at the skies. In an instant, the stars began to hurtle down towards the earth. The people on earth panicked and ran helter-skelter to escape whatever calamity they portended. Then, Skanda raised his arm again and the stars flew back to their original positions. Ganesha nodded in acknowledgement of his brother's prowess. He waved his danda in the air and instantly the moon turned green and gleamed from a pink sky. Skanda laughed out loud and waited while his brother turned things back to normal again. He then drew a circle with his finger and from within the circle rose a whirlwind, enveloping Ganesha in sand and hiding him from sight. When the storm settled down, they could see Ganesha standing unruffled, with his hands on his hips.

Ganesha motioned with his fingers to bring down a jagged bolt of lightning that engulfed Skanda in fiery tongues of scarlet and blue. But Skanda stepped out of the flames unharmed, his body glittering like gold. The brothers then assailed each other with boulders and huge trees, mountain peaks and volcanoes spewing fire. They unleashed a typhoon of astras and scorching chakras, glittering spears and pikes. Their bodies bled from a hundred wounds but they fought on without pause. Finally, Skanda raised his golden lance and Ganesha strode forward, his face grim, with his trident in his hand. Who could withstand the lance imbued with Durga's shakti? Who could survive the fiery trishul of Mahadeva? The devas cried out in fear and Ganesha's wives fell at Parvati's feet, imploring her to intervene.

12

Celebrating Love

Skanda threw his glinting lance at his brother. Ganesha halted its fearsome attack with his trident. Each brother strained his muscles to the limit, trying to overwhelm the other with his superior strength. Fierce sparks sprang from the friction as the weapons clashed together. Flames rose to engulf the skies and set fire to the seas. Brahma watched with fear as all creation was threatened with extinction. Surya went into hiding and Yama readied to harvest a mountain of lives.

And then, Ganesha moved his lips close to Skanda's ear. The devas strained to hear what he said, but the wind carried only a few words to them: Muruga, girl and elephant.

The two combatants stood frozen, and it seemed as if Time stood still too, waiting for the cataclysm. Karthikeya smiled then and backed away. His lance vanished as did Ganesha's trishul. Parvati's lips twitched with laughter and she embraced her three new daughters. Vishnu's smile assured the devas that the danger was past and that the world would return to normal again. The ganas turned cartwheels in joy, for they had been distraught at seeing the two sons of Shiva in conflict.

'We should have realized that they were sporting with us,' said Indra to Vayu, laughing, as Ganesha returned to their midst, his arm around his brother's waist. Siddhi cast Ganesha a smouldering look. Her husband would have to pay a price for teasing her. Buddhi's mind was busy wondering what Ganesha had said to Skanda to make him retreat. Riddhi was happy that her Sumukha was unharmed and joined her hands in gratitude to Parvati.

There was nothing to mar their happiness now. Like Krishna in Vrindavan, Ganesha too created many forms of himself to please the girls. He played the flute to serenade Buddhi and the tabla too when the three of them wished to dance. He roamed the forests with Siddhi on the back of his lion and brought Riddhi rare silks and rubies. He blessed his devotees who were celebrating Ganesha Chathurthi, for a whole year had passed since he had first met the sisters.

It was a challenge of another kind to keep his three wives happy. Buddhi happened to see a temple where he was worshipped with Siddhi and Riddhi, and asked him angrily why she was missing.

'You were already a part of me,' he answered softly. 'People who pray at this temple seeking jnana are in reality praying to you. As Krishna said to Radha in Vrindavan when she asked him why he would not marry her: "How can I marry my own soul?"'

'Does this mean that Buddhi is more important than we are?' demanded Riddhi, glaring at him.

It is easier to create a new world than to keep these three happy, thought Ganesha. But he would not have it any other way.

The girls laughed at him then and he understood that they had been teasing him. They looked down on earth and saw his many images, big and small, red and yellow, with one head and many. His devotees lovingly decorated the idols, placed them under colourful canopies and made sweet offerings. Each family had its own small idol of Ganesha that they bathed in honey, anointed with sandalwood paste and clothed in bright silks. And when the ten days of celebration were over, they carried the idols to be dissolved in the ocean or the river, and wept to see him go.

'Our god will return to us again next year,' said the priests as they performed the final aarti. 'Gajamukha helps us understand that all life must depart, only to be created again in a new form. We perform rituals and pujas, listen to stories that speak of his glory and realize the ultimate truth that he embodies. We learn the meaning that underlies our faith and keeps it thriving through the ages, transcending all boundaries. Bless us, divine son of Shiva, with your wisdom and your love!'

In the heavens, the devas too worshipped Ganesha: 'Twam Shakti Trayatmakah! O Ganesha, you are the embodiment of the three Shaktis—knowledge, desire and action. Bless us and guide us to bliss!'

MANDODARI

1

Strange Beginnings

She was submerged in water—foul, stagnant water that flooded her nose and her mouth. She panicked. Her heart seemed to stop and then start again, pounding faster than before. She gasped and more water flooded in. She could not swim. How could she survive? She spluttered and kicked out in desperation. The surface! She must get to the surface at once or she would drown. And how had she ended up here? She could remember a glorious world, filled with light and grace, where kindly eyes had looked upon her. That was where she belonged, not here. She was beautiful, blessed and admired, not someone meant to die in a noxious pond. Or perhaps, this was a nightmare that she would soon awaken from.

More water rushed into her mouth. She spat it out and flailed again. She was unable to breathe or call for help, her eyes were turning glassy, her body sinking to the depths. Where were the noble gods who had blessed her? Was this a trial to test her strength? If that were so, she was certain that she would fail . . .

No! She would not give up. She held her breath, clamped her lips together and renewed her efforts to raise her head above the water. But it appeared that she could make no progress. Her lifeless body would soon be eaten by sharks and fish.

And in that dark moment, she saw it. The water around her was lighter, brighter and shot through with sunlight. There was hope still! She kicked her feet out once more, filled with a grim focus. Her head emerged above the surface of the water. A harsh croak of triumph escaped her lips. She gulped down the air, fervently thanking the gods who had let her live. Something clammy curled around her foot and she shuddered as she shook it off. Her senses took in the murky pond she was in and the ugly creatures swimming around her. The dank smell made her nostrils twitch in distaste. Sheer terror overcame her senses. She dropped into a half-swoon and escaped into that rare world in which she had worn fine silks and her body had been anointed with crushed turmeric and rose water. She could literally smell her heavenly perfume, concocted from champaka, chandana, nagapushpa and other essences.

A loud grunt startled her from her reverie. Alas, not much had changed. She was still trapped in the water, her instincts screaming for her to flee. She knew without a doubt that death was coming for her. Her eyes scanned the waters in fear. The grunts were nearer now, battering her ear. Then she saw the giant turtle advancing on her, its jaws wide open, its sharp beak poised to mangle her flesh and bones. She pushed away in panic even as the turtle lashed out, raking its claws over her soft body. Her limbs thrashed furiously, but the enemy's jaws were clamped on her foot, grinding down into the bone, dragging her back towards its maw. She pulled desperately, ignoring the red-hot pain that lanced through her as she tore free, leaving part of her limb behind. She hid behind a forest of algae, but was it enough to shake her killer off? The turtle cruised slowly past, its head swivelling in search of its prey. She was safe for the moment, but she should get to land at once. Her foot was throbbing with pain. How badly was she hurt?

She looked down and shuddered as she saw not a dainty foot circled with a gold anklet, but the webbed foot of a frog. *No!* Her eyes must be playing tricks on her. She shut them tight and opened them again, gazing in disbelief at what she could see of herself. Instead of a slender, shapely body, she now had the gross form of a frog. The fair, perfumed skin of an apsara had been transformed into a mottled green. Her face probably featured bulging eyes and a snout. Then her tongue darted out of its own volition, wrapped itself around a disgusting insect and brought it back into her mouth. She gagged and spat it out. What was happening? She suppressed the scream that rose in her throat, knowing that her croak would bring back her foe. Was this her real world now? What had happened to the other one in Kailasa?

O Shiva, allow me to return to your radiant mountain, she prayed fervently. *Forgive me for the sins that have brought me tumbling down. Enfold me in your grace, great god!*

Once again, her memory took her back to the exquisite world atop a divine mountain—home to the wondrous Shiva and the divine Parvati. She saw Vishnu's beatific smile as he blessed her. How could she find her way back to that ethereal domain? She was sure that what she was seeing was not real. If she were only a frog, how could she have imagined that rare world in such detail?

And then she remembered . . . A wrathful goddess had cursed her with an upraised arm. A profound grief had cleaved her soul. A curse! That must be the reason for her being reduced to this state—desolate, broken, without hope.

She had been sent here to die.

In her moment of despair, she seemed to hear a strong, virile voice calling to her. 'Come to me, my love! Hold on to me and never let go,' he said. Her eyes brightened, her heart leapt with

joy. She recognized the voice of her saviour. She remembered
the warrior with arms so powerful that he could carry the earth
with ease. His eyes had burned into hers with a searing passion,
vowing to keep her safe forever.

And then, a savage wind had whirled her away. She had been
helpless, hurtling earthward, the curse turning her into a frog.

Where are you, great one? she screamed now. *Save me, for
without you I am nothing!*

But all she heard in reply was the keening of the wind in
the trees.

Many hundred years earlier, the asura princess Kaikesi had given
birth to a baby boy—a son like no other. She and her husband
Sage Vishrava had named him Dashanan, for he had ten heads.
'He is born under an evil star that makes him easily susceptible
to vanity and desire,' said Vishrava's father Maharishi Pulastya,
son of Brahma himself. 'However, I will watch over him and steer
him on to the right path.'

Soon, under his tutelage, the child dedicated himself to
intense study and prayer. After years of fierce effort, he became
proficient in the astras and shastras, in music and mathematics,
in astronomy and astrology.

'Your body and mind are pure, cleansed of the ten vices,' said the
proud Pulastya to his grandson. 'Your many heads now symbolize
your mastery of the four Vedas and the six Upanishads. Next, you
must learn to control the indriyas, the five organs of sense and five of
action. You will then become like Indra, lord of the heavens!'

Dashanan was a devoted son and a good brother to
Kumbhakarna, Vibhishana and Surpanakha. He quickly became

an expert in the Sama Veda, the most sacred and complex of the Vedas, and delighted the gods with his chants. He played the veena with exquisite skill and composed verses in praise of the Trinity. His deep study of the planets helped him interpret their movements and provide guidance to sages and kings. He also imbibed the intricacies of statecraft at the feet of Pulastya.

However, Dashanan's maternal grandfather, the asura Sumali, had a darker scheme in mind for Kaikesi's son. Sumali had chosen Vishrava to be his daughter's groom only because the sage was imbued with great potency due to his tapasya. He knew that the glorious child born of their union would wield power over the three realms and help Sumali fulfil his ambition.

'My people are eager to see my grandson, their future ruler,' said Sumali to Vishrava, seeking his permission to take the lad with him. The sage felt a stirring of unease but knew that he could not rightfully turn down the request. The asura king rushed his grandson away to a splendid palace he had constructed for him and lost no time in immersing him in pomp and pleasure. He showered Dashanan with priceless gifts and surrounded him with lovely women who pandered to his every whim. The young prince, used to an ascetic life, gradually began to enjoy and then to crave these sensuous delights. Memories of the tenets inculcated in him by Pulastya made him hesitate initially, but then he gave in to temptation, telling himself that he needed to experience these joys first before relinquishing them.

'Remember that you are young only once, sweet child!' said Sumali, encouraging him to indulge himself. 'Soon you will be a king and will be spending all your energies on arduous expeditions to extend your dominion.'

Dashanan's mind struggled to reconcile the disparate ideas of life promoted by his two grandfathers. 'Grandsire Pulastya warned me to shun worldly power and not allow pride and lust to cloud my mind,' he said to Sumali. 'He said also that if I can control my passions I can aspire to be like Indra.'

'Be *like* Indra?' scoffed Sumali. 'Listen to me and you will *become* Indra. You are young, handsome and powerful—not a dried-up ascetic like Pulastya!' He watched his grandson's eyes light up at the thought and smiled to himself. He had identified Dashanan's weakness and would have no qualms about exploiting it. 'You can yoke Surya to your chariot and make Yama stand guard at your door. You can take the beauteous Indrani to bed. Why, you can even rewrite your future as you please, for the planets of destiny will be your slaves.'

'How can I achieve all this?' Dashanan whispered, enthralled by this vision.

'Pray to your great-grandfather, Brahma. Seek the boon of immortality,' said Sumali. 'Then no god or demon can stop you.'

The skies soon echoed with Dashanan's fervent chants. Pulastya was grieved when he realized that his grandson sought worldly powers and not spiritual ones. Had all his efforts to attune his mind to virtue been wasted? On the other hand, Sumali watched gleefully as the intensity of Dashanan's tapasya shook Indra's throne and made the devas tremble.

A hundred years passed, but Brahma did not appear before the tapasvin. The intrepid Dashanan cut off one of his heads and proffered it as sacrifice. More years passed without reward and Sumali's grandson offered a second head to the fire. This too was fruitless and Dashanan offered one more head and then another, resolved to achieve his purpose or die in the effort. Finally, only one head remained. By now, Sumali was overwrought, tortured by the fear that he would lose his grandson entirely. He began pleading with him to stop the penance that he himself had suggested.

'No, grandfather!' replied Dashanan, his eyes glittering wildly in a face grown gaunt due to his prolonged austerities. 'Surely, the gods have never seen a penance so intense or a devotee so fierce. Brahma must acknowledge my greatness and grant me his boons. Further, it is not in my nature to retreat or accept defeat once I have set my mind on a goal.'

Dashanan closed his eyes for a moment and then raised his sword to lop off his remaining head. It seemed certain that the life of this luminous tapasvin would end that day. Sumali rushed towards him with a scream, but his grandson's sword had already started on its downward course. The devas watched with ashen faces while the sages fled in terror. The planets and the sun swerved from their positions while the creatures on earth felt a dark dread engulf them. What would happen when the rakshasa completed his sacrifice?

And then, an invisible force intervened.

Dashanan's hand froze in mid-air, though he strained every sinew to bring down the sword. He felt a fierce heat envelop him. Brahma appeared before him in a flash of incandescent light.

'Your devotion and sacrifices have pleased me,' said Chaturmukha, the god with four faces. 'What boon do you seek?'

Dashanan offered him worship and asked that he be made immortal. But the god replied that this was not a boon he could offer anyone. All creatures that were born had to die.

'Then make me impervious to my enemies—gods and demons, gandharvas and yakshas, serpents and wild beasts,' he said.

'So be it!' smiled Brahma. 'And as a further reward for your piety, I hereby endow you with power over divine and occult weapons. Use your gifts wisely, Dashanan.'

The next instant, Brahma disappeared as swiftly as he had come. The nine heads that Dashanan had sacrificed were restored to him, and they appeared to be even more magnificent than before. The rakshasa roared in triumph for he had gained powers through which he could make all the realms dance to his tunes. His arrogance grew, feeding on the extravagant praises that his asura followers showered on him. He unleashed the ambition that he had kept subdued for so long, sending the devas in swarga and the nagas in patala scattering in fear.

Dragging her maimed foot, tormented by strange memories, the frog maiden made her way carefully to the edge of the pond. If she wanted to discover the truth about herself she must first leave the foul-smelling water. She pulled herself onto land and carefully looked around. In the distance she could see two ascetics chanting mantras before a sacrificial fire. Perhaps these learned men could help her unravel her destiny if she could only make them understand her plight. She hopped forward as quickly as she could, but halted when she heard a rustling that set her senses jangling. A desperate leap took her to a hiding place behind a boulder. Now she could see the snake making its way forward, its dark body glowing with hideous red bands. She knew that the reptile was a frog's mortal enemy and was a thousand times more dangerous than a turtle.

The snake made its way towards a covered pot that was placed some distance away from where the rishis were engaged in prayer. She watched as it climbed up the side of the pot, forced aside the cover and dipped its head into it. A few moments later, it retreated and slithered away behind some bushes.

What was inside the pot? She hopped rapidly forward and saw drops of milk splashed on the ground. The milk had been poisoned and the rishis would die if they drank it. She had to warn them. But how? Her croaking would convey no meaning.

They would drive her away, thinking that she was tainting the sacred ground. She could turn away and leave them to their fate. But what if this was her chance to reverse the karma that had brought her here? She could sacrifice her useless life for theirs. Perhaps she would be born again as a woman and have the good fortune to marry her warrior. Her heart raced at the mere thought and she felt a new energy coursing through her. She was ready to face anything to make that possible.

The frog maiden hopped nearer the pot and tried to jump to the top. But it was too high and the sides too smooth. Her feet could find no grip. She tried again and fell back on the hard ground. The chants were growing louder, reaching a crescendo. The prayers were coming to an end. She looked around and spotted the stone on the farther side against which the pot rested. *Yes.* Using the rock as a step, she leapt, and plunged into the creamy milk through the gap created by the snake. The milk was frothing with poison. Her feet scrambled to keep her afloat, but soon the noxious fumes smothered her. She gasped for breath and knew that death was near. But her lifeless body would serve as a warning to the ascetics. They would be safe. Her weak croak of triumph floated in the air.

The rishis rose to their feet, their austerities completed. One of them moved towards the pot of milk, his throat parched with the heat of the fire and the fierceness of the chanting. He raised the pot near his face and retched as he saw the frog. He drew back in horror and smashed the pot to the ground.

'I curse you, greedy frog, for polluting the milk!' he said. Then he gasped as the motionless form moved and rose from the shards of clay, no longer a frog but a beauteous young woman standing with head bowed and hands joined in prayer. Tears ran down her cheeks as she realized that the rishi's curse had reversed the one that had turned her into a frog.

'Forgive me, great one,' she said in a voice that was as melodious as a veena. 'I had to do this to warn you that a snake had poisoned your milk.'

One of the rishis closed his eyes in meditation and perceived what had happened a little earlier while they had been absorbed in prayer. 'She speaks the truth,' he said to the other ascetic. When he found out that she did not have a name, he named her Mandodari, for she had been recreated from a manduka or a frog.

'We bless you with a happy life, divine maiden!' he said. 'You will have a valorous husband who is renowned in the three worlds.'

Knowing that an ashram was not the right place for her, the rishis entrusted her to Mayasura, the architect of the asuras, and his apsara wife Hema, who had long been praying for a daughter.

Mayasura and Hema took the young maiden into their home and hearts, viewing her as a blessing from the gods. They showered her with love and watched her beauty grow by the day. They saw that her piety and innocence gave her a glow that was almost unearthly. Soon, however, Indra summoned Hema to heaven and she was forced to leave her daughter in Mayasura's custody.

'You must find a groom worthy of her,' she advised Mayasura. 'Someone who will love and cherish her as she deserves.'

Mandodari wept at being parted from her mother, while her father sought solace from his own grief by beginning his search for the right groom for her. His daughter already knew who she wished to marry—the man she had glimpsed in her vision, the one she knew was meant for her. Watching her face clouded with yearning, Mayasura asked her to tell him what troubled her. But when she did so, he was unable to help her, as she did not know her suitor's name or lineage. Where was he? Was he even real?

'Do not fret,' Mayasura said to his daughter. 'I will find the finest groom on earth, the greatest warrior ever seen. He will adore you and you will soon forget your dream lover.'

Mandodari knew that she must listen to her father, though she was certain that her warrior was no dream. She felt in her heart that so many miracles had taken place in her life only so that she could be united with him. He was there somewhere, pining for her as deeply as she did for him. She heard his voice every day and saw his face every night. 'O, my king! How unfortunate I am to have lost you so soon after seeing you!' she mourned. 'Will I ever have the good fortune to see you again?'

2

Lankeshwara

Dashanan's fearsome powers grew by the day, and neither the devas nor the demons could stand against him. Egged on by his asura grandfather, Dashanan embarked on a campaign to subjugate the lords of the earth and the skies. In his arrogance, he listened neither to his father Vishrava's advice nor Pulastya's. He drove out his half-brother Kubera, the treasurer of the gods, from his beautiful island kingdom of Lanka, and occupied the throne himself. He destroyed ashrams, ravaged the richest lands and ravished women who he treated as the spoils of war. Knowing that he had won his powers through tapasya, he allowed no one else to conduct a sacrifice, for he feared that they would challenge his supremacy. He seized Kubera's immense treasures and his pushpaka vimana, a flying fortress that would obey his very thought and traverse the three realms. Mounted on his aerial chariot, Dashanan continued his depredations with impunity. His harem was soon filled with alluring women of every race, from glowing gandharva women to sensuous and earthy rakshasis, from mermaids of the sea to delicate woodland sprites. Apsaras sang his praises while sinuous nagakanyas pleased him in bed.

The king's sins grew by the day, as did his dark aura, seething around his many heads with malevolent power. 'I am invincible!' he gloated as he sailed the skies, looking for rare treasures to seize and new enemies to destroy.

One day, Dashanan's eyes lighted upon a mountain that glistened like a jewel, with facets of crystal, ruby, gold and lapis lazuli. He flew closer to its dazzling peak, only to have his chariot jerk to a stop in mid-air, as if it had encountered an invisible wall. The jolt nearly caused Dashanan to tumble headlong to earth.

An angry voice bellowed at him from the mountain peak. 'Did you think you could fly so arrogantly over the abode of Shiva, the god of gods?" asked Nandi, Shiva's attendant, who also served as his vaahana.

'So this is where your god hides in fear!' roared Dashanan in reply. 'I have heard of this Shiva, a mendicant without home or wealth, an ash-smeared ascetic who lives in a cremation ground! I know of his sons, the war god Karthikeya, and the elephant-headed Ganesha. But how dare you, a mere servant, address me so rudely? Know that it is only a moment's task for me to destroy your mountain, to kill your master and take home your treasures.'

'How you do rant and rave, rakshasa!' Nandi retorted. 'You speak recklessly about the Tandavamurti whose dance controls creation, preservation and dissolution. You mock his ardent devotee who guards his mountain and serves as his mount.'

'A devotee with the head of a bull! Look at my glorious form and then at your own misshapen one! Why, even your god is no match for me. My body is anointed with sandal paste while his is coated with ashes. I wear fine silks and jewels, whereas he wears animal hides, skulls and snakes. I come from a noble lineage of sages and kings, whereas no one even knows who his father is. I own everything that is precious and valuable, while your master owns nothing except a begging bowl!'

'Stop your foul words, Dashanan!' bellowed Nandi. 'You mock Shiva who is everything that is auspicious and eternal. He is the lord who bestows moksha on those who chant his name. He is Digambara who wears the sky as his garment. He—'

'Speak another word and I will cut off your tongue, beast!' interrupted the rakshasa. 'Look at the ghouls with long tails that come stumbling out of caves to confront me! Their faces are hideous, their bodies beastly. They howl and hiss and contort their ugly faces. Is this vanara army going to prevent the great Dashanan from uprooting this mountain?'

'Your insults exceed all limits, asura!' roared Nandi. 'Try laying rough hands on Kailasa and you will face dire Shiva's wrath. For my part, I curse that the kingdom you are so proud of will be destroyed by vanaras! And your rampant conceit will bring about your downfall.'

'The animal challenges me!' laughed Sumali's grandson. 'Watch now while I imprison Shiva and enslave his sons.' He bent low and clasped Kailasa in his outspread arms.

Shiva was in his cave, engaged in profound meditation. But Parvati, seated beside him, stringing a garland of lavender flowers, raised her head angrily on hearing the upstart's boast. 'My sons to be your slaves?' she fumed. 'The indomitable Karthikeya, who subdued Tarakasura and leads the deva armies? And glorious Ganesha, first among the gods? You will now face the wrath of Bhadrakali, rakshasa! You will tremble on seeing my mighty arms, my dreadful fangs and my eyes rolling in rage. I will shred your adamantine body as if it were gossamer.'

Suddenly, she heard a voice in her ear, pulling her back from the edge of wrath. 'Do not go before the rakshasa now, Parvati,' it said. 'His own actions will hasten his doom.' Parvati looked up into the radiant face of Vishnu who had appeared before her.

'Mother of gods!' he said, his voice gentle and soothing. 'You are the embodiment of peace, the refuge of all living beings. Hold back your anger, Shakti!'

She joined her hands together in reverence. 'Welcome to Kailasa, my brother,' she said, allowing his grace to calm her. 'I submit myself to your wisdom.'

But even as she spoke, the mountain shook under their feet. Again, Vishnu gestured to her to wait. They emerged from the cave and saw that Dashanan had carried out his threat to uproot Kailasa. Mountain goats and deer scattered in fear. The sages in their ashrams stopped their chanting and stared in horror. Shiva's fierce ganas rushed to gather their weapons. Nandi furrowed the ground with his mighty hooves and lashed his tail, awaiting Shiva's command. The devas gathered above, watching their foe attack fierce Rudra's domain.

'O great Shiva! Awaken now to kill the demon and free us from his tyranny!' they prayed.

The skies exploded with a fierce light as Shiva opened his eyes. His indignant roar shattered mountain peaks and set the seas aflame. His body glowed with the light of a thousand suns. The emerald serpents on his body spat poison. The trident in his hand blazed with supernal power, ready to shear off Dashanan's heads. The ganas sent boulders flying towards the assailant. Nandi bellowed, seeking Shiva's permission to kill Dashanan.

But Shiva had the power to annihilate the universe with a glance. He needed neither Nandi nor the ganas to quash the foolish asura. The dire god knitted his eyebrows and pressed lightly down on the mountain with his little toe.

At once, the mountain extended stony roots to surround the rakshasa and hold him captive. Dashanan felt as if he was pinned down by the weight of the whole earth and her creatures. He roared in pain and pushed at the walls of rock that imprisoned him, but to no avail. Trapped as he was beneath Kailasa, his enormous powers were useless.

He struggled through the day and the night, exerting all his strength, but to no avail. Days passed and then months. His agony grew unabated until finally he realized that he could free himself only through Shiva's mercy. He had to show the three-eyed god that he was repentant.

Once he had decided on this path, Dashanan plunged into prayer just as fiercely as he had fought earlier. He subdued his ego and focused his energies on devotion. He chanted verses from the Sama Veda that were closest to Shiva's heart. He then composed and sang the Shiva Tandava Stotra, extolling the god and his cosmic dance in verse. The music reverberated through heaven, earth and patala, binding man and god, animal and bird in its exquisite rhythms. Shiva listened, rapt, with his eyes closed. Dashanan then created the Rudra veena, using one of his heads as the gourd, one arm as the beam and his veins as the strings. His song, set in Raga Kambhoji, was majestic in gait and drenched the world in devotional fervour.

Dhimid dhimid dhimi dhvanan
mrudanga tunga mangala
Dhvani krama pravartita prachanda tandava Shiva

'I worship Lord Shiva, whose dance of creation is in harmony with the fierce dhimid-dhimid-dhimi that comes from the auspicious drum,' he sang.

Shiva's heart was softened by the music, and he raised his toe to allow Dashanan to free himself. Then he appeared before the rakshasa on the mountaintop in order to accept his worship. Parvati remained out of the rakshasa's sight still, at Vishnu's insistence.

Delighted at his success in winning Shiva's grace, Dashanan conjured up a drum, a flute, a trumpet and a conch shell that he played with his many hands and mouths, creating a rhapsody the likes of which had never been heard on earth or in heaven. So enchanting was the music that even the serpent around Shiva's neck swayed to the rhythm. The ganas listened spellbound while Nandi shed tears of rapture. Fierce Rudra now became gentle Ashutosha—easily pleased by his devotee's faith. His eyes closed in ecstasy. His trident glowed with a white radiance, calmed by the sublime cadence of the song.

Shiva opened his eyes as the song ended and glanced with favour upon the repentant rakshasa. 'I bless you, my son. Henceforth, the world will know you as Ravana—the one with the terrifying roar,' he said.

Ravana! A splendid name that befits my grandeur! thought the rakshasa, delighted that he had gained Shiva's favour.

'You have won me over with your mystic melodies, and for that I reward you with my invincible moon sword, Chandrahasa,' said Shiva. 'I will grant you another boon as well, so tell me what you most desire.'

Ravana's ego blinded him and he decided to ask for Parvati, whose incomparable beauty was renowned in the universe. She was the mighty daughter of Himavan and the embodiment of Shakti. With her by his side, his prowess would surpass even that of Shiva.

Parvati sensed his unworthy thoughts. 'He pretends to worship Shiva while he lusts after his wife. I will burn him to cinders,' she muttered.

'Wait just a little longer,' urged Vishnu. 'Shiva is now a slave to the demon's music and he will be vexed if you should harm him.'

The rakshasa knew that he had to be devious if he wanted Parvati, for Shiva adored her and had made her half of himself in his form of Ardhanariswara. So he kept up his pretence of humility and said, 'By your grace, I now possess the greatest treasures of the universe, Maheshwara. I have Brahma's astras, your moon sword and Kubera's pushpaka vimana. My desire now is for a wife as beautiful as yours!'

'But that cannot be,' said Shiva. 'No goddess or mortal can ever be as beautiful as Parvati. Ask for a different boon, Ravana.'

But the rakshasa was adamant. He knew that Shiva would be forced to give up Parvati as he could not retract his promise. He lowered his head to conceal his lustful eyes and twitching lips.

'Does he really think he can hide his thoughts from me?' fumed Parvati. 'Did my lord not call Ravana his son? That makes the rakshasa my son as well, and he commits the foulest of sins by lusting for his own mother. I should have killed him earlier and not held back, Vishnu. If I do so now, the asuras will mock my lord, saying that he is unable to grant Ravana's boon. But what other course remains? How will the realms survive the sacrilege if the demon were to seize me? The seas will dry up and the planets will spiral to a fiery end. My eyes burn and my weapons fly to my hands. I can never allow this beast to touch me!'

Her trident pulsed with fearsome power as she raised her arm. The watching devas cowered as the universe trembled on the edge of annihilation.

The next moment, something flashed from Vishnu's hand and wrapped itself around the prongs of the trishul. It was an iridescent garland of unfading ocean lotuses. Parvati turned her burning gaze on the blue-hued god. Did her brother expect to deter her still? *No*. He could not stay her hand any longer.

As her lips tightened in anger, one of the blossoms from the garland spun free, glinting like Vishnu's chakra as it sailed forward. The flower was transformed into a maiden of divine beauty who stood before Shiva with her head bowed.

'This must be Parvati!' whispered Ravana, as he gazed at her exquisite face and form. The maiden's skin seemed to be woven from moonbeams. Her face was radiant like the lotus from which she was born. Her eyes were bright and liquid like a fawn's. The soft smile on her lips held the three realms in thrall. Her limbs were shapely, long and golden. A delicious fragrance of sandalwood and aloe wafted towards him, bringing him the promise of heady delights. Her anklets tinkled melodiously as she moved forward gracefully to offer worship to Shiva.

'Salutations, great god,' she said, her voice clear and sweet like a koel's.

Ravana was in a trance. He ached with the desire to clasp her in his arms, to carry her away to his palace, to shun the world forever and lose himself in her caresses. He could hardly wait for Shiva to grant him his boon. He stood breathlessly on the sacred peak of Kailasa watching the apsara. She raised her eyes then and looked at him.

3

The Rapture

Long, long ago, before Time began, there was only the great god Narayana, reclining over the waters of the cosmic ocean on the coils of the serpent Adisesha. From Narayana's navel sprang a lustrous lotus, bearing four-headed Brahma, entrusted with the task of creating the world and all its creatures. Brahma created Purusha, the primal man, within whom was embedded all life. This Purusha, who had a thousand heads, eyes, arms and legs, encircled the earth from all sides and transcended it. The visible world was only a quarter of his vastness and the remaining three quarters lay hidden in the celestial sphere. His soul was in repose and free of fear and desire. However, Brahma soon realized that a creation without fear or desire would not act. And without action, the world would remain barren of life.

The Creator took up his great sword and split the Purusha into two. With this stroke he created night and day, darkness and light, sky and earth, life and death, male and female. The two halves yearned to become one again, and from their embrace was born all life in pairs—horses, lions, cattle, birds, snakes, fish and ants. The fierce desire of men and women to join together transformed them into Kama and Rati, the god and goddess of love. The whole world became their playground and their rapture gave birth to Shringara, the poetry of love. So powerful was this fervour that it flared higher when the lovers came together and also when they were apart. Poets sang joyously of a passion that was sated when indulged and at the same time left one hungering for more.

When the gods themselves were maddened by Shringara, how could a rakshasa withstand its allure? Just one glimpse into the maiden's eyes set off a tempest within Ravana. A blinding light enveloped him, cleansing his soul with its fierce purity. The evil aura that clung to him was battered, twisted out of shape and dissolved into nothingness. Ravana's powerful shoulders trembled like they never had before god or man, and he stared unblinking at her. His ego bowed to a force greater than itself, suffused by the transformative energy of love.

The maiden looked back at him, entranced. The very air between them seemed to throb with ardour. Her tender limbs quivered with yearning. Her body ached to get closer to him so that she could be enfolded in his arms.

'Give me this beautiful maiden as wife,' Ravana said to Shiva, his voice hoarse. He wondered for a moment whether this was Parvati or someone else. But he was so enraptured by her beauty that he dismissed the question as soon as it arose in his mind. He would die if he could not make this woman his own, and at the soonest. It did not matter who she was or from where she hailed. He forced himself to wait for the god's reply.

The lord of Kailasa smiled at the blue-hued god who now stood beside him. 'You have always granted boons out of your infinite mercy, only to see them misused,' Vishnu said softly to him. 'I have come to help you unravel the knot!'

'Maybe Ravana will be redeemed through his love for this maiden,' Shiva said. He turned his gaze on the woman born through Vishnu's grace. 'Your creation is lovely,' he said, 'perhaps as charming as the Mohini avatara you took to rescue me from another asura! I would even say that she is the most beautiful woman who ever lived, except . . .'

But before he could finish speaking, Parvati appeared before him in a rage, unable to listen any longer to his words praising the maiden. She gazed angrily at the woman whose body was curved and sensuous, her lips perfectly formed, her face more luminous than the moon. And a terrible curse erupted from her lips.

'Be gone to earth and live your life as a frog, strumpet!' she cursed. 'Do not imagine that your coquettish eyes will snare my lord.'

Shiva shook his head in regret and said, 'You have spoken in haste, Parvati! I merely wished to say that no woman can compare in beauty or grace with you, the queen of my heart. Alas! You have cursed an innocent soul for no fault of hers.'

Parvati stood chastened, realizing that she had erred by giving in to a jealous impulse. Ravana exclaimed in dismay as the maiden he loved spiralled down to earth in the body of a frog. His goddess transformed into a frog? How could this happen?

'Do not leave me, my beloved!' he wailed. 'O Shiva, restore her to me!'

Shiva raised a hand in blessing. 'You will find your soulmate and rejoice in a love that is eternal,' he said.

The distraught Lankeshwara plunged to earth, desperate to reclaim his lustrous beauty. His conquests were forgotten, his many queens faded from his mind. All his thoughts were now focused on the one woman who held his heart in her delicate hands.

Ravana searched relentlessly, disregarding food and sleep and forsaking the luxury of his palace to roam the four corners of the world. But the earth was huge and her creatures infinite. To find a frog that was not a frog, to rescue her from wherever she was and transform her again into the apsara he loved—this was a daunting task even for him. But he persevered, as he needed her for his very survival.

His quest was frenzied, his forays endless. Where was she now? Was she even alive? If she were still a frog, she could have fallen prey to one of the many enemies of her species. How could he live on if he never found her?

Tired of roaming the earth, frenzied, his efforts so far in vain, Ravana decided to rest awhile in a lush forest where deer roamed free and brilliant birds chirruped in the branches. He sat with his back against a giant coral tree, feeling troubled and fatigued. His eyes were unseeing as he relived again his fleeting moments of bliss in Kailasa. Seeing that apsara before him, dreaming of a life with her—that had been more significant to him than even receiving Shiva's boons. He felt dejected, and wondered if he could go on living if he failed to attain her love.

And then he heard a voice . . . her voice! Was it . . . could it be . . . ? His pulse raced. He had heard his apsara speak just a few words, but he was certain that he could recognize her voice even in his sleep. It was her . . . it must be her! Providence had somehow reversed the curse and restored her to her natural form.

He jumped to his feet, impatient to look upon the girl's face. He saw her slender arms first and then the edge of her bright red garment. He waited in agony to find out if it was her. And then her face emerged like a full moon from behind the clouds as she pushed past a hibiscus bush, pausing to pluck one iridescent bloom and tuck it behind her ear. She heard his loud gasp and looked up swiftly. Her eyes were trapped by the fierce ardour of his glance. A delicate blush stained her soft cheeks and she looked down in confusion, only to look up again in a fever of anxiety. Surely, he was not a mere illusion conjured up by her passionate dreams! Her heart thudded under the silk she wore. This radiant face was certainly the one that had haunted her memories. She had yearned for him, though she knew neither his name nor his parentage. He belonged to her previous life, if that was what it was, when she had lived among the gods. She saw now that he too had eyes only for her. Was good fortune smiling upon her again that she had been granted another opportunity to attain bliss?

Ravana was almost beside himself with joy. His long journey had ended with success. His greatest penance had been rewarded. He had found his apsara who could raise him to ecstasy with a mere glance from her entrancing eyes. He would seize her in his arms and fly away, before fate intervened to separate him again from the woman who anchored him to life, to love and to happiness.

As he stepped forward eagerly, Mayasura walked into the clearing behind his daughter. He glared at the intruder at first and then softened his gaze when he saw that the warrior was magnificent and that he had eyes for no one but Mandodari. The rakshasa's ornate jewels, his splendid sword and the arrogance of his stance revealed to the father that this stranger was no commoner. His majestic face and form showed that his ancestry was noble and that he was accustomed to rule.

'Greetings from Mayasura, king of the danavas and architect of the asuras,' he said, welcoming the stranger. 'And this is my daughter, Mandodari.'

Ravana woke from his contemplation of Mandodari's blushing face and nodded in acknowledgement. 'I am Ravana, king of Lanka, and lord of heaven and earth,' he said. Then his lips murmured her name with reverence and love: '*Mandodari. A name as beautiful as she is.*'

Tearing his eyes away from Mandodari, Ravana respectfully addressed Mayasura. 'I must have your daughter as my wife, O king!' he said. 'I will make her queen of my heart and of the three realms. The sun, the moon and the planets that determine destiny—they will all offer her homage. And Indrani herself will wait on her.'

Mandodari stood silent, her eyelids fluttering, snatching glimpses of his face and listening to the passion throbbing in his words. This was what she had been waiting for; this noble soul was the one for whom she had been created. The curse, her life as a frog, her death and rebirth were all a prelude to her life with Ravana. *Shiva be praised, for gazing upon me with favour. Noble Vishnu, bless me once more with your gracious smile*, she prayed.

'Give her to me in marriage, Mayasura,' Ravana asked again, weakened by desire, his impatience starting to break through his composure. If Mayasura refused, he would have to crush him. There was no way he would allow himself to be separated from Mandodari ever again.

A voice from the heavens answered him, loud and clear, startling the birds and silencing the winds. 'You invite doom by seeking to marry her, Ravana!' it said. 'The daughter born from her womb will cause your death and the destruction of your clan.'

Mandodari was thunderstruck and looked fearfully at Ravana's face. Would he still wish to marry her after this prediction? Even if he did, would it be right to bring down doom upon the warrior who stood firm and tall like a banyan tree? On the other hand, had Shiva and Vishnu not already blessed their union?

'The gods have warned us in time,' said Mayasura, his face pale. 'It would be foolish to let you marry my daughter and condemn you both to a terrible fate. Go your way, Ravana, and may destiny guide you to another maiden as beautiful as my daughter.'

Mandodari's eyes filled with tears, making them glisten like liquid silver. She looked piteously at Ravana, a question in her eyes. Why was destiny snatching him away each time he came near? Why were the gods playing so cruelly with them? Her heart swung between panic and defiance as she wondered what she should do if her suitor still wished to marry her. But did he?

Ravana felt himself pulled irresistibly into the depths of her magnetic eyes. He needed her like the night needed the day, like darkness needed light. Why should he forgo his pleasures because of the fears of an old asura and the warning of an unseen presence? He had absolute faith in his prowess and the boon that Shiva had granted him. Besides, he had never taken kindly to being told what not to do. Perhaps that was why he had rebelled against Pulastya and his edicts. His ego prompted him to forcibly take whatever was forbidden to him. He tore his gaze away from Mandodari's face, raised his head high and spoke firmly.

'No voice from swarga or patala can prevent me from marrying the woman I love,' he said. 'I will take on the very gods in order to make her mine. I will destroy any force that may come between us. Marry me, fair maiden, and rule my heart and my kingdom!' Ravana stood erect, with his legs braced as if to counter a challenge. His eyes gleamed with the thought of battle, for he was always eager to display his dominance.

Mandodari was thrilled that he had sought her consent, not her father's. She stared intently at him as she wondered if she could trust him with her love and her life. What she saw there gave her strength and confidence. Her heart told her that she could risk everything for just a few moments in the arms of her love—this elegant warrior who had stolen her heart with just one impassioned glance. She nodded in acceptance.

And at that significant moment, Hema descended from heaven. Mandodari rushed to embrace her mother, but her delight did not last long.

'Are you sure, my child?' asked Hema. 'The Lankapati is indeed a splendid suitor, but do you wish to challenge fate so rashly?'

It appeared as if her mother too was against her marriage to Ravana. Had the gods sent her down to warn her daughter? Mandodari began to ponder again. Was she indeed making the right decision? Would she be standing one day over her fallen husband regretting this? But equally, did she want to be haunted for the rest of her life by the thought that she had thrown away her one chance at happiness? She was torn between reason and emotion, fear and love. Tears trickled down her cheeks as she looked pleadingly at the godlike asura.

'Do you not trust me, Mandodari?' he asked her, fearful that she would retract her consent. 'Look at my broad shoulders, my potent weapons. See how I control the very elements.' With one raised arm, he sent Surya plunging into the sea and brought up a brilliant moon in his stead. And in a move to silence his doubters, he summoned a fierce wind to lift Hema into the air.

'No, no!' Mandodari's voice rose in fear. 'Do not harm my parents who are merely concerned for my well-being.'

The wind set the apsara gently on the ground again while Ravana looked intently at his chosen one, waiting for her answer. Mandodari's thoughts were in a whirl still. On one side were her parents, who cared for her and wished her nothing but happiness. Their fears were real, based as they were on a dire prophecy. However, on the other side was her love for Ravana that had raged within her unabated for as long as she could remember. She was impatient to join him in the glorious life that he promised.

Why should she not seize her happiness with both hands? What was the alternative? A dispirited, miserable life with another groom chosen by her parents . . . She could not bear that.

'I will marry you, Lankeshwara, though the gods should stop me. Fate has not brought us together again only to tear us apart. Together, let us challenge destiny!' she said firmly.

Ravana's joy leapt out at her like a warm flame, touching her body with its exuberance. Her parents appeared to be slowly reconciling themselves to her decision. They began to make preparations for the wedding. Mayasura conjured up a magical canopy in the forest and the ceremony was performed by the ascetics of the forest. The two had eyes only for each other and felt no regret that their only guests were the spotted deer and the chirping birds.

Soon, the newlyweds took their leave of her parents, with Ravana summoning his pushpaka vimana to carry his bride to his island kingdom. The sight of the magnificent aerial chariot left the bride spellbound, for it was as high as a small hill and was festooned with jewels and silver bells that tinkled melodiously as it flashed across the skies.

'My vimana shines like the sun during the day and like a brilliant moon at night,' said Ravana proudly as he noticed her wondering gaze. 'It is as fleet as my thoughts and can travel unhindered through heaven, earth and the netherworld.'

The mystic craft flew so swiftly that the hills and vales below were reduced to a blur, for the rakshasa was eager to take his bride home. The emerald island of Lanka appeared below them, with its gleaming turrets and jewelled mansions. His courtiers and his other queens hurried to greet their emperor when they landed smoothly within the walls of his vast palace. But they were able to catch only a quick glimpse of the beauteous Mandodari before Ravana carried her into his inner chambers.

The new queen looked in amazement at the gold walls, the windows framed with diamonds and the floors of jade. Many beautiful women waited to serve him, their eyes alight with passion. They pined for his touch, for his prowess in bed was legendary and he had mastered the sixty-four ways of the Kamashastra. But today, he had no eyes for anyone but Mandodari and dismissed them with a snap of his fingers.

The king wooed Mandodari with exquisite patience and skill, awakening her desire slowly until it blazed fierce and strong. He clasped her by her waist, brushed a kiss on her petal-soft lips, stroked gently down her arm and watched as she shivered and sighed. He teased her with his lips and his many hands, nibbled on her smooth cheeks and made her moan in pleasure and pain. Soon, she too began to caress him with her soft hands and fragrant lips.

Days passed and months while the two were locked together in a sensual journey, completely lost to the world. He dressed her in shimmering silks only to undress her again in haste so that he could glory in her perfumed skin and her lush body. They lay entwined in green meadows, in hidden caves and on the tops of mountains from where they could view his boundless domain. They wandered in a haze past crystal pools and exotic gardens where songbirds chorused a divine symphony. They traversed scented forests on the back of the mighty, four-tusked Airavata, the elephant that Ravana had seized from Indra. The Lankapati never tired of bringing his queen new gifts—Rati's radiant earrings or Indrani's necklace of rubies.

Mandodari garlanded him with wild jasmine and yellow kadamba flowers, and inflamed him with her lovelorn glances and youthful desire. The air was heavy with the perfume of sandal and aloe, and peacocks danced amidst the fragrant clouds. It appeared as if the world had been newly created to celebrate their union and that all its creatures were caught up in the ecstasy of love.

The devas on high watched and marvelled that a rakshasa so fierce could be so tender. Would the power of love tame and transform the master of darkness? Or would his passion shrivel up and die as his heart was so cruel and lustful?

The lord of Vaikunta looked down at them all, deva and demon, and smiled.

4

Folly

Ravana found that the more he indulged his passion for his lissom queen, the more he desired her. He observed Mandodari raptly as she combed her long, rippling tresses and coloured her lips with the juice of red berries. He lurked behind the lavender tree with its emerald leaves and purple blossoms to watch her bathe in a silvery stream. At times, he stayed away only so that he could enjoy the sight of her pining for him, unable to eat or sleep. He laughed as he watched her cool her heated senses with a jewelled fan or whisper her love for him in the ears of the hamsa bird. She fed golden corn to a handsome black buck that she called her 'Beloved rakshasa'. And when he finally returned to her like a tempest, they came together in an explosion of delight.

Loathe to be parted from her, Ravana had her sit beside him in court, where she showed that she was as loyal as she was loving, and as intelligent as she was giving. Her devotion to the gods and her king was unfailing, and she did everything she could to ensure that his life was peaceful and blessed.

'We have never seen him so content,' said the courtiers who had often faced his blistering rage. 'His ambition seems to have been curbed by his passion for his queen.'

The alluring women in his harem were distraught and watched Mandodari with jealous eyes. 'The king ignores us all, lost in the charms of his new wife,' they whispered. 'Is she a sorceress that she has cast such a powerful spell on him?'

'Be careful, my queen,' said Mandodari's devoted maid to her one day. 'His wives plot your downfall and will stop at nothing to win him back.'

Mandodari nodded, knowing that this girl Kumuda was the only one she could trust in a palace where loyalties shifted every day. She had rescued the orphaned girl one day and brought her to the palace with her. Kumuda had repaid her handsomely since then, dedicating herself completely to her well-being.

Realizing that Ravana's insatiable urge to dominate and conquer new lands led him to sinful acts, Mandodari invented a war game to occupy him. It came to be known as Chaturanga for it featured four kinds of forces: elephants, horses, chariots and foot soldiers. She also attempted to gradually reshape his brutal nature with tender words. She told him that he had been blessed with many hands so that he could help people, and that his ten heads were meant to guide him on the right path.

However, this was not easy to achieve as Ravana was naturally vain and aggressive. One day, when he and Mandodari were worshipping Shiva by the river Narmada, the waters rose suddenly and violently and carried away his offerings. Ravana sprang up in wrath and ordered his men to find out what was behind the disturbance.

'King Kartaviryarjuna is bathing with his wives downstream, my king,' they said fearfully when they returned, knowing how

Ravana would react. 'He has blocked the river with his thousand arms so as to make an immense pond for his queens to play in.'

'A thousand arms!' Ravana exclaimed, furious that someone should challenge his own might.

'The sages say that Kartavirya has been blessed by Dattatreya, who embodies the Trimurti, and that none but Vishnu can defeat him' said Mandodari in a soft voice.

'I will soon expose their foolishness!' roared Ravana. 'A thousand arms or ten thousand—Kartavirya will pay the price for disrupting my prayers. Am I not the mightiest of kings, blessed by the great Shiva?'

'Your boon protects you from the devas and the demons, not from a human, my love,' Mandodari reminded him, fearing for his safety.

'A human king pitting himself against the emperor of emperors?' shouted Ravana, angry that his wife doubted his prowess. 'Your words prove that women lack judgement, Mandodari. You shudder at your own shadow and then bring your foolish fears to me.'

Mandodari said nothing more, realizing that Ravana would not stop now. He sallied forth in his vimana against his foe and roared a challenge. 'Kartaviryarjuna! You parade your powers before your wives by restraining a river that cannot fight back. Fight with me instead—paltry human!'

Kartavirya untangled himself slowly from the embrace of his wives and smiled mockingly at his challenger. 'Ravana! Come down from your vimana so that I can answer,' he said.

Bristling at his enemy's insolence, Ravana jumped down on earth and came forward with his mace in his hands. His foe picked up his own mace and charged at him.

The maces met in mid-air and both kings strained their formidable muscles to overpower the enemy. Kartavirya managed to deal a quick blow that knocked Ravana off his feet. But the rakshasa quickly recovered and hurled his mace at his enemy's chest, making him stagger on his feet. The two took up other fearsome weapons and continued the fight. Kartavirya's queens watched in fear as the battle continued through the day and the night with neither able to prevail. They fought with swords and iron clubs, with boulders and trees, until both of them were bleeding from a hundred wounds. Kartavirya expanded his form to dominate the earth and the sky, but Ravana roared in defiance and enlarged his own body to match his foe's. Angry that Ravana had dared to challenge him before his wives, Kartavirya resolved to put an end to the battle. He used his thousand arms at the same time to hurl spears, lances, axes, cudgels and spiked clubs at Ravana. When the rakshasa was fully engaged in blocking this fusillade, Kartavirya bludgeoned him to the ground.

The Lankapati sank to the ground in a swoon and woke up hours later—in his foe's dungeon. What a devastating blow this was! What would Mandodari think of his defeat, especially when she had warned him not to attack Kartavirya? The wound to Ravana's ego was greater than that to his body. He strained at the iron chains holding him captive and roared in wrath. His only hope was that his troops would have set out to battle the king of the Haiheyas.

Rescue came to him, however, from an unexpected direction. A few days after the encounter, Kartavirya's capital Mahishmati received a great visitor—Sage Pulastya, Ravana's grandfather.

Kartavirya bowed low to the sage and offered him a reverent welcome. Pulastya put forth his request. 'O Kartavirya! You are indeed unequalled in prowess for you have defeated my grandson whose dominion extends to the heavens. Ravana has now learned his lesson and will never oppose you again. Please free him from your prison, noble king,' he said.

The king of the Haiheyas acceded graciously, telling the sage, 'Mahishmati is blessed by your visit, Wise One, but you need not have gone to all this trouble. I will honour your slightest wish and a mere message from you in future will suffice to make me obey.'

The chastened Ravana was set free at once. The two kings clasped hands in friendship before the sage, swearing never to attack each other again. The Lankapati returned to his capital where Mandodari soothed him with her attentions and secretly hoped that his aggressive tendencies would be curbed by this debacle. She also worshipped the gods fervently, hoping that her piety would lighten the burden of her husband's karma.

'O Parvati!' she prayed. 'Your exalted love transformed Shiva from an ascetic into a loving husband and father. He honoured your devotion by making you half of himself so that the world could worship you both together. I pray that my love too may change my lord and turn him firmly towards the righteous path. Divine mother, bless me with powerful sons so that I may satisfy my husband's desire.'

That night, Mandodari was startled awake by a nightmare. She heard again the heavenly voice that had predicted doom if Ravana should marry her. Was this a reminder that she herself would be the cause of his downfall? She tossed and turned, praying that she should never give birth to a daughter. Her restlessness awakened Ravana who soothed her with his tender embrace.

'What is it you fear, my love?' he asked her, but she remained silent. 'What can assail the queen of the indomitable Lankeshwara? I will never allow anyone to harm you, precious

one. And you in turn must shield me with your love and
your purity.'

Mandodari let go of her fears for the moment. Indeed, was
she a frog still that she should tremble so? Her husband was
blessed by Shiva and ruled the planets that determined destiny.
No harm could ever touch them.

'Tell me that you love me,' she pleaded then. And he did so,
with his words and caresses. 'There is no place in my heart for any
woman but you,' he said.

Mandodari was soon with child and was greatly relieved
when the royal astrologer said that the offspring would be a
boy. Ravana ordered the planets to take positions in the most
auspicious houses on his son's birth chart, thereby ensuring that
he was immune to all dangers. Knowing that this would make
the rakshasa clan invulnerable and extend their evil reign forever,
Shanideva extended his leg into the next house at the exact
moment that the child was born. An angry Ravana punished
Shanideva by maiming his foot, but could do nothing to alter his
son's fate.

Ravana named the newborn Meghanada, because his voice
was loud like thunder. The child grew rapidly as was natural
among the rakshasas. He trained rigorously under the asura guru
Shukracharya to master the astras and the dark arts of sorcery.
Not satisfied with that, he embarked on severe penances to the
gods to acquire their blessings. Pleased with his ardour, Agni
blessed him with the power to turn invisible and gifted him an
invincible chariot drawn by tigers. Brahma gave him his most
powerful weapons. Armed with these, Prince Meghanada arrived
at the gates of Amaravati to challenge Indra to battle. Indra was
unable to kill him even with his thunderbolt, and the other devas
fled before the prince. Meghanada bound the celestial king with
his occult power and dragged him through the streets of Lanka.

'Glorious son, you will henceforth be known as Indrajit, the conqueror of Indra!' exclaimed his proud father.

Ravana had two more sons with Mandodari—Atikaya and Aksha. He had many sons from his other wives as well, but his dream of having a daughter did not come true. Unused to being deprived of anything, Ravana began to obsess about what he perceived as a void in his life.

'I have everything I desire,' he said to Mandodari. 'Everything except a daughter.'

'Why crave a daughter who will cause your death, my lord?' asked Mandodari, her face clouding over at the mere thought.

'Do you think I live in fear of a voice?' asked Ravana. 'The reality is that I am eager for a new challenge, as my shoulders grow weak with no enemy to fight against.'

Ravana studied astrological charts over the next few days, consulted his priests and finally decided to perform a yagna that would result in the birth of a daughter. Brahma would not be able to turn down his request when he had Mandodari beside him, for her piety and purity were unmatched on earth.

To his shock, however, when he spoke to Mandodari, she refused to join him in the sacrifice. 'The fear of the prophecy keeps me awake most nights,' she said to him. 'How can I pray for a daughter, when it means that I could lose you, my lord? Ask me for anything but not this, I beg you.'

Ravana was stunned for a moment. Then he flew into a rage. He sprang to his feet and hurled the heavy throne he had been seated on at the mirror in her chamber, splintering it into a thousand shards. Angry still, he drew out his sword and slashed at the canopy over her bed, bringing it down with a crash. Her maids came running, saw his contorted face and fled. Kumuda alone stood watching from the doorway, kneading her hands in distress.

Mandodari retreated to a corner of her chamber, looking at Ravana with shocked eyes. She had never seen his rage at such close quarters and that too directed at her. Tears ran down her cheeks as her mind raced to find a way to placate him. Should she capitulate? What if her refusal should cost her his love? How would she survive?

Ravana attacked her then with violent words. 'Have you forgotten your duty to me as a wife and as a subject?' he railed. 'Do you not know that the punishment for defying the lord of the three realms is torture and death?'

Mandodari attempted to explain that her refusal sprang from love and not from disrespect. But he silenced her with an angry roar. Was this why he had married her, in order to add another slave in his harem? Was it not her duty to counsel him when he chose a disastrous path? If this was what he expected of her, it would be better if he ended her life that very day. She was not willing to agree with him on everything and he owed it to their love to at least listen when she spoke. She looked up at him, her face set in grim resolve.

Thwarted in his desire, enraged at her unaccustomed defiance, yet unable to lay violent hands on her, Ravana finally said, 'If you will not give me a daughter, there are many who will. I will find one as pure and lovely as you are, if not better.' He stormed out of her presence, leaving her chamber and her mind in shambles.

His other wives were delighted when they heard of their argument. 'You are no ordinary man, but the king of kings, with many noble princesses and apsaras as your queens,' said one of them. 'Choose one of us and we will gladly accept the honour to perform the yagna by your side.'

'Banish Mandodari who has shown herself to be stubborn and unworthy of your love, great emperor,' said another jealous wife.

However, their attempts to provoke him had just the opposite effect on Ravana. He would not tolerate any criticism of Mandodari and he ordered them to leave him alone. He prowled the far-flung corners of his kingdom, venting his rage on the weak and the young, destroying ashrams and performing dark rituals to augment his powers. Everywhere he went, he looked for a challenger, someone he could defeat to reaffirm his supremacy in the eyes of the world.

On one of his rampages, Ravana heard of Indra's son, the vanara king Vali, who ruled undefeated in Kishkinda. They said that Vali's favourite sport was to toss huge mountains in the air and catch them again in his arms. Vali was also armed with a boon by which he gained half his enemy's strength when he faced him in combat.

Unfazed by what he had heard, Ravana resolved to kill Vali by stealth while the vanara offered worship to Surya on the shores of the four seas. He crept up behind him when Vali began his prayers by the southern ocean. But Indra's son sensed him approaching and trapped Ravana's neck under his arm while he continued with his rituals. When he had completed his ablutions, Vali rose into the skies like Garuda, with Ravana still pinioned under his arm, and flew to the western ocean. The rakshasa flailed desperately, trying to escape, but was unable to do so. Still gripping him, Vali flew to the northern and the eastern seas, submerging Ravana when he stood waist-deep in the water and chanted his mantras. His worship completed, Vali flew to Kishkinda and there dropped the rakshasa to the ground, pretending to notice him only then.

'O, a toy for Angada!' he exclaimed, reducing Ravana in size so that he could tie him on top of his son's cradle.

The Lankapati realized that he would never succeed in freeing himself from this mighty vanara and decided to throw himself at his mercy. 'O king!' he said. 'Your strength and your flight through the air have left me dumbfounded. I erred in thinking that I could kill you by deceit and have realized that it would be foolish to have you as my enemy. Let us be allies, great Vali. Let us fight no more until the end of time.'

The magnanimous Vali laughed heartily on hearing this and embraced him in friendship. He gave Ravana the respect due to an honoured guest and showered him with rare gifts.

When he returned to his own kingdom, Ravana chose to interpret this encounter and the earlier one with Kartavirya in a manner that suited his own conceit. He claimed that these were victories rather than defeats, for he had managed to neutralize his biggest foes. Now he could rule unimpeded, without fear of defeat.

The rakshasa preened and postured, and paraded a bevy of beautiful women he had seized in his rampages around the world. Mandodari spent her days shedding bitter tears, experiencing his petulance for the first time. Why could he not understand that her refusal to perform the yagna with him was based on her love and her fear for his life? What if he replaced her in his affections with another woman? She could not survive his rejection . . . She would die!

5

Cursed

Ravana soon began to enjoy his old life, indulging in debauched amusements. 'This is the way an emperor should live!' he told himself. 'Besotted by my new wife, I suppressed my natural instincts and led an arid life. But did Mandodari appreciate my sacrifice? No. She grew so complacent that she spurned my desire for a daughter. I love her still, no doubt, but will not give up my pleasures anymore. She must see the error of her ways before I accept her again.'

At times though, he recalled her face when he had declared that he would cast her aside for a more beautiful woman. He had seen the blood drain out of her face in shock. She had been a devoted wife after all and had indulged his every whim, except for one. Her refusal this time too stemmed from concern for his life. Mandodari watched over him now with the same care that Pulastya had shown during his childhood. And he knew deep in his heart that he could never be happy when he was away from his frog princess.

However, Ravana soon chased away these uncomfortable thoughts and told himself that he had done nothing wrong. It was Mandodari who should make the first conciliatory move. He could never surrender to anyone, least of all a woman.

The rakshasa now focused his resentment on families that enjoyed the love that he himself had lost. He amused himself by separating wives from their husbands and children, crushing their protests in his bed or winning them over with his gifts. He abducted and defiled young girls and gave full vent to his hedonistic impulses.

His grandfather Pulastya came to him one day and reminded him of the days when his mind had been unsullied. 'You curbed your senses, performed penances and acquired boons that helped you conquer the realms,' the sage said. 'But alas, your senses are now taking their revenge by controlling you.'

Ravana was respectful to Pulastya while he was with him, but once he had returned to his ashram, he unleashed his wickedness once more.

On one such expedition, he was attracted by a bright glow radiating from the sacred Pushkara forest. He descended to the ground in his vimana, eager to find the source of this light. It was here that his fate caught up with him, in the form of the enchanting Vedavati.

Vedavati was a young tapasvini meditating upon Vishnu in order to be united with him. She was none other than Goddess Lakshmi born on earth as the daughter of King Kushadhwaja. The king in his conceit had stopped worshipping the goddess who had blessed him with good fortune. An angry Lakshmi had left him, leaving him prey to calamities and loss. The rains failed and the land dried up, the royal treasury became empty, his enemies attacked and the king was driven from his throne and kingdom. Kushadhwaja then embarked on a severe penance to placate the goddess. She finally took pity on him and promised that she would be born as his daughter.

Soon afterwards, the king's wife gave birth to a miraculous child who chanted the Vedas as soon as she was born. Hence, they named her Vedavati, and with her blessings they regained their fortunes and their kingdom. The goddess, having kept her promise, left the palace to begin severe penances in the forest, wishing to return to her lord in Vaikunta. This was where Ravana chanced upon her.

He saw the divine maiden who glowed with the lustre of a loftier realm and was spellbound by her incredible beauty. Her garb was simple but her face and form were so lovely that he grew dazzled and lovelorn.

'Who are you, fair maiden? An apsara or a goddess? What do you do in this fierce forest, all alone?' he asked. But Vedavati's eyes remained closed and her lips continued to chant the sacred mantras. 'Marry me and be my queen,' Ravana persisted, growing more impatient by the moment. 'I am Ravana, king of Lanka, and I offer you a life befitting your youth and beauty.'

Vedavati's eyes flew open and rage shimmered in them. 'How dare you address me in such terms?' she asked, her voice fierce. 'I am Princess Vedavati and I will marry no one but the lord of the universe, the great Vishnu himself. Leave my presence at once, asura.'

'You are speaking to none other than the lord of the universe, foolish maiden,' Ravana scoffed. 'Your Vishnu is nothing compared to my strength and my wealth. Give up your fruitless penance and come with me so that you may enjoy pleasures beyond imagination. Sweet Vedavati, your lips are meant to be kissed, your body to be caressed . . .'

'Raging fool!' Vedavati cried out, cutting him short. 'You rant without knowing that you face certain doom!'

'If you will not come with me willingly, I must take you by force,' snarled Ravana as he grabbed her by her hair. Vedavati rose to her feet, her wrath surging forth in a wave towards him. Her hand chopped down like a sword to lop off the tresses that he had touched.

'You have defiled me, rakshasa,' she said, 'and you will soon face the consequences of your lust.'

He leapt back as a fierce fire rose between them. Vedavati stepped into the fire, her heart fixed on the radiant lord reclining on Adisesha.

Thwarted by a woman again, Ravana exploded into a frenzy. He ravaged the forest, killing the innocent animals that roamed there. Then he soared through the realms looking for a woman who would satisfy the desire that Vedavati had aroused in him. This time, an apsara caught his eye—Rambha, the queen of the apsaras.

Rambha had been sent to earth to disrupt Sage Vishvamitra's penance as it threatened Indra's throne. But Vishvamitra had grown angry when she interrupted his meditation and cursed her to become a stone for a thousand years. The unfortunate Rambha had languished as a stone, waiting to be released from her present state and from her life as an apsara when she was used by the gods to attain their own ends. She dreamed of a gallant lover who would desire her for herself and cherish her forever. Would she ever be so fortunate?

And then, when she was finally restored to life, the first man she encountered was the gallant Nalakubara, the son of Kubera.

His ardent wooing and noble manner convinced her that he was the man she had been waiting for during her endless vigil. They were soon married, only to have their idyll interrupted by the vile Ravana.

A full moon shed its silvery light on the celestial garden where Rambha was gathering fragrant yellow champaka flowers to make a garland for her beloved. Ravana could hear the lilting songs of love sung by heavenly singers. And before him was a beauty whose charms had captivated the gods. How then could a rakshasa resist her? Rambha was slender yet curvaceous, delicate yet sensuous. Her shapely limbs were golden, anointed with sandal paste. Her dark hair flowed like a torrent down to her hips, glinting with white jasmine blossoms, like the midnight blue sky studded with stars. Delighted to come upon such a prize, Ravana floated lightly to the ground and obstructed her path. The doe-eyed maiden glanced at him and joined her hands together in respect.

But respect was not what the asura craved. 'Who are you and where are you headed, so beautifully adorned?' he asked in his resonant voice.

'Do you not know me, great king?' asked Rambha. 'I am Rambha, the wife of Nalakubara, your brother's son. I am on my way to meet my husband.'

Ravana watched entranced at the way her lips moved and the graceful sway of her body as she spoke. Blinded by lust, he ignored her words and stepped closer and grabbed her hand. 'You may not go anywhere!' he growled. 'Stay with me and cool my body that is heated with passion. We will attain bliss together, uniting our skills in the magical arts of Kama.'

Rambha struggled to free herself, her eyes filling with helpless tears. 'It is your duty to protect me, O king!' she said. 'It is not dharma to treat your daughter-in-law in this fashion.'

'You speak as if you are Nalakubara's wife alone,' he leered. 'Are you not an apsara who shares her bed with many men at Indra's behest?'

The rakshasa seized her trembling body in rough arms, silenced her protest with cruel lips and took her by force. Finally satiated, he flew away with a triumphant smile. Soon, Mandodari would hear about his tryst with the beauteous apsara. She would be hurt, no doubt. He felt sorry for a moment, but then his arrogance took over. Did his queen think that there was no one else to satisfy his passion? He had been a slave to her love and she had spurned him. She had to suffer now until she realized what a great prize she had lost.

A distraught Rambha carried the story to Nalakubara who pronounced a terrible curse on the king. 'If Ravana should ever violate a woman again, his head shall shatter into a thousand pieces,' he said.

And the gods whispered, 'Tathastu!'

Outside Ravana's palace, his guards cried out in fear as the royal flagstaff splintered and toppled with a crash. Mandodari woke up with a moan and heard the curse thundering against the walls. She was soon informed of Ravana's misdeeds. His other queens gloated that she too had been cast aside, just as they had been when Ravana had married Mandodari.

'Did you think that your beauty was so dazzling that he would remain forever under your spell?' they mocked. 'What was so special about you that he should give up his old ways?'

Mandodari could not help but feel guilty that she had not been able to stop his downward spiral. Perhaps if she had agreed to the yagna, he would have remained faithful. With his powers and her prayers, they could have challenged fate. But she had been obstinate and had ended up losing him entirely. An uncertain prophecy had vanquished the certainty of love. She had been a fool and betrayed the very cause for which she had been born.

It was Kumuda who finally roused her from her anguish by appealing to her intellect. 'Is the king totally free of blame, my queen?' she asked. 'He forgets his promises to you and refuses to acknowledge the love that prompted your decision. You knew that his well-being was more important than his desire for a daughter. What has happened now is merely the result of his uncontrolled lust.'

When the maid left her so that she could rest awhile, Mandodari pondered sadly about her future. From being the beloved wife of an emperor, she had descended to being the discarded mistress, the object of mockery and pity. She felt hurt, angry, desperate and heartbroken—all at the same time. More than anything else, she felt betrayed. He had violated her trust in him. But was it his fault or hers that she had believed him when he had probably sworn eternal love to each of the beauties he had wooed? Not Ravana alone, she too had been vain in thinking that she was superior to his other wives. She felt a deep pain in the pit of her stomach as if he had physically assaulted her.

She dismissed her attendants and paced to and fro, reflecting on her dismal fate. She no longer had the strength to listen to tales of Ravana's depravity or watch his headlong rush towards disaster. Maybe it would be better to die now than to agonize over his downfall. But the sages said that those who killed themselves would be condemned to endless suffering in naraka. And what of her sons who would be shattered at losing her? Her thoughts conjured up images of her firstborn, Meghanada, valiant Atikaya and her youngest child, Aksha . . . If she were to die now, they would come fully under the sinful sway of Ravana.

But her wounded heart forced her to return again and again to thoughts of death. Even naraka would be better than the life she was leading. Now there was nothing she could do and nothing to live for. She needed something that would kill her silently, without attracting anyone's attention.

Poison. That was what she needed. Her mind flitted at once to the pot that was stored in a dark alcove in her bedchamber. Ravana had killed numerous ascetics and sages and stored their blood as a means to acquire their powers through occult rites. He had chosen to hide the pot in her antapura as her bedchamber was forbidden to everyone except him. He had warned her too to keep away from the potion, as it was the deadliest poison on earth.

'I will drink this potion,' resolved Mandodari, her face pale yet determined. 'It is fitting that I should die by the fruits of Ravana's sins, the darkest of his crimes. Maybe the shock of my death will bring him back to the path of virtue. If I cannot live for him, I can at least die for him. My love then will not be futile.'

Her eyes overflowed with tears as she lifted the pot in her hands.

6

Torment

Mandodari closed her eyes tight as she tilted the pot and poured some of its contents into her mouth. The taste and smell of the blood, together with the horror she felt at what she was doing made her retch dreadfully. She stifled her cries with a supreme effort of will and put down the pot with trembling hands. But a fierce moan erupted unbidden when she wiped her lips and saw the dark blood on her hand. What had she done? How could she have drunk this awful brew? And why was she alive still? She had willingly sought death despite her fears that she would be cast into a world of unending torture.

Perhaps she needed to drink more of the vile potion, for she could not stop now. She had to complete what she had started before she was discovered by her maids or by her husband. Mandodari shuddered. She knew that Ravana would suffer immensely when she died, for he did love her. But he would also regard her action as an affront to his supremacy, for he regarded her as his possession, to live or die as he commanded.

What if he came in now before the deed was complete? Perhaps he would kill her with a fierce blow so that he could tell himself that her death had been determined by him. Or perhaps he would use his dark powers to revive her, just so that he could torment her every day.

She lifted the pot with a trembling hand to her lips again, only to have it snatched away. Had Ravana arrived, summoned here by her thoughts? She whirled around, bracing herself to confront his fury.

'How could you do this, my queen? Why should you sacrifice your life to pay for the king's sins?' It was Kumuda who stood before her, her eyes overflowing with tears. She wiped Mandodari's lips with a wet cloth in a desperate bid to erase the effects of the poison that was even now coursing through her body.

Fond Kumuda, so young and so loving. The daughter I will never have, thought Mandodari. *I am happy that it will be her face that I see before I die.*

'Permit me to call the physician, my queen!' Kumuda said desperately. 'It is not too late to save you.'

Mandodari reached for her hand and held it tight. 'Allow me to die, Kumuda,' she pleaded. 'I cannot stand by and watch as the curses snatch him away. I am unable to shed my guilt for spurning him when I knew well that his ego could not tolerate such a blow.'

'But he is the one who sinned against a wife who will die rather than see him suffer!' Kumuda replied fiercely. Her clear young eyes discerned the truth that her king could not.

'If you love me, you will obey my last wish!' said Mandodari even as she felt a strange languor envelop her mind and body.

Ravana, who was far away in patala, caught up in the embrace of a lustrous naga princess, was overcome by a strange feeling. He pushed the princess away, his eyes drawn to a dark corner of the bedchamber where he could see a luminous figure. Was it Mandodari? He looked closer, but now he could only see the curtains fluttering fiercely in the wind.

Perhaps his guilty heart had conjured up a vision of his wife. But his reason told him that he was not at fault. Mandodari had erred by mistrusting him and choosing to believe a voice emanating from the deceitful gods. Did she think that she knew better than he did? Had he not assured her that he could meet any challenge when he had her beside him? He had realized soon enough that the maiden who had captivated him was not Parvati. But that knowledge had not constrained him from loving her and telling her that he was more blessed than Shiva. In the end, though, Mandodari had betrayed him. Why should he waste time thinking about her when he could be enjoying the caresses of the nagakanya? He buried his face in the maiden's neck, losing himself in the fragrance of her body and the allure of her silken limbs.

Mandodari felt as if she was floating, watching herself as she lay on her bed, in readiness for what was to come.

'Om Namo Narayana! Om Namo Narayana!' Her mind filled with the resonance of the supreme mantra that awakens the divine power within. She could see a vision of Lord Vishnu, radiant in yellow silk, holding the conch, the chakra and the mace, smiling as he lifted a hand in blessing. Her body was infused with a glorious energy, uplifting her mind and soul.

In her trance, she saw Sage Gritsamada gathering durva grass, a plant that had been rendered sacred when drops of nectar had fallen on it during the churning of the eternal ocean. The sage extracted the milk from the durva and began a fierce tapasya to Lakshmi. But why was she seeing these mystic visions? How did she even know who the sage was? Mandodari then saw her ten-headed lord make his way stealthily into the ashram, carry off the milk and add it to his pot of blood. She moaned and sat up slowly in her bed, discovering that her body was strangely heavy. Her eyes opened wide when she saw that her belly was swollen as if she was with child. How was that possible? Had Ravana performed some occult rite to compel her to have his daughter? Perhaps it was too late even now to counter the prophecy. Or was all this a hallucination caused by the poison she had drunk? Mandodari shook her head to clear the cobwebs shrouding her mind.

She then heard the soft gurgling of a child and felt a touch on her midriff as if from a small hand or foot. She saw the perfectly formed child lying by her side, a beautiful girl with eyes like lotus petals and lips like rosebuds. Had she travelled to another dimension where she had delivered a child miraculously without pain? Was it due to Vishnu's blessing or to the magic of this newborn?

Mandodari saw Kumuda staring awestruck at the child and felt a breeze swirling around them, bringing with it the fragrance of the parijata flower. The child kicked her again and she realized that this was no dream. The infant was smiling at her as if to say that everything had happened as it should.

Ravana's queen touched the child's petal-soft cheek while her mind wrestled with the turn of events. How had the poison not killed her but brought new life instead? Was the infant an imp from the netherworld who had come to torment her? No, this child was divine. Nothing evil could ever be part of her. Perhaps this was the effect of the milk extracted by the rishi from the durva grass. She had heard that the grass was so potent that it sprouted again after it was plucked. Perhaps its powers of fertility had dispelled the effects of the poison.

'Who are you, wondrous child, who came so magically from my womb? The daughter I ached to hold but knew I could not . . .' she murmured, lifting her up in her arms and clasping her close. She saw the infant opening her tender lips seeking to be fed, and helped her find her breast.

'Is this the daughter prophesied to bring doom upon our king and our people?' whispered Kumuda. 'The one you swore would never be born?'

Mandodari wilted as she heard the words. Her shoulders slumped. Her joy was now swamped with fear. 'She is so precious, Kumuda. Look upon her sweet face and tell me how she can cause harm. Maybe the fates will spare my lord, as this little one was born not from him, but from the poison I drank.'

She was torn between her love for Ravana and the gross injustice to the child if she were to kill her. Kill her? How could she even think of such a dastardly act? A child so beautiful could not embody someone's death. She would keep her close, keep her safe. Maybe this was a chance given to her to reclaim Ravana's love. Maybe with prayer and penance they could defeat the prophecy. Hope lighted up her face only to be quenched at once.

'But no,' she continued. 'The blood of the sages was the fruit of Ravana's cruelty. The durva milk too was snatched from a noble ascetic. So Ravana is responsible for whatever happened when I drank the brew. And the little one is indeed the daughter I swore I would never have.' Her face twisted in anguish. 'What will happen now? What should I do?'

Mandodari knew that Ravana would view this child as a blessing and the fruit of his prayers. He would look at the skies with a challenge in his eyes, asking the gods to defeat him if they could. He would show the world that prophecy or not, Ravana was invincible.

'Fate directs me to get rid of my child,' Mandodari whispered. 'But how can I do that?' She shuddered and saw her own horror reflected in Kumuda's eyes. 'Why are the gods forcing me to choose between my child's life and my husband's?'

'You cannot think that the two lives are equal. He is steeped in sin and she is so pure,' protested Kumuda. Then she clapped a hand to her mouth, afraid that she had gone too far. The queen had never permitted anyone to speak ill of her husband. But Mandodari was too distraught to pay attention to her words.

'It is not just my husband's life that is at stake. The prophecy predicted the ruin of our clan,' she murmured, forcing herself to think. 'Preserving my child's life could result in the death of many. But how can I give her up? How can I fail her when it is a mother's foremost duty to protect her child? I am truly cursed. Do I have any choice but to let my child go, to pay for my sins and those of my lord? Alas, my daughter, you are cursed too, for you were born from my womb!'

Mandodari clutched the chortling infant close, trying to find a way out of her dilemma. A sudden thought flashed into her mind and she began to grapple with its ramifications. Maybe this was the solution to preserve her child and also ward off the prophecy. She sprang to her feet to put her plan into action at once, before her husband should return. She had fed the child for the first and the last time and now gave her a sleeping potion so that her cries would not awaken her attendants. Around the child's neck she fastened a gold chain with an enormous blue sapphire, the gem favoured by Saturn, the dominant planet at the time of the child's birth. Her lips murmured obeisance to Shanideva who was the lord of life and fortune, and the teacher of the hard truths of life. She placed the little one in a jewelled casket, closed the lid and slipped out quietly. Kumuda followed her queen, racked with grief, her muffled sobs the only sound in the night.

The queen set the casket afloat on the dark sea behind her palace to be carried far from her husband and her people. Then, when she saw the swift current bear the casket away, she cried out in a frenzy of grief and ran into the water to retrieve it. But it was already beyond her reach and Kumuda dragged her back to the shore.

'Let me go,' sobbed Mandodari. 'I must have been demented to think that my child could survive the thundering sea with all its dire creatures. What an evil mother I am that I cast her away in this fashion! I am as guilty of killing her as if I had throttled her myself.'

Her lips moved in a desperate plea to the gods. 'May foam-bedecked Varuna protect you, my dearest,' she wept. 'May fierce Vayu be gentle and transport you to a safe harbour. May the Trimurti grant their protection to this abandoned child. May nourishing Earth guide you to someone who will love and treasure you. Little one, so tender, so helpless, so small! Forgive this cruel mother who will pay for her wickedness by spending her remaining days in pain. Still I hope that you will be sheltered by another woman who will love you as you should be loved. Your face is that of a goddess, though this ill-fated mother will never see it again. Go with Vishnu, my love!' she sobbed, straining her eyes for a last glimpse of the casket.

She collapsed then on the moonlit sands, until Kumuda came to her and clasped her in her strong young arms. Mandodari clutched at the girl, incoherent in grief. 'All will be well,' Kumuda said softly. 'Your child will have a better life than she ever could in the palace of a sinful king. Come, my queen, let us return to the palace before the other maids discover our absence.'

The unfortunate mother took tottering steps back to her bedchamber where she collapsed, bidding Kumuda to keep everyone away. 'My husband will return soon,' she whispered, her eyes wide in fear. 'If he should discover that I cast away the daughter he has been longing for . . . O Ravana, my king! How will I ever look at your face again knowing what I did?'

Ravana could sense that his wife was calling to him, for she was still the queen of his heart. He saw her in his mind, tears spilling from eyes dulled with pain. She tossed and turned on her bed and wept fitfully. He heard her cry out, 'My love, my beloved!' Was she calling to him or was it to someone else? He gnashed his teeth at the mere thought.

'No, she can never be unfaithful. She loves me,' he roared, startling the naga princess and making her draw back from him in fear. He sprang out of the velvet bed, his clothes in disarray, his eyes red. He quickly set himself in order and snatched up his moon sword. 'I am coming to you, Mandodari!' he shouted, as if his voice could span the world and reach her ears.

Mandodari awoke from her torpor and called out to Kumuda who had fallen asleep on the floor at her feet. 'He is coming, he is coming!' she gasped. 'Remove all traces of what happened here. Help me adorn myself so that he does not suspect that there is anything amiss. Help me, dear one, or all will be lost. My life and yours are in peril!'

7

Temptation

Mandodari rushed to cleanse her face and change her raiment while Kumuda returned the pot of poison to its hiding place. The girl swiftly straightened the bed and helped her mistress remove all traces of her recent ordeal.

Soon enough, there was a flurry of activity and the sound of heavy footsteps and voices raised in praise of the emperor. Ravana strode in hurriedly, his eyes rolling as they scanned every corner of the bedchamber. His face was sombre and his manner fierce. He wanted to let his wife know that he was still angry with her. He watched impassively as Mandodari performed an aarti of welcome and sprinkled flowers and fine perfumes over him.

'What news, my love?' he asked her, noting that she looked wan and avoided his eyes. Was she distressed that he had been seeking the company of other women? Did she not realize that this was the consequence of her obstinacy? He had nothing to apologize for. 'Are you hiding something, my queen?' he asked again, his voice a low growl. Mandodari raised fearful eyes to his face, revealing that she was no longer his blithe queen who boldly expressed her feelings. Had he hurt her so much with his behaviour? His tender feelings warred with his anger and resentment. He had given her his heart, and in return he expected total obedience.

Seeing his reddened eyes and the way he clenched his fists, Mandodari hastened to answer. 'I have done nothing except to await your return, my lord,' she said, a tremulous smile on her lips. 'You know well that my sole purpose in life is to adore you.'

Ravana heard the sincerity in her voice, but his suspicions were not lulled completely. He would have his spies question her maids. Where was Kumuda, who was his queen's confidante? He spotted her, peering at him from behind the massive door of the chamber. The girl's eyes dropped when she met his fiery gaze and then she raised them again to stare at him. He sensed now that there was something she knew that he did not. He would allow them to think that he had been fooled and confront them again when they were unprepared. No one could betray the king—not unless they wished to lose their heads. His nostrils flared as he smelled a faint fragrance that was alien to him. What could it be? Had Mandodari performed some rituals to bring him back to her? He was pleased with the thought that she was repentant. He quickly folded his queen in his arms. After all, she had no one but him and would not like the thought of him in the embrace of another woman. He heard the sob that erupted from her lips.

'I am back, my love. Do not fear. You will never lose me,' he murmured. Her clinging arms and tender kisses cast their spell on him again as they always had.

Ravana decided to stay awhile in Lanka and forget his wanderings. His beloved was eager to please him and he could see in her renewed ardour the young girl he had wooed and won. But some inner sense was still warning him not to let down his defences. Was there a threat to his kingdom perhaps? But who would have the audacity to confront him?

He called his spies to him the next day when he was seated in his court with Mandodari and sought a report on everything that had happened in his absence. They shook in terror as they informed him that all was well and that they had performed their duties diligently. Even as they were speaking, his restless eyes lighted upon his queen and he saw how her face had paled. At once, his suspicions flared up.

'Leave us!' he barked at his ministers and courtiers. When Mandodari rose to her feet, he beckoned her closer by raising an imperious finger. *Does he know?* she wondered. *Does he suspect?* But how was that possible, that too when several days had passed after his return? Perhaps one of his spies had told him something. Or one of the rakshasis standing guard around her antapura had heard an infant's cry. She stifled the sob that rose from within at the thought of her child at the mercy of the stormy seas. *Where are you, my little one? Will I ever see you again?* She saw her husband's keen eyes studying her and wondered how to distract him.

Ravana surprised her by pulling her roughly onto his lap. When she looked up at his face, startled, he said gruffly, 'May I not show my love for my queen from whom I have been parted for so long? Do you not desire it too, my love?'

She forced a smile and lifted her hand to touch his face gently. 'How can you even ask me this question, lord of my heart?' she replied. 'I was merely surprised that you chose to express your affection in open court.' She reached up to kiss him lightly on his cheek and then fluttered tiny kisses down his tense jawline, trying to soften him.

He turned her face upward with one huge hand and directed a hard, probing stare into her eyes. 'I hope my absence has made you think hard and deep, my wife,' he said, his voice a sibilant whisper. Her lips trembled and she clasped her hands together to hide their trembling.

'Yes, my love. I have spent my days praying that we are never parted from each other again.'

'That will depend solely on your actions, my beloved!'

What does he mean by that? she wondered. No one knew what she had done. No one except Kumuda. And Kumuda would never betray her.

Mandodari lowered her eyes, seeking desperately for some way to allay Ravana's suspicions. If he gained even an inkling of the truth, he would most likely attack her and then set out to look for his daughter. Whether the child was alive or not, calamity would certainly follow. He would never forgive his wife for what she had done. Her lips quivered. Maybe she should have braved fate and kept her daughter close. She could have at least enjoyed a few blissful days before he discovered the truth.

Ravana looked down at her bowed head, his mind in turmoil. Was he being foolish to suspect that she was hiding something? Did he not know that his chaste queen would never seek another man? Maybe her jittery manner was due to her guilt over driving him away with her obstinacy. Perhaps he himself was to blame in some measure for having stayed away so long. Whatever the cause, he could see that her usual exuberance was missing. There was a sadness in her manner that she was unable to conceal however hard she tried. But he would have to discover more before he confronted her.

'You may go,' he said to her then, and watched dourly as she walked away. He summoned Ketu, his bodyguard, with a quick clap of his hands. 'Bring me the queen's maid, Kumuda,' he ordered.

Soon, the young girl stood before him, eyes wide in terror and her whole body trembling as Ravana glared at her. 'Tell me what happened when I was away,' he demanded. 'Why is my queen so wan and pale?'

'There is n . . . nothing to tell you, great king,' she whispered. 'You know well that your queen is purer than the Ganga, and more devoted than Arundhati, the chaste wife of Sage Vashista.'

'Answer my questions alone!' he roared, standing up to tower over her. 'I do not need a maid to testify to my queen's loyalty. I know well that it is her pure heart that shields me from harm, not my armour or my valour.' He was silent for a moment, shocked by his own confession. Mandodari's love had made him humble, and this was a weakness that he could not allow.

He pulled Kumuda's head up by her hair and glared into her eyes. 'I know that you are hiding something,' he said. 'Reveal the truth now or you will suffer!'

'My queen was in agony because you left her, my king,' she stammered then. 'You know as well as I do that her every moment, her every thought is focused on you.'

He nodded, happy to hear her reinforce his own belief. 'Do not fear me, Kumuda,' he said softly, freeing her from his grip. 'Show me your loyalty and I will reward you generously!'

Was he asking her to spy on her mistress for him? She looked at him in confusion, unable to keep pace with his moods. He smiled then and his forked tongue hissed out of his mouth, making her stumble backwards in fear.

He grabbed her shoulder, shouting, 'Tell me what she is hiding. This is your last chance to confess, you fool!'

Kumuda cowered before him like a mouse cornered by a snake. He pulled out a dagger from his waist belt and drew a long line with it down her arm. She screamed in pain and stared at the blood spurting out in a swift stream. 'I . . . will not betray . . . my queen,' she said finally, unsteady on her feet as her senses began to fail.

'That means that there is something to betray!' he exclaimed, shaking her fiercely again.

'You must trust her, you must!' the girl whispered. Her eyes blazed then in a final spark of rebellion. She would speak up for her queen who had saved her from evil men such as the one standing before her. 'Do you not know that she is a hundred thousand times superior to you? You were never worthy of her love and loyalty!'

Ravana was dumbfounded for a moment and then he exploded in incendiary rage. He stabbed the girl in the chest with terrible force. Kumuda uttered a gurgling cry and collapsed, just as Mandodari came running in, having discovered that Ketu had dragged the girl away.

'Kumuda!' she screamed, falling to the ground beside the lifeless girl and placing her head on her lap. 'How could you do this?' she shouted at Ravana. 'You killed an innocent who knew nothing but her love for me! Your ungoverned rage has changed you into a beast, Ravana! No prayers of mine can salvage your cruel soul anymore!' Her tears fell unheeded as she closed Kumuda's eyes with a trembling hand.

But Ravana's rage was unabated as he could not accept that he had been thwarted by Kumuda's courage and loyalty. 'Tell me what she wouldn't. You must!' he roared. Mandodari raised her head and glared at him.

She laid her shawl on the ground like a pillow and gently lowered Kumuda's head onto it. Then she rose to her feet, majestic like a lioness protecting her young. 'What have you accomplished by killing her?' she asked in a low, fierce voice. 'What is it you doubt? My love or my chastity? It is you who deserted me to roam the world to defile women and add to your evil karma. I have remained in your gilded prison, besieged by spies and jealous queens, pining for you. You have returned now after months of absence only to insult me.' Her voice rose as her anger increased. 'Are you still the man I married, the one who

searched the universe until he found me? Are you the gallant who
defied my parents and the voice from the gods in order to marry
me? All I see now is a demented rakshasa whose hands are stained
by the blood of innocents and whose aura is dark with sin. I am
weary and desolate. Leave me alone so that I may grieve my loss.'

There was silence then while Mandodari stood with her head
bowed. There was nothing he could say in reply. He paused in
thought for a moment and then walked away.

Days and months passed. An impenetrable wall had risen
between Ravana and his adored queen. Mandodari still felt his
eyes watching her every movement. He stationed more guards
around her chamber, and a fierce rakshasi took Kumuda's place
in her antapura. She often saw Ketu lurking in the shadows or
threatening her maids. But there was nothing for him to discover.
Kumuda had taken her secret with her.

Ravana brought home young princesses from many foreign
lands and cavorted with them before his wife's eyes. But she
remained listless, tortured by her own pain and guilt. She
screamed in her sleep, feeling the dagger pierce her own breast.
'You died for me, sweet Kumuda,' she moaned. 'Forgive me, dear
one, for I could not protect you.'

Now Ravana was always angry, always aggressive. His vanity
would not let him accept that his own wife defied him with her
silence. What had he not given her? Had he not brought her the
rarest treasures on earth and heaven? Had he not proclaimed
to the world that Mandodari was more beautiful than Parvati
herself? And then, she had repaid him by denying him a daughter
and keeping secrets from him.

Yet, he could not lay rough hands on her, for he still
remembered the sweet-faced innocence that had captured his
heart in Kailasa. He recalled his delight when he had found
her again in the jungle, after he had almost given up hope. Her

startled eyes had met his and the deep blush that had stained her creamy cheeks had matched the hibiscus she wore in her hair. Ravana yearned to return to those idyllic days when love had not been marred by doubt and suspicion.

It was then that the fates intervened. A visitor to their palace brought him some news that would change the course of their lives forever.

8

Beauteous Sita

Ravana sat resplendent like Surya, on a throne hewn out of a magnificent emerald that he had discovered in a fierce jungle guarded by black panthers. He wore ten glittering crowns on his heads. A massive necklace studded with giant rubies stretched from one ten-armed shoulder to the other. His chest was bare, revealing the deep scars he had received in his battle with Indra, caused by his enemy's thunderbolt and by his elephant, Airavata. Surya and Agni stood before him with their hands folded in respect; Vasuki, the emperor of the nagas, stood reverently before him with an offering of precious gems. Mandodari sat beside the king on his throne.

A rasping wail broke the fearful silence that prevailed in the court. A huge woman with straggling hair and a harsh face bounded in like a dark wind.

'Surpanakha!' gasped the courtiers, who knew her reputation for ferocity. Then they noticed that her ears had been chopped off and that only a mangled stump remained of her nose. Which man or beast had been responsible for this foolhardy attack on the rakshasi?

They had heard that Ravana's sister was living in the dark forests of Dandaka with her asura cousins, Khara and Dushana. With them resided many dire demons, who killed and ate men and animals with equal relish, and destroyed the ashrams of the sages who lived there. Why had she come here now after so many years?

'So the great Ravana sits here making love to his unworthy wife while his sister is abused and mutilated?' she taunted.

Ravana's hand flashed to his sword, but then he satisfied himself with a warning growl. 'Speak with respect to your king and his queen,' he said. 'Have you forgotten that it was Mandodari who supported your marriage to Vidyutjihva, the scion of my enemy clan?'

'Yes, I remember. Perhaps it is you who has forgotten that you killed my husband when you invaded the Danava kingdom in your quest to become emperor!' she retorted. 'And then, when I raised my voice in protest, you banished me to the Dandaka forest.'

'Why do you speak of things that are long past?' asked Ravana, his voice scornful. 'Tell me why you are here now or return again to your foul lair.'

'I came here with the hope that you still had some love for your sister,' said Surpanakha, her chest heaving. 'Do you not care to find out what two humans did to me? Or do you prefer to remain ignorant of everything that goes on beyond the doors of your harem? Your monstrous ego clouds your senses. Your artful ministers and spies tell you only what you want to hear. Meanwhile, a huge calamity is waiting to happen.'

'Tell us, sister,' Mandodari intervened softly, knowing that her husband would not hesitate to throttle his sister if she continued in this vein. 'The king is always eager to know what is happening in his kingdom.'

'Then listen!' said Surpanakha. 'A lone mortal razed our clan in the forest, killing fourteen thousand rakshasas, including our cousins Khara and Dushana.'

'Tell me about this man,' said Ravana, his face as still as a snake's before it attacks.

How can he be so calm? wondered Surpanakha. Did he know already what had transpired in Dandaka? And was that derision in his eyes? Maybe he had heard of her disgrace. Her fists clenched and then loosened. She must be crafty if she wanted events to unfold the way she wanted.

'The man's name is Rama and he is the son of King Dasaratha of Ayodhya,' she began, her tone softening as she recalled the stranger's glorious form. 'He wears a hermit's garments, but his body is powerful and his arrows fly like lightning. Though he spared me from attack as I am a woman, his brother was not so noble. A magnificent warrior like his brother, Lakshmana maimed me cruelly and without cause.'

'Without cause? What tales you tell, adored sister!' Ravana mocked. 'Did you not flaunt yourself before the brothers in the form of an apsara, trying to seduce them? And then, when this attempt failed, you tried to kill Rama's wife so that you could take her place. Lakshmana attacked you only then and you ran to my men seeking to avenge your humiliation. If you had told me how desperately you needed to bed someone, I would have sent you a hundred rakshasas, sister. Now, my brave cousins and my men have been sacrificed at the altar of your lust.'

Someone has told him everything. Surpanakha trembled. Even being his sister would not protect her if he grew wrathful.

Ravana's eyes glared at her and his forked tongues darted out of his mouths with a hissing sound. She shuddered, realizing that she had made a mistake. Now all was lost.

'Our uncle Akampana came to me with your shameful tale,' he said. 'To what depths have you sunk, Surpanakha?'

His contempt slashed at her like a whip. Rage and hatred flared high in her breast. She had to humble not just Rama and Lakshmana but also her cruel brother. Ravana had blighted her happiness by killing her husband. And he dared to speak of her lust when all the realms were agog with tales of his escapades. She would provoke him to fight against the valiant humans, for if there was anyone who could kill Ravana, it was they.

Her eyes glinted. She knew how she could ensure this.

'Forgive me, brother,' said Surpanakha, casting down her eyes and looking penitent. 'I spoke hastily, disappointed as I was in my quest. Akampana brought you only part of the tale. The reason I approached Rama and his wife in the forest was that I was thinking of you, as always. I wished to regain your affection by bringing you a rare gift—the most beautiful woman on earth.' She cast a quick glance at his face and looked down again to hide her smile. She had seen desire spark instantly in Ravana's eyes when she had mentioned the woman. 'I told Rama that I was the sister of Ravana, the conqueror of the three lokas. I told him that his wife Sita belonged with you in your palace, and not in the wilderness with him. I exhorted him to surrender her to you, telling him that you would reward him with riches beyond imagination.'

Ravana listened to her with rapt attention while Mandodari felt a dark sense of foreboding. 'Do you know what they said in reply, Ravana?' asked Surpanakha, her eyes fixed on his face. 'The brothers laughed uproariously and mocked me. "My wife to be given up to a rakshasa king?" jeered Rama. "Tell this pretender that his days will be numbered if he were to cast even a single glance at my Sita. He may call himself emperor, but that is only because he has not faced Dasaratha's sons in battle. Run away now, rakshasi, if you wish to save your life."'

Ravana's eyes smouldered when he heard what Rama had said. Who was this puny human who dared laugh at Lankeshwara? He would go to Dandaka at once with his army and destroy the human and his brother. Before he left, however, he would gather all the information he could get about Rama.

He encouraged Surpanakha to tell him more, and she was happy to do so. 'When the brothers refused my friendly overtures, I took the form of an apsara so that I could get close to them and then kill them. After that, Sita would be helpless and I could bring her easily to you. Such is her beauty that it captivated even a rakshasi like me. Her lustrous skin glows like a magnolia blossom. Her lush body is more inviting than an apsara's. Her lips are scarlet like the petals of a hibiscus. A treasure like her belongs in your harem, Ravana. I would boldly say that Sita is worth a thousand Mandodaris!'

Surpanakha saw Ravana's face darken at her gibe at Mandodari and hurried to turn his thoughts in the right direction again.

'You will find it easy to slay the brothers, no doubt, but I have a better plan in mind,' she said. 'The best way to take revenge on Rama for killing our rakshasas is to abduct his wife. He loves her desperately and will roam the jungles looking for her. Meanwhile you can delight in the caresses of the beauteous Sita. Even if Rama manages to follow you to Lanka, it will be child's play for you to kill him and his brother.'

Ravana nodded slowly, turning over the plan in his mind and finding nothing to quibble about. Having planted the notion in his head, Surpanakha decided to retreat. 'I will return to Dandaka and await your coming,' she said, bowing to him and tossing a scornful glance at Mandodari before leaving the court.

'Pray listen to me, husband,' said Mandodari, seeing how his face had been transformed at the idea of another conquest.

'Remember Vedavati's curse and Nalakubara's. Sage Pulastya too warned you that abusing a woman would destroy not just you but also our children and grandchildren. Do not pay heed to your sister's words which spring from her desire to avenge her husband's death at your hands. Think twice before making an enemy of a man who has singlehandedly routed your fiercest fighters.'

'Are you done speaking or is there more, foolish woman?' stormed Ravana. 'You insult me with your doubts and your carping criticism. I forgive you because it is in the nature of women to weaken men with their cowardice and foolishness. How can a curse bring down mighty Ravana? How can two feeble men vanquish an emperor who has never been defeated? Remember also that my mighty brother Kumbhakarna and our valiant sons fight by my side. Leave me now, my queen, and reflect on the many occasions when you have failed me.'

'How easily you say that I have failed you, my lord!' Mandodari said, biting her lips to keep from crying. She walked away quietly, her head held high, for she had done what she had to. The future lay hidden in the mists of time. She could only pray that Ravana did not tempt fate with his actions.

Ravana sped to his uncle Maricha, who dwelt in the Dandaka forest, and forced him to play a role in his diabolic plan. 'You will take the form of a brilliant golden deer and entice Sita, uncle,' he said. 'When Rama follows you in order to capture the deer for his wife, you will lure him and his brother far away. I will use the opportunity to seize Sita.'

Maricha feared Rama's prowess, but could not turn down the command of his demon-king. He transformed himself into a deer and carried out his role to perfection. When Rama followed him deep into the forest, Maricha called for help in Rama's voice. A panicky Sita forced Lakshmana to go to his brother's aid, leaving her alone.

Ravana then crept close to Rama's ashram and looked for the maiden whom his sister had described in such ecstatic terms. He saw Sita's feet first, so dainty and graceful that he could hardly lift his eyes from them. She came out of her hut then, and he gazed spellbound at her. The moon was gleaming brightly in the skies, but before him shone another moon that was even more brilliant. Sita's skin was the froth of the cosmic ocean. Her long hair rippled like the Ganga in spate. Her neck was graceful like Vishnu's conch and her body seemed sculpted from deep sea pearls. Her doe eyes glowed with the light of sapphires and set his heart on fire.

But something about her made Ravana pause before approaching her. Sita had a rare incandescence like that of the sacrificial fire, and he heard Mandodari's voice in his head, warning him to back away. 'Slake your desire if you must, but only with women who will gladly surrender to you, my king,' she seemed to be saying.

However, Ravana was drawn irresistibly to Sita as if they were tied by a mystical bond. So powerful was her spell that he wondered for a moment if this was the eternal love he had been promised by Shiva.

He could not stop himself, nor did he want to. He would seize her now and not give room to fanciful notions. Sita was but a woman like many others he had wooed and won. She would soon forget the hermit Rama when she reigned by his side.

Ravana took one step forward. And then another. He snatched her up in his arms and carried her struggling to his aerial chariot.

Sita screamed for help. 'Rama, save me! Lakshmana, where are you? Beloved peacock, bring my lord to me. O mighty devas, will you not save me from the demon?' she cried. She tried to leap from the chariot as it climbed into the skies but Ravana held her down fiercely with a warning hiss. His forked tongues and fangs terrified her into silence.

Onward flew the demon over hill and dale while Sita sobbed, wondering how her Rama would find her. And below on earth, the rivers wept as they thundered down mountain slopes. Tigers and lions tore at the shadow of the passing chariot with fangs and claws. The giant bird Jatayu obstructed the rakshasa's path, but lost his wings and later his life. Sita said a prayer for the valiant bird and cast her jewels to the ground one by one so that they would guide her Rama in his search.

The chariot flew over the turquoise ocean to arrive at Ravana's jade island with its soaring walls and towers. However, Sita could see nothing as her eyes were blinded by tears.

'Stop weeping, beautiful one,' said Ravana. 'Look upon the empire that I lay at your feet. Behold the mansions I have built for my queens. One shines with the lustre of pearls, another glows with the light of amethysts. I will build you a palace that glitters with diamonds. Forget your mortal husband who lives like a beggar in the forest, chased out of his kingdom by a weak king and his vicious wife.'

Sita sobbed, realizing that she was now completely at Ravana's mercy. The chariot descended in a beautiful garden and several rakshasis appeared at his command to take charge of their prisoner. 'You will stay in this ashokavana until I build you a palace,' he said.

He turned away reluctantly then, realizing that his new conquest had made him forget Mandodari and all his promises to her. He would now direct his energies towards convincing his wife to accept Sita so that the three of them could live peacefully together.

However, when Ravana entered his wife's chamber, Mandodari fended him off with raised arms and horrified eyes.

'What have you done?' she shuddered. 'The stench of evil clinging to you overpowers my senses.'

'Sita, the fair daughter of King Janaka, is now held safely in the ashokavana just beyond our palace gates,' he said, unwilling to describe Sita as another man's wife. 'I have abducted her and brought her here to be my wife and your sister.'

'Alas, you have forgotten Vedavati and my warning to you,' said Mandodari. 'The wives of all those who died in your battles and all the women you forced apart from their loved ones curse you. And now, you have exceeded all bounds by abducting the wife of Rama, who the world believes is Vishnu himself! Do you not realize that in your desire to embrace this woman you embrace death? Give her up before it is too late, my lord. Seek Sita's forgiveness and return her to Rama. Or prepare to face your doom!'

Ravana flinched as he saw a spectral form standing behind her—that of his wise grandfather. He heard Pulastya echo her warning. 'Alas, your lust and pride hasten your ruin, Ravana,' the sage whispered to him. His grandfather loved him deeply as did Mandodari. Was he erring in flouting their counsel?

Ravana was disturbed, but not enough to retract his plan. Rama and Lakshmana had attacked his sister and mocked his prowess. If he were to return the woman to them now, the world would taunt him and say that he was afraid. If Dasaratha's son was so brave, he could come to Lanka and rescue his wife.

'I will rip out Rama's entrails and hang them on our fortress gates as a warning to those who defy me,' he swore to Mandodari. 'Maybe then you too will realize your husband's might, for you insult me every day with your doubts.'

'Be careful not to allow your arrogance to blind you to reality, my king. I remind you again that your boon does not protect you from men.'

'Whatever you may say, I will not step back!' he roared, annoyed by her persistence. 'Sita may protest at first but will soon succumb either to my lures or to my threats. Come with me now to see her and you will realize that her presence in our kingdom is not a curse but a blessing. She is the crown jewel of my conquest, and by abducting her I have delivered a killing blow to Rama.'

'Snatching a woman by force or stealth is not an act of valour, Ravana. She is not an object of lust or a means to settle scores with your enemy. Your foolish act endangers not just you but all our people as well. You have invited the wrath of a colossus among men, and this can only lead to horrific bloodshed.' Mandodari's voice was loud and clear. She would speak the truth regardless of consequences. It was a risk she had to take for Ravana and her people.

'Speak respectfully, woman,' barked the Lankapati, his face red with rage. 'If anyone else had spoken to me in this manner, I would have struck off their head in a trice. Do not forget your wifely duties to honour and obey your master, Mandodari. Remember that an ideal wife is one who serves her husband faithfully while he lives, and becomes a Sati, burning herself on his pyre when he dies!'

Mandodari's face was grim as she replied. 'A Sati is one who follows dharma, not one who worships at her husband's feet and kills herself at his death. The first Sati was Shiva's wife, who immolated herself when her father Daksha insulted her husband. She did this because she no longer wished to live on as Daksha's daughter. She was born again as Parvati, the daughter of Himavan, and married Shiva again. Another Sati whom we revere is Savitri, who followed her husband Satyavan to the netherworld when he died and persuaded Yama to restore him to life. These women are goddesses to be worshipped, not sacrifices offered to the fire. The scriptures you have studied prescribe that a noble wife is to be honoured for her wisdom. Even if you refuse to accept my advice, I will speak the truth, for it is my duty as a queen to prevent carnage.'

But Ravana was not listening to her, as his mind was filled with a vision of Sita. 'Her face, her eyes, her magnetic voice!' he exclaimed. 'I no longer consider her a conquest but as the breath that sustains my life. Her radiance pervades every particle of my body. I will be her slave and carry out her every desire—except to restore her to her wretched husband.'

'So what should I do now?' asked Mandodari, her voice rising. 'Should I welcome another man's wife into our bed and tell her that I would be delighted to share my husband with her? Perhaps you expect me to convince her that this was what was meant to be. Will you marry her now by the rites of gandharva vivaha where a man and a woman marry for love, though their families disapprove? But wait. That would need Sita's consent. Do you have it?'

Mandodari laughed out loud as if she had lost control of her senses. Perhaps she had. She felt deranged, broken and dead—except for the pain that twisted her heart and spread its tentacles to every part of her body. Her eyes were pools of pain. She had grown gaunt with grief and the endless fasts she'd been observing to try and stop her husband's sinful behaviour.

He could hear the anger in her voice and the underlying heartbreak. But he was helpless.

Mandodari had grown calm, and her voice dropped to a whisper. 'I have shared a lifetime of love with you, my king—perhaps even two lifetimes if we count the exquisite moments in Kailasa when we thought that we were created for each other. And because of that, I will still do my duty and counsel you whether you accept it or not. Let Sita stay in the ashokavana until she comes to you willingly, my king. Do not let the curses take you from me and our sons.' She bowed her head and tottered away in grief.

Would Ravana, obsessed with the exquisite Sita, listen to her?

9

Vayu's Son

Months passed. Sita remained obstinate, impervious to both threat and lure. Ravana found himself strangely unable to take her by force. Was it because he feared the many curses cast upon him? No, the great Ravana feared nothing. Perhaps it was because even a rakshasa like him could not bear to coerce her. Sita made him remember his younger, purer days under the tutelage of Pulastya. Why, she even made him recall his early, idyllic years with Mandodari when he had been content to be the lofty soul of her dreams. Sita was perfect, an ideal that his nobler self urged him towards. She made him yearn for a world of peerless beauty from an exalted time. Further, even his occult powers warned him not to violate the fierce shield that her chastity had cast around her.

However, Ravana still came to see Sita every day. His heart leapt each time he glimpsed her radiance in the middle of the dark rakshasis, like a flash of lightning among black clouds. Would she ever turn to him like the bright sunflower that smiles in the light of the sun alone?

'He seems tender. Can a monster be tender?' whispered Trijata, a rakshasi whose heart was pure though she served a demon. 'She flouts him, yet he remains gentle. He threatens her and then finds excuses for her obstinacy. His wrath appears to be newly tempered with humility.'

Trijata saw Ravana pleading with Sita once more. 'Give up your loyalty to the outcast who can never match me in wealth or splendour,' he said. The woman merely turned her head away in answer. 'I lay my head at your feet, my goddess,' he whispered then, matching his action to his words. The rakshasis gasped as they saw how the tyrant king abased himself before the mortal woman.

Sita sprang backwards in horror, unwilling to allow even his breath to touch her. 'How can you compare yourself to my Rama?' she asked in anger. 'You are a vile creature who stole me by stealth, whereas my lord is pure and will free me with his valour. The more I see of you, the more I understand why all this had to happen. The righteous prince of Ayodhya was born to defeat evil and establish dharma. My suffering is merely an offering in the yagna that he performs to save the world.'

Ravana sprang to his feet and glared impotently at her. He had humbled himself to no avail. Why was he pleading with a woman who represented everything that was opposed to his own inclinations? It was time to put an end to her insolence.

'I give you one more month to submit to me!' he roared. 'At the end of that time, I swear that I will have you cut into pieces and feast on your flesh.' He stalked away, his hands clenched and his face grim. Sita buried her face in her hands and wept, wondering if she would ever be united with her Rama again.

The war of words was witnessed by Hanuman, the mighty son of the wind god Vayu, from his perch on a tree in the ashokavana. Hanuman was the wisest of the vanaras in the retinue of the monkey king Sugriva who had allied with Rama. Vayu's son had crossed the seas to Lanka looking for the luminous Sita whom Rama had described in worshipful terms.

'The silver moon is sullied by spots and the rose by its thorns, but Sita's wondrous form is unmarred,' Rama had said to him. 'And her voice is sweeter than the warbling of the parrot and the koel.'

Hanuman had looked high and low for Sita in the fortress city of Lanka but had failed to find her. He had seen the bejewelled Mandodari asleep on a canopied bed and wondered if this were Sita, for her beauty was as flawless as Rama had described. But he had realized that Rama's wife would never sleep so peacefully in captivity and had continued his search. *Had Ravana killed her because she refused to submit to him or devoured her in a rage?* he wondered. Or perhaps he held her captive in another realm. Finally, his prayers guided him to the ashokavana where he saw her surrounded by rakshasi guards while the rakshasa king stood in front of her.

Vayu's son came before Sita after Ravana had left, bringing her hope that she would soon be rescued by her lord. 'Tell my Rama that I have but one month to live,' sobbed Sita. The vanara then set out to destroy the vana, uprooting all the trees and shrubs, until only the tree under which she rested remained upright. The rakshasis fled to their king to tell him of this potent intruder, and he sent his palace guard commanded by his son Aksha to capture the monkey.

Prince Aksha, who was just sixteen years old, wielded his bow like Indra and shot endless arrows that struck his foe like thunderbolts. However, Hanuman was impervious to all weapons due to Brahma's boon and shrugged them off his body with ease. Aksha fought on relentlessly, even winning the admiration of his foe. But Hanuman knew that he must end the battle with the dauntless prince if he wished to complete his mission. So when Aksha flew into the air and raised his mace to attack Hanuman, the vanara snatched him up in one giant arm and smashed his head against a stone wall. 'Bless your brave heart, young prince!' he murmured as the rakshasas set up a fierce wail mourning the loss of their bright star.

When Mandodari's guard brought the awful news of her son's death, she let out a piercing shriek and fainted. Her maids revived her, and she finally opened her eyes with a moan. She saw a sombre Ravana standing before her, with nine of his ten heads having gone into hiding.

'Take comfort, my queen, that Aksha died a hero's death, fighting the enemy valiantly,' he said, his voice hoarse with grief, yet trying to maintain a brave face.

'Yes, I am comforted that my sweet Aksha, whose smile brightened my days, lies with his head shattered!' she said, excoriating him with her mockery. 'I am delighted that I will no longer hear his clear voice regaling me with his latest exploits. What a triumph for you that he died facing foes whom you dismissed as puny! No, I forget. He did not face the "weakling" Rama or Lakshmana but their vanara messenger who was himself powerful enough to kill our son and our troops. Nevertheless, I am comforted that my dauntless Aksha gave up his life for a father who has dharma on his side!' She broke down then, weeping as if her heart would break.

Ravana struggled to think of arguments to counter her disdain, but then walked away with his head lowered. His thoughts flew to Pulastya and he imagined how outraged he would be when he heard that Dashanan had sacrificed his half-grown son to satisfy his lust. For a moment, he wondered if Surpanakha had set him on a disastrous path because she was envious of his good fortune. After all, he was a powerful king living amidst adoring wives and sons while she herself lived alone in the forest. Perhaps her visit that day to tell him about Sita's charms had been part of an elaborate plan to cause his downfall . . .

No. He shook his head in denial. His sister was no match for him in intelligence. Nor could the great Lankeshwara be defeated by a mortal. He would triumph as he always did. Aksha's death would fuel his rage and help him decimate his enemies. Surpanakha too would die if he discovered that she had plotted against him.

Ravana strode to his court showing no signs of grief over his dead son. He summoned his firstborn Indrajit and ordered him to capture the monkey that had killed his brother. 'Bring him to me alive,' he said. 'I know that it will be a simple task for the one who defeated Indra.'

Indrajit smote his chest with a powerful fist, swore to seize the creature and sallied forth to confront Hanuman, who was seated atop a giant tree waiting to complete the mission he had been sent on. A fierce war erupted between the two. Hanuman flung huge rocks and missiles at the prince, only to have them shot to dust by a tempest of arrows. Indrajit finally let loose an astra given to him by Brahma. Hanuman knew that the astra had the power to hold him for only a moment. However, he allowed himself to be bound, as he wanted to be taken before Ravana. After that, he would return to Rama and convey the news of Sita's imprisonment. He would tell him that Sita remained resolute despite Ravana's pleas and threats.

Indrajit hauled the vanara, trussed up in the coils of the astra, before his father. Hanuman took in the glittering crowns on Ravana's ten heads, his powerful shoulders and his mien of dominance. He heard the verses the priests sang in praise of the king, describing the boons he had received from Shiva and Brahma.

'Who are you? Why are you here?' Ravana growled, his hands itching to take the monkey's throat between his hands and squeeze his life out of him. 'Speak now or face my wrath.'

The vanara stared at him without answering and Ravana rose from his throne and raised his foot, ready to kick the creature senseless.

'Stop!' shouted a voice he knew well. It was his weakling brother Vibhishana, who was always quoting the scriptures to him. 'We are bound by dharma to treat our enemy's messenger with respect,' said Vibhishana.

'Respect!' growled Ravana. 'I will show this creature respect by killing him!' Before that, he would slice off the vanara's ears and nose as a fitting reply to Lakshmana's assault on Surpanakha. He bent threateningly over the monkey with his sword raised. Then he flew back in shock as the binding coils of the astra vanished and the monkey vaulted to his feet and bared his teeth. Some courtiers tittered when they saw the king's shock and Hanuman joined them, chattering in glee. Mandodari rushed into the court to see the vanara that had killed her son, and stood watching with a deep unease.

Ravana signalled to his guards to drag out and kill those who had dared laugh at their king. Then, ignoring Vibhishana's cry of protest, he raised his sword over the vanara's head.

Hanuman sprang back with a light step and laughed again. 'Listen to me, rakshasa,' he said. 'Know that I am not an ordinary vanara that you can kill easily. I am Hanuman, the servant of Rama, born on earth to vanquish you. No astra can hold me, for I am blessed by Brahma himself.'

Ravana grew still, waiting to discover what he could about his enemy before making his next move. Hanuman continued to speak. 'I belong to Vali's clan. Yes, the same Vali who pinioned you under his arm and carried you effortlessly over land and sea.

Rama killed this magnificent vanara with a single arrow and made Vali's brother Sugriva the king. Dasaratha's sons will soon be here with Sugriva and his army if you do not release Sita. When a single Hanuman can cause so much devastation, imagine an army of many thousand vanaras, each more valorous than I am! If Rama's humble servant can cause such havoc, envision the plight of your people when he himself comes to fight you! How will you counter his astras that killed your fiercest demons?'

Hanuman looked at Ravana's intent face and continued persuasively. 'Mighty king, I have come to ask you to restore Sita to her husband. She is the flame of truth, the fire of chastity. She could also be the instrument of your doom. Give her up now and the merciful Rama will spare your life. Return to the glories of your days when you worshipped Shiva and Brahma, and imbibed the scriptures at the feet of Pulastya. The punya you earned through righteousness has been exhausted and you must now face the consequences of your lust and ego. Do not invite doom upon your island of jade, proud rakshasa,' he said.

Ravana glared at the vanara, his dark aura twisting and pulsing over his head. 'I tamed the elephants that bear the earth aloft,' he said. 'I uprooted mighty Kailasa, home to three-eyed Shiva. Do you think I will tremble now before monkeys and men?'

Hanuman was moved to pity by the rakshasa's foolhardiness. 'If you think Brahma's boon will protect you, remember that you did not seek protection from humans or animals, as you considered them too lowly to pose a threat. But now, these two have joined forces against you. Turn away from sin, rakshasa. Release Rama's noble wife. Or you will face certain death!' Hanuman's voice rang out sonorously. But Ravana's ego overwhelmed his powers of reasoning.

'Kill the monkey!' he snarled. His guards ran to capture the intruder. Hanuman soared to the ceiling to evade them.

Vibishana argued again against killing an emissary and Ravana modified his command. He ordered his servants to set the monkey's tail on fire.

Vayu's son allowed the men to catch him and carry out the command. He then vaulted out of the royal court and set Ravana's mansions, his gardens and his palaces ablaze with his burning tail.

The prelude was over. The blistering war would now begin.

10

Carnage

Rama had crossed the seas and arrived in Lanka. Mandodari was afraid, for she had seen the losses they had suffered at the hands of one vanara. Now there was an ocean of monkeys at their gates, clamouring to lay rough hands on their people and their wealth. She attempted once more to convince Ravana to let Sita go. 'The woman refuses to accept you, despite all your pleas and threats. Why court death for someone who has no regard for you or your valour?' she asked, but her husband merely turned his face away. 'Rama is no ordinary mortal, not when he has shown such prowess,' she tried again, but Ravana turned on her in fury and cursed all women.

Soon afterwards, the Lankapati donned the golden armour created by Brahma that he had snatched from Indra. On his feet he wore anklets whose sound made the worlds tremble as they knew that savage Ravana was near. He swaggered out of his palace to mount his massive chariot and lead his army to battle. His war banner bore the emblem of a human skull, showing his contempt for the human race and warning his mortal foes to keep away. Ravana was a formidable sight, with a body that was adamantine like a mountain. His arrows flew like a molten river, while his mocking laugh thundered in their ears. He looked like three-eyed Shiva surrounded by his ganas, come to destroy the world.

'Foolish monkeys!' Ravana called out in challenge. 'Did you think you could fight with sticks and stones against an army of rakshasas bristling with weapons? Are your hairy arms and fists, your big teeth and chattering tongues sufficient to vanquish the lord of the realms? Indeed, I fear that my glory will be tarnished by confronting such feeble foes.'

Along with Ravana came his commander Prahastha, in a chariot that had iron scythes mounted on its axle hubs, and was drawn by hideous green snakes. Their monstrous army streamed out of the city gates like the flood at the end of time. Hordes of demons armed with gleaming swords and shields fell upon the monkeys who fought back with boulders and branches of trees.

Hanuman charged at the Lankeshwara who attacked him furiously, remembering that his son Aksha had died by this vanara's hand. Hanuman struck him fiercely with an uprooted tree, but Ravana smote back with his mace and stunned him. When Hanuman rose again, the golden chariot had vanished and the vanara roared in anger at having lost sight of his foe. Angada, brave Vali's son, spotted the demon's chariot in another corner of the field and charged forward. Ravana reeled back from the force of his blows but recovered soon to drive Angada away and slay a thousand vanaras in revenge. The vanara leaders converged on him, but he vanished quickly from sight, using his powers of sorcery.

Angered by the rakshasa's devious attacks, Lakshmana set out to confront him. 'Do not flee from us, Ravana!' he roared in challenge. 'Stand and fight if you are a warrior.' Ravana replied, not with words, but with serpent astras that hissed through the air. However, Lakshmana's arrows cut away their burning heads so that they became powerless. Lakshmana then broke the bow that Ravana wielded, provoking the demon to invoke a howling Shakti astra. Lakshmana swooned under its power and Ravana descended on him to kill him. Hanuman flew between them like a shrieking tornado and drove off the rakshasa with fierce blows. He carried the warrior in his arms to Rama who healed him with his divine touch.

'I will destroy Ravana myself,' swore Rama. 'He will pay for all this bloodshed, for wounding Lakshmana and for abducting my precious Sita.'

'Allow me to be your chariot,' said Hanuman and the two rose in the air like a whirlwind. Ravana saw the enormous vanara flying through the sky and aimed his occult arrows at him, knowing that Hanuman had to be killed if he wished to defeat the enemy. The arrows flew thick and furious, obscuring the noonday sun for a while, making it appear as if night had fallen. But the mighty son of Vayu remained unharmed by the shafts. An angry Ravana directed his arrows at the vanara army, laughing uproariously as the monkeys fell in droves, screaming piteously. Flushed with triumph, the demon turned his attention to the man seated on Hanuman's back.

The vanara may be impervious to my arrows, but not the weakling mortal on his back, he thought as he strung his bow in readiness. He stared intently at the man Sita pined for—the one who stood between him and happiness. He would destroy him and make him regret the day he had set foot on the sacred soil of Lanka.

Hanuman flew closer. Ravana's eyes met those of Rama. He saw the luminous face, the furious gaze, the splendid body and the powerful arms holding a bow that glittered like Shiva's Pinaka. The rakshasa's vision blurred, blood rushed to his head and his heart raced uncontrollably. He heard a loud ringing in his ears that made him shriek in pain. He pressed his hands down on his ears and shut his eyes tight, unable to bear the onslaught. The noise died suddenly and was replaced by a sepulchral silence. Ravana opened his eyes in fear. It appeared as if the earth had split apart and swallowed all life in the few moments when he had been paralysed. He could see no battlefield, no warriors, no Hanuman—nothing but the piercing gaze of his foe. The two of them appeared to be locked in a duel that had no beginning or end. Ravana's legs folded under him and he held on to the chariot's sides for support. Sweat broke out on his brow, and the arrow in his hand dropped without his volition. His spine seemed to be broken, weighed down by the burden of his sin.

'Face your death, rakshasa!' shouted Rama, sending ten arrows flying from his bow. The arrows flashed with a fire that put to shame the Kalagni, the fire of the final day. They tore off the diadems Ravana wore on his ten heads, proclaiming to the world that the asura's reign was coming to an end. Ravana's faces grew dark now, like a night without the moon. More arrows flew from Rama's bow, the Kodanda, and grievously wounded the rakshasa's horses and his charioteer. Still Ravana stood motionless, watching his foe in a daze. Rama's arrows carried away his enemy's bow and shattered the canopy of his chariot. Another fusillade broke the wheels of the chariot, leaving it just an empty shell. The vaahana sank to the ground with no one to guide it. The demon's guards, shocked to see their master's plight, flew to him and sheltered him from Rama's attack. Hanuman descended as well so that Rama could confront the demon on land.

Rama's arrows cut a crimson swathe through Ravana's guards and soon the Lankapati was revealed standing all alone, still staring at his foe. Rama drew one last arrow from his quiver.

The earth hushed. The skies filled with devas and rishis come to witness this epochal moment. Rama fitted the arrow to his bow. The rakshasa remained frozen, making no attempt to defend himself. Thunder split the skies and a fierce downpour drenched the two combatants. *Was Indra celebrating the imminent death of his hated enemy?* wondered Hanuman. *And why was Rama hesitating to kill the rakshasa who had stolen his wife?*

Then, Rama inexplicably returned his arrow to his quiver and lowered his bow. He stared silently at Ravana for what seemed to be an endless moment. Then both armies heard what he said in the jagged silence: 'You are tired after a long day of battle, Ravana. Go home and return tomorrow.'

Ravana reeled in shock, his heart riven by the words as they never could be by an arrow. He was broken, distraught, humiliated. His ego lay shattered and he stood defenceless before the world. Unable to reply or to even stand erect, the emperor turned away to return to his palace.

Lankeshwara. Lankapati. Trilokadipati. All the names used to eulogize him were now meaningless. Overturned by one man who had humbled him in front of all his people. What force had paralysed him when he had needed to act, to fight, to slay his foe? It had to be the curse on his head. Nay, the many curses that he had incurred. His ten heads murmured among themselves. 'Nandi cursed me when I laughed at his animal head and Vedavati when I laid rough hands on her. Nalakubara predicted my doom when I ravished Rambha. Ages ago, King Anaranya said that a scion of his solar dynasty would kill me and Rama is his descendant.'

The central head, the one in which his ego resided, spoke up. 'Stop moaning like a wretched woman. Have you forgotten your most potent weapon, the supreme warrior whose roar threatens to shatter the earth and the skies?' The other heads nodded, baring their fangs in glee. 'We must wake up Kumbhakarna!' they shouted. 'Bring on the deathless hero!'

Ravana sent slaves armed with conches and drums to wake up his brother, who spent half the year in deep slumber. Kumbhakarna feasted on enormous amounts of food and slaked his lust with numerous young women before striding to his brother's court.

'Greetings, adored brother!' he said to Ravana. 'Tell me who I must kill for you—devas or nagas, danavas or Yama kinkaras.'

'Brahma's boon protects me from them all, brother,' replied Ravana. 'It is a human prince named Rama, his brother Lakshmana and their army of monkeys that you must fight. They seek to rescue Rama's wife Sita whom I abducted from their ashram in Dandaka. When you were lost in slumber, our foes wrought great havoc on our army, killing my precious Aksha, Prahastha and many thousand rakshasas.'

Kumbhakarna's face grew sombre. 'How calmly you speak of a colossal tragedy caused solely by your lust and pride! Were these not the vices grandsire Pulastya warned you against? Did wise Vibhishana not advise you that we cannot win a war waged in support of wrongdoing? However, it is not too late. Surrender Sita to her husband, brother. Reclaim the nobility that I know resides deep in you.'

Ravana could not bear his brother's harangue and flew into a rage. 'Cowardly Vibhishana has joined hands with my enemies,' he shouted. 'Do you wish to do the same, Kumbhakarna? Where is the valour in asking me to surrender to my foes? I sought your help as I thought we shared an understanding that is beyond time. But it appears as if you are afraid to take up the challenge. Do not fret, brother! Go back to your women, your wine and your feasting. If you will not fight, I will myself. I swear by the sacred throne of Lanka that the great Ravana will not lose! He will fight for what he desires to his last breath.'

The courtiers trembled as they watched their king rage. But Kumbhakarna stood unmoved, his eyes unflinching. Ravana glared at him for a moment and then looked away. His nine heads withdrew into one. His voice was low as he whispered, 'I became numb when I saw Rama, my brother. Dasaratha's son denuded me of my weapons, my chariot, my pride. And as a crowning insult, he advised me to return to the field the next day when I had recovered from my defeat. Imagine the imperious Ravana standing crestfallen before an army of men and monkeys! Dishonoured, diminished, debased . . .' He stopped, choking on the words. He sighed and continued to speak. 'And yet, I cannot bear to let go of Sita, Kumbhakarna. She is my heaven, my earth, my life and perhaps my death as well. Gladly will I give up my kingdom if she will grant me just one smile. I am tied to her by a bond that I cannot untie, however hard I try. O, first of rakshasas! Only you can fight for me and restore the glory of our people.'

Kumbhakarna could hardly believe that his invincible brother had been humbled by a mere human. And that an emperor famed for his prowess with women had been spurned. He felt compassion arise where earlier there had been anger. He said gently, 'Adored Ravana! I swear by my love for you that I will kill Rama this very day. And I will kill his brother and their vanara hordes. Then, the woman you desire will come to you herself so that you may be together forever.'

Ravana's eyes were moist as he rose to embrace his brother and kiss his cheek. He placed around his neck a massive gold chain with a giant ruby that he had brought from patala. The warrior took his brother's blessings and resolved to slay the kshatriya brothers or give up his own life.

Kumbhakarna stepped over the high ramparts of the fortress city and uttered a war cry that was so fierce and unnatural that the vanaras fled, buffeted by the sound. He strode forward, trishul in hand, looking like Yama himself. The earth lurched under his feet, shuddering in fear. 'Where are you hiding, foolish prince?' he bellowed. 'Come before me and fight. Or flee from the field before I kill you!'

'It is my brother Kumbhakarna,' whispered Vibhishana to Rama and Sugriva. 'His hunger is insatiable and he will devour you and the entire vanara army if he is not stopped!'

Sugriva led the attack with a fierce war cry and his vanaras converged on the giant, armed with rocks and trees. Kumbhakarna's trident spewed fire in one hand, reducing them to ashes, while with the other hand he grabbed and thrust them into his mouth and devoured them. Hanuman hurried to divert Kumbhakarna's attention and almost collapsed when the rakshasa struck his chest with his trishul. However, he recovered quickly, grabbed the trishul and broke it on his knee. Now Rama confronted the rakshasa and his arrows sheared off his foe's right arm and shredded his armour. Kumbhakarna took up a massive sword in his other hand but Rama unleashed a typhoon of arrows that broke the sword and tore off the arm holding it. Two more arrows shot off his legs. 'Onward for Ravana! Onward for Lanka!' cried Kumbhakarna, his torso still advancing like a mountain, with blood pouring in torrents from his severed limbs.

Ravana's brother knew that his death was moments away, yet the blaze in his eyes remained undimmed. He fixed his eyes on the radiant face of Rama and whispered a plea: 'Take my life, great one, but do not let the world lay eyes on my shattered visage. Send my head whirling to the depths of the ocean with your final arrow.'

Rama nodded and sent forth Vayu's astra, which tore through the air, carrying off the rakshasa's head that still roared in defiance and plunged it into the depths of the ocean. The giant's body crashed to the ground, heaving still in defiance. The rakshasa army wailed at his loss while the vanaras hushed in reverence to the indomitable warrior.

The news was quickly carried to Ravana who at first refused to believe it and then broke down in grief. Mandodari came to her husband and looked pleadingly up at him, a silent question in her eyes. But it seemed as if Ravana had decided to follow his path to its inevitable end, whatever that may be.

Ravana's son Atikaya took the field next, looking like another Kumbhakarna in his lightning-swift chariot. He fought bravely, reaping the lives of his foes like a whirlwind let loose on the field. He rebuffed Lakshmana's astras with his own flaming arrows, leaving the kshatriya totally spent. Night was falling and Lakshmana decided to use the Shakti astra to put an end to the brave youth. Mandodari's dauntless son tried to shatter its blazing power with a hundred arrows of his own, but fell lifeless as it struck his chest and consumed him with its fierce power.

Ravana sat alone through the night, grieving for his brother and the sons he had lost, horrified that this war could claim such a monstrous price. Dawn broke, but it seemed that even the sun could not lighten the darkness that prevailed. Vultures and other birds of ill omen circled Ravana's fortress as if sensing that corpses would soon be littering the streets of the capital. The city walls were crumbling and echoed with the wails of the rakshasis who had lost their husbands and their sons.

It was at this hour of dismal gloom that mighty Indrajit came to his father who sat dazed, with his head buried in his hands. Ravana's tears were spent, his heart was emptied of all emotion. His course was set; he knew that disaster and death awaited him, but he would not retreat.

Indrajit strode confidently forward, his courage reinforced by the thousand battles he had won. His gaze was fiery and his face fixed in grim resolve. 'Do not despair, father,' he said, his voice thunderous like the skies on a stormy night. 'Though our foes have killed mighty Kumbhakarna, though the skies may fall and the seas rise to heaven, I swear that I will not return unless I bring you the heads of Rama and Lakshmana.'

Ravana saw a shadow move behind Indrajit and saw that it was Mandodari. She joined her hands to him in prayer and sent out a silent plea: 'Spare me my firstborn. Do not send my Meghanada into battle. Do not sacrifice him too, my king.'

Her prayer was in vain. Ravana would not grant her this wish. He raised his hands in blessing over Indrajit's bowed head. 'Victory be yours, my son!' he whispered, holding back the tears that threatened to flow from his eyes.

From the shadows rose a piteous wail, a sound of primeval grief. Indrajit heard it too and turned to see his mother standing there, her eyes blank and unseeing. He touched her feet to seek her blessing, his mind engaged already in devising battle plans that would ensure his victory. Mandodari could not speak, but clasped his wide shoulders in her arms and clung to him. She knew that she should not dishearten her son when he strode out to face his enemies. They would not listen to her, father or son. She would have to stand by and watch the final scenes unfold. She watched him go, the last of her sons, until she could see him no more.

She hurried away then, bent over in grief, unwilling to say anything to her husband who appeared broken too. Had he also realized that he would never see his brave Indrajit alive again? If he had, then why had he let him go? There were no answers. Even her questions appeared futile. She could not speak to Ravana. She had no comfort to offer him. The reality was that she could not even bear to look at him. Their love appeared now to be a mirage, a dream that she had woken from. She would take refuge in Vishnu, her god, the protector of the universe. But how could the great lord of Vaikunta protect her son from Rama, believed to be Vishnu himself?

Ravana watched her go, his heart wracked with pain. Mandodari had given up on him when she never had before, though he had wounded her many times with his actions. He wanted to explain to her why he did what he did. But could any explanation be sufficient when it entailed sacrificing your sons, your country, your love? The ghastly train of events had been set in motion when Surpanakha had told him of Sita's beauty. His fate had been determined when Rama had shorn him of weapons and sent him home, shamed before the eyes of the world. Events had progressed too far now to be remedied.

Do not ask me anything. Just say that you love me still, Mandodari. Tell me that you will stay with me no matter what. That we are in this together . . . Stand with me, my love, for you are all I have in my darkest hour.

But he would not say this to her. At best, it would make her look at him with pity. And he could not bear to have her pity the husband who had promised to lay the world at her feet.

Indrajit burst into the field roaring, threatening, laughing, terrifying. Ravana watched from the ramparts as his son rained havoc on the monkeys that ran screeching for cover. His arrows flamed blue and green and scarlet as he took on Rama and Lakshmana. Maybe he would win. Maybe he would survive. Maybe he would have a son still to call him father . . .

Mandodari's son flashed like a comet trailing fire and destruction. He conjured up a monstrous cloud from which erupted a hundred thousand arrows like molten lava. Rama and Lakshmana quickly intervened to draw the arrows towards themselves, thus lessening their impact on their army. But the power of Indrajit's sorcery was so great that all the vanaras slumped to the ground in a deep sleep, as did Lakshmana.

Then Rama too fell unconscious. And with him swooned the gods—as well as virtue, truth and compassion. Mother Earth wept and a gentle rain fell from the skies, in an attempt to revive Kaushalya's divine son.

Vibhishana looked in horror at the fallen army. He himself was protected from Indrajit's maya by the power of his tapasya. But all would be lost if he could not rouse the kshatriyas from their torpor.

He saw a solitary figure rushing towards him, crying out for help. 'What shall we do now?' sobbed Hanuman. 'How will we live when all those we love are dead?'

11

A Mother's Grief

'Not dead. Not dead!' said a feeble voice. Hanuman turned eagerly to see who offered them such hope. 'You can save them, Hanuman. Only you!' the voice said again.

He hurried closer and saw that the voice belonged to Jambavan, mighty king of the Himalayas, who had been born as a bear in order to assist Rama in his battle. 'Bring the healing herbs that grow on the mountaintop that rises between Kailasa and Meru,' said Jambavan. 'They will rouse all those who lie here in a swoon that resembles death.'

Meanwhile, the rakshasas rejoiced, hailing Indrajit as the conquering hero and carried him proudly on their shoulders to his father. Ravana embraced his son, delighted that Indrajit had wiped away his father's shame and reaffirmed their supremacy. Mandodari hurried to the temple to make offerings of thanksgiving.

The great Hanuman flew across the oceans and over land until he reached the snow-capped mountains of the north. Unable to identify the plants that Jambavan had described, he wrenched the whole mountain from the earth and carried it to the battlefield. The magical fragrance of the herbs was sufficient to revive Rama, Lakshmana and the vanaras—not just those who were in a daze but those who had lost their lives as well.

The vanaras turned in unison towards Ravana's city to attack their enemies who were celebrating their apparent victory with dance and drink. They swiftly set mansions and gardens aflame, awakening those who were sunk in a drunken stupor. The rakshasas panicked when they saw what they believed were vengeful spirits and fled.

Indrajit marshalled the troops and led them in an attack against the intruders. Gradually, the rakshasas reclaimed the ground they had lost and set up guard posts to ensure that the vanaras did not slip in again.

When the sun rose the next day, Lakshmana set out to slay Indrajit. Indrajit's arrows were like flaming madness, but Lakshmana mocked them saying that they were like frail lotus stems. He broke Indrajit's bow in two with one mighty arrow and then assailed him with many more that pierced his face and body, covering him in a swirl of crimson. Finally, Lakshmana took up the Aindraastra and invoked the power of Indra.

'I worship you in the name of dharma,' he said. 'I invoke you in the name of my righteous brother Rama!'

Lakshmana released the astra which flamed through the air and removed Indrajit's head from his neck. Meghanada's thunderous voice would be heard no more. The rakshasas wailed in grief as their prince's body crashed to the ground.

The waves attacked the shore, again and again. The moon was dimmed by sinister clouds. Mandodari sat alone on the dark sands, wanting to throw herself into the maw of the sea. She would gratefully embrace the waters for it seemed as if her daughter was calling to her from its depths. The gods had already punished her by taking away her sons. Now she had nothing to live for. Her dying here at the very spot where she had abandoned her child would be the final price she would pay for her sins.

She had lost so much over the last few days. If she could only stop Time . . . rather, reverse it. Maybe this time Ravana would listen to her counsel. He would realize that the wise thing to do would be to send back the viper that he harboured in the ashokavana. But alas! Time stopped for no one, least of all for the ill-fated mother of three sons who had been sacrificed for their father's lust.

'Sita!' she exclaimed, hatred pulsating in the two syllables. *What did my king see in you that he did not find in me or in his other wives?* Her heart filled with anger at the woman she had refused to meet all these months. But her avoiding Sita had not helped in any way to deflect the danger to Lanka. Proud Ravana had been reduced to a desperate supplicant seeking the favours of a captive. It was Mandodari's duty to help her husband that kept her on the shore when her heart yearned to end it all.

It seemed as if her thoughts had reached out to him, for Ravana came looking for her. Looking at the stubborn set of his jaw, Mandodari realized that he was not ready to back down. She refused to rise to greet him as she always did or offer him comfort with her soft words and gentle touch. Ravana noticed the marks left on her cheeks by her tears; he noted the rigidly clenched jaw and the fierce challenge in her eyes. He was silent, waiting for her to speak her mind.

'Indrajit, the last of my sons, my firstborn, the fruit of our love—bloodied, beheaded and forfeited for your lust. Is she worth the sacrifice, my lord? Is your Sita worth the price of your brother, your people, your sons? And soon, your kingdom and your life? What remains then, my king? Is this the meaning of the eternal love you swore? You said that it was the rakshasa custom to take other women to your bed. But there would be room in your heart for me alone. Alas, you have killed my love, Ravana. You have destroyed me. But I will do my duty still, counsel you as a righteous wife, plead with you to repent. Do not hold another man's wife against her will; do not immolate your people in the fire of your desire. Surrender now to the divine Rama, who I am convinced is Vishnu born on earth. Return his wife to him and beg his forgiveness. It is not too late, my lord. We will perform penances together to redeem ourselves and our land from our sins.'

Her words shook the Lankapati. It was true what she'd said. He had broken his promises to her, yet she remained true to him. He had snatched away her precious sons, yet she was willing to fight for his soul. However, he could not surrender. Not now. He could not forfeit his dignity and the fame he had won over many years and battles. He chose to die the way he had lived, with his head held high.

Ravana spoke gently and persuasively. 'If what you say is true and Rama is a god, remember that my boon from Brahma protects me from all devas. On the other hand, if Rama is merely a fierce kshatriya, remember that I am the mightiest of warriors, undefeated in war. Either way, I am invincible, protected by the moon sword that Shiva gave me. Give up your baseless fears, my love, and I promise to slay my enemies and return unharmed. And if Sita still remains obstinate, I will have her killed and consume her flesh at my victory feast. Support me in my quest, my queen.'

Mandodari stared at him aghast and then slowly rose to her feet. 'Ahankara—a monstrous ego!' she whispered. 'It is your conceit that hastens your doom, O king. You have wasted your whole life seizing treasures, subduing people and tyrannizing the three realms. Your quest has always been to impress everyone with your wealth, your learning and your strength. Do you know what your grandsire Pulastya said to me soon after our marriage? He said that I must help free you from the hold of the ten vices that control your actions. Lust, anger, attachment, greed, pride, envy, selfishness, injustice, cruelty and finally, the worst of them all—ego. You now have one last chance to rise above these and realize the divinity within you. Take my hand, my lord, so that we may step away from our doom. Take my hand . . .'

Her voice shook. Her hand rose towards him in a desperate plea. Would he listen? Would he allow love to win over his ego?

Ravana gazed deeply into her eyes, a profound sadness in his own. 'I must go,' he said. 'I must summon my occult powers before I enter the battlefield. Farewell, my love.'

As he turned away, he heard a deep sigh behind him. It was the sound of a body relinquishing its soul, giving up its breath to death. Would he ever see his Mandodari in this life again?

Ravana began a fierce ritual, invoking Chamunda, who held dire weapons in her twelve hands and was adorned with skulls and serpents. The dreaded goddess lived in cremation grounds and was accompanied by fiends and goblins. She was the rakshasa's guardian deity, the mistress of tantra and the occult arts. She was the one whose blessings he needed to complete his mission. He fed more ghee to the sacrificial fire and intensified his prayers.

Far away in the enemy camp, Vibhishana felt the reverberations set up by Ravana's sinister chants. He shuddered as he sensed the evil vortex being created by his brother's dark prayers.

Vibhishana summoned Vali's fierce son Angada to him. 'My brother has begun a potent sacrifice that will make him impossible to defeat,' he said. 'If Rama is to win against Ravana, it is essential that you stop Ravana from completing his ritual. Hurry to his palace at once, for our fate hangs in the balance!'

Angada hastened with his sena to disrupt the sacrifice. His monkeys created havoc in the palace, bringing down pillars, driving out Ravana's guards and harassing his queens. However, they could not enter the circle of fire within which Ravana sat, closing his mind to everything except his tapasya. The monkeys dragged the women in his harem before the king and threatened to carry them away, but still, Ravana remained focused on his chants. Finally, Angada pounced on Mandodari herself and dragged her by her hair before Ravana.

'You abducted Rama's wife. Now see what I do to your queen,' he jeered. 'Your Mandodari—so pure, so chaste, so beautiful—is now in my power!'

Ravana stuttered for a moment, then continued relentlessly on. He needed just a little more time to complete the prayers that would make him invincible. Angada grew agitated as Ravana's chants began rising to a crescendo. He could see the dark shape of a demon with many arms and eyes of fire emerging from the altar. He had only moments before the monster came to life. Angada howled fiercely and tore at Mandodari's clothes in an attempt to shock Ravana. 'I will ravish her before your eyes, Ravana!' he screamed.

'Save me, my king. Do you not see my desperate plight?' the queen cried. Ravana opened his eyes and saw how his beloved Mandodari struggled in the hold of the giant vanara. He closed his eyes again, speeding up his chants that were now close to completion.

'O Ravana! Is this how you show your love for your wife?' she screamed again. 'You are a coward then unlike Rama who fights fiercely to rescue his Sita!'

Her gibe struck Ravana to the core, but he continued with the sacrifice, his twenty arms flashing in his haste to complete his oblations.

'Beloved Meghanada! Valiant Indrajit! Would you have let your mother be abused in this way?' she wailed. 'Come back to me from your warrior's heaven, sweet prince. Save your mother who has no one. No one but you.'

Her plea to her dead son stirred Ravana as nothing else could. He rose with a dark oath, spun away from the altar and grabbed his sword. 'I will kill you, monkey!' he howled. 'I will slice off the arms that torment my queen.' His sword flashed out like an arc of fire, slashing Angada's arm deeply. The vanara shrieked in pain and bounded away, with the others following in his wake. Ravana let them escape as he had something more important to do. He gathered his weeping wife in his arms and stroked her head gently. 'My queen, my Mandodari,' he sobbed. 'Forgive me, forgive me.'

Her weeping quietened. Ravana's face grew grim again. He had to leave now to complete what he had started. The sun was already rising in the east. He would kill the invaders that day or die. His arms dropped and he stepped away from his wife.

'No, my lord. No!' she screamed, discerning his intention. But he was gone, with not a single glance back at her. He had left without seeking her prayers for his success and long life.

Mandodari wept. She stormed at fate. 'O Shiva! Bless your devotee. Protect him on the battlefield,' she cried out. And then she turned her steps towards the woman she blamed for all that had happened. Sita. The object of her hatred. The embodiment of Lanka's doom.

She would strangle her with her own hands.

Mandodari hurried to the ashokavana, stumbling in her haste. The rakshasis guarding Sita moved hastily away at their queen's imperious gesture. The angry queen saw the woman in a tattered saree, sitting on the ground with her head bowed in her hands, the very picture of despair. Her hair hung unkempt and loose, covering her face. Her body was frail, as if it would disintegrate in a puff of wind. For a moment, even Mandodari's heart filled with pity for the captive's plight. Sita had been snatched away roughly from the man she loved. Surely, she must have expected to live a long, fulfilling life by his side. Instead, she had been brought to this alien land where she lived among foul rakshasis. Mandodari felt a reluctant admiration stir in her heart for this woman who had stood firm against a mighty king.

And then, the queen came to herself with a start. A horrific image flashed into her mind—that of a bloodied simha kundala, an earring shaped like a lion's head. She had had it made especially for her 'little lion', for that was what she had called her youngest son. The earring was all that remained after Hanuman had dashed Aksha's head against a stone wall and smashed it. Before her eyes now was the woman who had caused Aksha's death and Atikaya's and Indrajit's. This frail-looking woman was not an object of pity. She was deadly, like the halahala poison that lay hidden in the ocean of nectar. When Sita had arrived in Lanka, she had brought with her death, disaster and the end of Ravana's love for his queen.

A bitter laugh escaped Mandodari's lips. 'What did he see in you?' she hissed and saw Sita's body jerk in shock. Tear-filled eyes looked up for a moment before her hair covered her face again. 'The apsaras of Indra's court dance for my king. Princesses from distant kingdoms pine for him. And then he brought *you* home to consume everything that is fruitful in our land. I have lost all that I cherished!' Her voice rose then in rage. 'Look at my face, Sita. Look at Ravana's queen Mandodari. Tell me what you have that I do not. You are still an unformed girl, with neither experience nor wisdom to equal mine. I have survived immense travails and emerged stronger in love and life to be a worthy partner to the king. Did you think that you could come and take over my king and my kingdom?'

The figure sat motionless, as if turned to stone. Mandodari continued to speak, her voice hoarse now and agonized. 'I thought that Ravana would return to me as he had many times earlier, once his obsession with you was past. But that was not to be. He declares that he will die rather than give you up. Do not think however that your Rama, a mere boy, will succeed in defeating Ravana, the king of kings, however hard he may try.'

Her mockery of Rama aroused Sita from her dejection as the queen's earlier anger could not. 'How dare you compare my valorous prince to a debased demon?' she retorted, glaring at Mandodari. 'Your king and his hordes will certainly be crushed by my Rama. Why, I myself could have burned Ravana in the fire of my chastity.'

'You speak glibly, woman, for words cost nothing. If your virtue endows you with such power, why did you not burn him when he abducted you? Or when he attempted to force you into his bed?' stormed the queen. 'If you had killed him, I would have gladly died with him, for at least my people would have been saved. My kingdom would have prospered under my son Indrajit.

What held you back, Sita? Your presence here has brought my mighty kingdom to its knees. Your allure has destroyed my glorious island with its mansions spangled with gems, and its gardens bursting with flowers. You are responsible, Sita, for the death of my sons and for my losing the king's love. And you must pay the price for it. I will kill you with my own hands, crushing your head like we crush the head of a poisonous serpent! Say your prayers, Sita, and bid goodbye to your Rama.'

Mandodari rushed at Sita in a frenzied attack. Sita tried to back away from her but it was too late. The queen grabbed her by her shoulders and shook her. Her eyes glared madly and her hands rose as if to throttle the prisoner. The earth shook under their feet as if it were being torn apart. Was this how the battle would end, with Sita being killed by Mandodari, thereby taking away the very purpose for which the armies fought?

12

The Secret

Sita tore herself free from Mandodari's grasp and almost fell, weakened by her fast during her captivity, when she had eaten merely what was needed to keep her alive. But then she drew strength from her defiance.

'What depths will you plumb, rakshasi?' she cried out. 'Can you not understand a wife's love or her husband's sacred duty to protect her? The rakshasa you call the king of kings insulted my prince by abducting his wife. Rama must avenge the insult by fighting and killing his foe himself.'

'Are you a prize then to be won in the war?' Mandodari ranted. 'Does it gratify you that our husbands fight over you?' But even as she spoke, the queen felt a strange unease that prevented her from engaging fully in the war of words. Was Sita a sorceress perhaps that she could cast a spell on anyone who approached her? Mandodari forced herself to focus on the need of the hour. A terrible tragedy was unfolding even as she wasted time in futile arguments. She appealed again to this frail yet fierce woman.

'I beg you Sita to help me save the ones I love,' she pleaded, joining her hands together in prayer. 'I do not know why fate brought you to our shores. Maybe you are the fruit of all the curses Ravana incurred with his sins. Or perhaps you are Vedavati reborn to take vengeance on my husband. I do not care about the past, but wish merely to stop the ghastly bloodshed. We have suffered too much—yes, both of us. You are held captive by rakshasis and separated from your Rama. I have lost my husband's love, my three sons and countless subjects. Listen to me now and I will help you escape. I will send my own personal guard to escort you to your prince. It is in our power to stop this war, for we women are wise and have the zeal to do anything to protect those we love. I pray to you, Sita, have mercy upon us . . . have mercy!'

Sita drew closer to the woman whose manner had changed from arrogant to humble. She touched her shoulder with compassion as Mandodari sobbed uncontrollably.

'I cannot accept your offer, my queen, though my heart aches for you,' she whispered, stroking her head. 'If I had wanted to escape, I would have done so when Hanuman offered to carry me on his back to my glorious Rama. But I have come to realize that I am but an instrument to destroy the demonic burden on earth. It is my duty to stand by Rama as he completes his mission. And yours is to try and save your husband from the doom that he is determined to embrace.'

Suddenly, Mandodari grew still and her sobs were replaced by silence. Sita stopped speaking and saw the queen staring at her, transfixed. What had happened to her, wondered Sita. Were her senses disordered by her losses? Mandodari placed her arms around Sita and hugged her close, though her prisoner shrank in fear and astonishment. 'Who are you?' she asked Sita. 'Where were you born? What is your lineage?'

'I am the daughter of King Janaka of Videha,' said Sita, held in thrall by the other's expression. The two now stood close to each other, talking in whispers while the rakshasis watched and wondered. 'My father named me Sita as he found me in a furrow when he ploughed the earth during a yagna. When Sage Narada came to our court, he told us that my mother had been forced by circumstances to set me adrift on the ocean. The sea god Varuna had saved me and entrusted me to Bhudevi who in turn ensured that I would be found by the king. But why do you ask?'

'This sapphire pendant around your neck!' whispered Mandodari, grabbing it fiercely so that Sita was dragged closer. 'Who gave this to you?'

'This was round my neck when my father found me and is the only link to where I came from,' said Sita. 'I have worn it always, hoping one day to find my mother and ask her why she so cruelly abandoned me.'

'It was the only way I knew to protect you before I set you afloat, my child. Forgive me, forgive your accursed mother!' said Mandodari as she drew Sita again into a fierce embrace. 'I have caused you so much pain, dear Sita. And to meet you now in such desperate circumstances! What an unnatural mother I must be to not know that my child was so near!'

'It was you then . . . it was you who cast me away?' asked Sita, trembling at the revelation. The thought that followed next was too monstrous for her to acknowledge. If this queen was her mother, was Ravana then her father? 'Am I so cursed that my own father lusted for me?' she asked, her voice hoarse with distress.

Mandodari shook her head in fierce denial. 'You were born from me, but not from his energy,' she said. 'The most that could be said is that you are the fruit of his sinfulness, come to claim his life. Allow me, daughter, to explain what transpired.' Her eyes widened then as another memory returned. 'A heavenly voice predicted that my daughter would cause Ravana's death! So I am the cause of this tragedy, for I hid the secret of your birth from

my king. O my child, I must go to him at once. I must warn him
that you are his daughter in spirit if not in body. He will set you
free at once, for I know him well. Forgive me, beloved Ravana.
Do not enter the battlefield before I can speak to you.'

Mandodari ran from the garden as if Yama's messengers
were after her. She must save Ravana. She must confess the truth
that could save him.

The demon army marched out of the fortress gates like a mighty
flood, their banners casting dark shadows that swallowed
the light of day. The rhythmic pounding of their feet on the
trembling earth sounded like Shiva's tandava of destruction. But
the rakshasas saw dark omens and dreadful visions that foretold
doom. They saw a headless corpse obstructing their path, its pale
arms swinging at them in a frenzy. Jackals howled at the palace
gates and the sun was attacked by stars though it was day.

However, the dauntless Ravana was everywhere—on land,
in the air and in several corners of the field. The elements did
his bidding, snared by his occult powers. Flames danced around
his head and lightning crackled in the hair that tumbled to his
shoulders. The rakshasa danced like Yama himself, his fury
a crimson tide that charred his foes like the fire in cremation
grounds. The wind wailed a dirge for all those fated to die that
grim day.

The devas saw the avatara confronting the asura who was
girded with boons from Shiva and Brahma. 'It seems like a fight
between mighty Garuda and the thousand-headed Adisesha,'
they whispered. 'They look like two of the mammoths bearing
the world, readying for a clash that will end in the destruction

of the universe. Who can win when mighty Shiva and Vishnu fight?'

'Do not forget that this is not a fight among equals but a fight between good and evil,' said Shiva. 'Rama must win or the three realms will be destroyed.'

Indra sent down his own vaahana with the charioteer Matali and a quiver of supernal arrows so that Rama could fight the rakshasa on an equal footing. The chariot shone brilliantly and was hung with shining rows of weapons. It was drawn by fleet horses with silvery manes and lightning hooves. However, Rama hesitated to mount the ratha, wondering if it was yet another of Ravana's illusions. Sensing his doubt, the celestial horses chanted the Vedas softly and Rama bowed to them and mounted the chariot.

The arrows of the avatara and the asura clashed in mid-air, sending the vanaras whimpering to cover while the rakshasas stood transfixed. Their astras hurtled forth like thunderbolts, destroying the tallest summits and setting the eight directions on fire. Their chariots flashed over the seven seas and continents, the seven mountain ranges and worlds. Their wheels turned so rapidly that those watching on heaven and earth could not tell which was Rama's chariot and which Ravana's. Meteors fell down, rain clouds dried up, the earth stopped its revolution and not a single wave ruffled the oceans.

Ravana unleashed the Tamasa astra from which emerged monstrous arrows tipped with fire and blood, and arrows with the faces of asuras, goblins and cobras. Rama destroyed them all with his own astra blessed by Shiva. Ravana could no longer see Rama but only his Kodanda from which the arrows flew like a river of fire. He grew weaker by the moment, as if a heavy burden was crushing his limbs and his head.

Desperate to end the war before he collapsed, Ravana took up his trishul, his weapon of darkness, and hurled it at Rama.

Rama's death appeared certain as the flaming weapon hurtled towards him, but at the last moment, the prince countered it with a Shakti that incinerated the trishul.

Rama's arrows continued to find their mark on the rakshasa's body while Ravana faltered in his attack, benumbed by a vision of Vedavati's angry face. Mandodari's voice rang in his ear, telling him that he was making a huge blunder. He felt weak, burdened by the immense losses he had suffered. Indrajit, Aksha, Kumbhakarna, his loyal guard—so many deaths that he could have prevented. Nevertheless he would fight on, to the very end.

Rama's masterly arrows broke Ravana's flagpole, tore through his armour and took off his crown. The final one sheared off Ravana's head and sent it flying through the air, still howling.

'The demon is dead!' shouted the vanaras, erupting in cheers. 'Victory to Rama!' But then they retreated in fear when they saw a new head emerge from the bloody stump of Ravana's neck, roaring vile challenges. The Kodanda twanged and another arrow scorched the air and carried away the new head. But this too was replaced by another, more hideous and wrathful. Strangely, whenever the new head howled its defiance, the others that had been torn off earlier also roared, no less loudly.

The rakshasa could not be killed. And the sun was rapidly sinking to the west. Night approached—the night of the new moon, when Ravana would become invincible. Was this the night when virtue would be vanquished?

13

The Setting Sun

Must I behead him ten times to destroy his ten heads? wondered Rama as he continued his attack. But ten heads emerged, and twenty, and a hundred, before Rama realized that this was a futile endeavour. The asura was standing still, though he was weakening rapidly due to his grievous wounds and the terrible loss of blood. Suddenly, Ravana swooned and the next moment, he and his chariot both disappeared, whisked away by his skilful charioteer.

Rama descended to the ground in his ratha and Sugriva said to him anxiously, 'If we do not find a way to kill him before night, Ravana will be unstoppable. He will kill you and earth will be plunged into ruin.'

The vanaras chattered in agitation. Rama and Lakshmana were greatly disturbed. Were they fated to lose their battle after sacrificing so much? Would Sita be bound hand and foot and delivered to the rakshasa's bed?

Vibhishana looked thoughtful and then told them a story that he had heard when he was young. 'They say that Shiva gave

Ravana a potent astra and told him to keep it safe, for it was the only weapon that could kill him,' he said.

'I must find it then, without delay,' said Rama. 'As Sugriva warns us, there is very little time before Ravana's strength grows beyond our own.'

'The astra must be hidden in Mandodari's chamber, for she is the only one he trusts,' said Vibhishana. 'Hanuman must go to her in the guise of an ascetic to win her confidence and then snatch the weapon.'

The vanara turned himself into a gaunt ascetic and appeared before the distraught queen. 'The king's life is in your hands, O queen!' he said. 'Vibhishana has revealed the hiding place of the astra that is the only one with the power to kill Ravana. Hurry! Hide it elsewhere before Rama's spies come here looking for it.'

Tortured by guilt, tormented by fears for Ravana's safety, Mandodari ran quickly to a crystal pillar in her chamber and removed the astra that was hidden within. Hanuman returned to his vanara form, leapt forward and seized the astra.

'No!' screamed Mandodari, running towards him to retrieve the weapon. 'Have pity on me, vanara, and give it back!' In her desperation, she held out a basket of choice fruits to him in exchange for the astra.

Hanuman laughed gently down at her from his perch near the ceiling. 'O queen, of what use are these fruits to one who cherishes Rama, the Parama Phala—the ultimate fruit of wisdom?' he said. The next moment he had bounded through the doorway and vanished, hastening to give Rama the astra.

The dazed Ravana had been revived and he returned to the battlefield to face Rama. He raised the Chandrahasa in a final show of defiance. But the sword vanished from his hand when touched by Rama's arrow, for it could not be used against a righteous opponent.

Ravana gasped and trembled when he saw Shiva's astra glinting in the kshatriya's hand like the fire of annihilation. The next moment, it was shrieking through the air in a fiery arc. It pierced the rakshasa's armour and cleaved his stomach. Ravana swooned from the agony and his life began to seep out of his body. The weeping charioteer brought his ratha down to earth.

The vanaras watched fearfully and exploded in joy when Ravana did not rise to his feet again. 'Ravana is defeated! Rama has destroyed the rakshasa!' they whooped in delight. Rama joined his hands in respect to a worthy foe who would have been invincible if not for his vices. Mourners from Lanka's capital flooded the field, looking for their loved ones. Moans and wails rent the skies.

Many of Ravana's women had grown to love his passion and magnificence. They came now in their hundreds to weep over the fallen emperor. 'How are we alive still when our king lies dying on the harsh earth?' they sobbed. 'Are you not the lord of the eight directions, the warrior who lifted Kailasa in his arms? How can death claim you when you are master of Yama himself? You protected your wives with valorous arms and high walls. But now we are bereft, exposed to the harsh light and wind and to the avid glances of commoners. How can you bear to see all this happen, O lord? Take us with you, great soul!'

Meanwhile, in the palace, Mandodari's attendants waited for their queen to acknowledge their presence. But she was lost in prayer, tears streaming down her cheeks. Finally, one of her maids clutched the queen's shoulder and shook her until she looked up in a daze.

'Dearest queen, we have dreadful news for you,' the girl said.

Mandodari reeled back, her hand outstretched as if to ward off a blow. She gasped, her face turning red and then ashen. Her eyes clung to the maid's, a fearful question in them.

'Yes,' the girl nodded in reply.

'O great king! My protector, my soul!' sobbed Mandodari.

'The guards have arrived to take us to him,' said the maid, helping the queen rise to her feet. Mandodari's eyes were unseeing and she clasped the maid's hand so tightly that the girl bit her lips to stop herself from crying out. A chariot waited, the one Ravana had made especially for the queen—with horses white as the ocean's surf. Around the queen's neck were huge pearls brought as tribute by Varuna, vying with the sheen of her skin. Ravana had always liked her to wear white, for it highlighted her purity. 'Your innocence and luminous beauty drew me to you and made me fall in love,' he had said. She had worn white thereafter, foregoing the brilliant colours that she liked herself. The white was however embellished with gems of varied hues—rubies, emeralds and amethysts. And her chamber was always vibrant with gorgeous flowers that were yellow and pink and red. Their love had been so complete that his likes had become hers and her wishes had become his.

Mandodari sobbed now, realizing that white was also the colour of death and mourning. It appeared now to be cold and desolate, as her life had become. How could she bear to look upon the warrior king lying bloodied on the field, his body torn by arrows? Perhaps she would never hear his voice again, or feel his touch. He was her companion, her soulmate, the one for whom she had been created. Was he alive still or dead? She was too afraid to ask.

'We must hurry,' said the guard escorting them. 'Our emperor holds on to life, as if waiting for his queen.'

'Fly like the wind then!' she ordered, a flash of red sparking her cheeks. She would see him then, say her final farewell. She would weep over him and then join him in death.

'You have killed the rakshasa!' shouted Lakshmana as he rushed to embrace his brother. Then he looked askance at Rama who was strangely silent, showing no signs of elation.

'He is not a mere rakshasa, Lakshmana,' said Rama. 'Ravana was Brahma's great-grandson and won great boons from him and from Shiva through his austerities. His knowledge of the Vedas and Upanishads, of statecraft and astronomy are unmatched. Go to him now and garner his wisdom to guide us after he is gone.'

Bowing his head to his brother who could see virtue even in his deadliest foe, the obedient Lakshmana went to stand near Ravana's head and sought his message for the world. However, Ravana turned his head away without answering. Seeing this, Rama hurried to him and stood by the rakshasa's feet with his hands joined in respect.

'Lord of the three worlds, learned Ravana, share the wisdom you have gleaned with the mortal who stands before you,' he said.

Ravana's eyes grew moist as he looked upon Rama's face. 'Sri Rama!' he said. 'You stand at my feet as a student should, unlike your brother. You are indeed worthy of receiving the knowledge I have gathered over my long life. Your humility when you are yourself the abode of all wisdom shames me, for it was arrogance that brought about my downfall. I had wealth, learning and the blessings of the gods. I had the love of a wife who was not just devoted but was also wise and strong. Fool that I was, I craved more, wishing to reduce all that was noble to my own level. I had the opportunity to do good, but squandered my blessings through greed and desire. I committed the ultimate sin of abducting Sita, not realizing that she was glorious Lakshmi herself. Now I lie here, having lost everything, my kingdom, my sons, my dignity and my life. And if there is one lesson that I have learned through my experiences, it is this:

'Good and evil thoughts arise in our minds every day. It is easy to embrace evil which is alluring, but difficult to do good, for it requires immense self-control. We defer good deeds and find excuses for our behaviour while rushing to give in to our temptations. I knew well that abducting your wife was sinful, but I did so readily. I avoided facing you, though I knew in my heart that you were my redemption. This then is my message to all men. Control your ego and your senses and choose the right path at all times, for you never know which day will be your last.'

He wept as he joined his hands in reverence. His ten heads, his twenty arms, his occult chariot and his golden mansions had no value now. All he craved was forgiveness from the lord of lords.

14

Will Love Triumph?

The queen's chariot made its way swiftly to the edge of the field from where Mandodari ran to Ravana who lay on the harsh earth, his body covered now with flowers that concealed his wounds. Though he was in great pain, he had refused any potions that would cloud his brain.

Mandodari's cry of anguish silenced the other mourners who watched sorrowfully as she raised Ravana's head to her lap. It seemed as if Ravana had yoked all his spiritual powers in order to stay alive until he could see her one last time. His eyes lighted up and his hand lifted slowly to wipe her tears.

'Alas! Your body is torn by arrows as if Rama sought to root out your mighty spirit,' she sobbed. 'Or did he pierce you so deeply to find out if a part of you still loved his Sita? I shudder to see the arms that held me close lying powerless and to see your eyes glazed with pain. How I wish that we could live out the rest of our days in peace, sharing the pain of our losses . . .

'. . . If only your sister had not come that day to tell us about Sita . . . If Sita had not come out of her hermitage to welcome you . . . If you had looked upon Rama first and realized the purpose behind his birth . . . If, if, if . . . Alas! Kaala and karma wait for no one, deva or danava.'

The rakshasis and the vanaras stood watching helplessly, moved by the intensity of her grief. Ravana's eyes were closed and tears spilled out in an unending stream as he knew that the time of parting was near.

'There is a final "If", my king,' Mandodari continued. 'If I had told you the dreadful secret that I concealed . . . we could have avoided this tragedy. But I discovered the truth too late to save you, to warn you . . .' Ravana's eyelids rose slowly and he struggled to keep them open amidst the pain. 'Sita is my daughter, born of the poisonous brew of sages' blood that you had stored in my chamber, Ravana. I drank the potion one day in an attempt to kill myself, for I feared that you no longer loved me. But the milk of the durva grass that you stole from Sage Gritsamada and added to the pot saved me. The sage's penances to acquire the lustrous Lakshmi as his daughter bore fruit in my womb. But sinner that I am, I concealed this from you and set our daughter afloat on the ocean.' Mandodari wept uncontrollably, consumed by guilt. 'It is I who brought about your fate, my lord. Fool that I am, I thought that casting the child away would remove the threat to your life. Forgive me, oh forgive me!' she wept.

'No, my love,' Ravana replied. 'I was the one who betrayed you. I have a secret too, the secret of why I was rendered helpless when I saw Rama on Hanuman's back. I realized soon afterwards that my opponent was the lord I had served for many yugas. Rama was the great Vishnu with the infinite arms, whose eyes are the sun and the moon—the one who pervades earth and heaven and dazzles the three realms with his radiance. I had run amuck in pursuit of pleasure, deluded by lust and greed, forgetting the One who is the final destination. I failed to realize that earthly desire can never be quenched and that it can only trap you in an endless cycle of birth and death. If I had been wise, I would have turned instead to Narayana who is the ultimate bliss.'

He gasped in pain and Mandodari moistened his throat with some water. Sugriva and Angada, Hanuman and Vibhishana, Rama and Lakshmana had all moved closer to the dying warrior. Rama's face was gentle as he listened to his penitent devotee.

'My past life was revealed to me in a flash,' continued Ravana, in a final burst of strength. 'Kumbhakarna and I were then Vishnu's gatekeepers named Jaya and Vijaya. We had stopped Brahma's sons, the Sanat Kumaras, without knowing who they were. And they had cursed us to be born on earth. When we begged for forgiveness, the gracious Vishnu told us that we could choose to live seven lives as his devotees or three lives as his foes. Wishing to return to him sooner, we chose to live three evil lives. We were born first as Hiranyakashipu and Hiranyaksha and were slain by Varaha and Narasimha, avataras of Vishnu. And once I discovered who Rama was, I resolved to die by his hands alone. Only then could I be redeemed from the sin of abducting the divine Lakshmi, the Shakti I worshipped every day in Vaikunta. I had laid rough hands on the Devi who had incarnated with her lord in order to destroy evil.'

'She chose to suffer like no woman before her, only to lessen the earth's burden of wickedness,' said Mandodari. 'I held her in my arms for a few moments and hope that her divine touch may free my soul too from sin.'

'I understand now why I could not let her go, for without her I am nothing,' whispered Ravana. 'My bond with her is eternal, but my rakshasa eyes failed to discern the truth. I kept her captive even after I discovered that Rama was Vishnu, only so that I could offer him my life. Now my second life of sin comes to an end and just one more life remains before I can return to Vaikunta.'

'If you knew that Rama was the avatara, could you not have surrendered to him, my king? Why did you continue the fight to the bitter end?'

'By holding all the evil forces together, I could help Rama destroy them completely,' said Ravana. 'My life and death would also help mortals understand the results of leading a sinful life of indulgence. This was the least I could do when my god and goddess had chosen to be born as humans and suffer pain and separation, just to show us that we too can aspire to perfection.'

Ravana moved a hand feebly in her direction and she clasped it in her own and raised it to her lips. 'To do this, however, I had to turn my back on you and your wisdom, my heart,' he said. 'I realize now that I was so strongly drawn to Sita because I saw you in her, for she is your daughter. Seek her forgiveness on my behalf after I die. Tell the goddess that I will return to Vaikunta one day and be her slave for eternity. May my end show the world that virtue will ultimately triumph over evil.'

His eyes blazed as he relived again the last moments of the battle, when Rama had sent Shiva's astra hurtling forward, lighting up the farthest corners of the universe. Ravana had seen Vishnu's Sudarshana chakra blaze forth from Vishnu and join its force with the astra. The divine weapon had entered his chest, quenching the power of his boons and the pride in his heart. It had then flown through the spheres to the cosmic ocean to wash away the blood and then returned to Rama's mystic quiver. How blessed he had been to be granted this vision!

He saw that his Mandodari was speaking, her body shaking with grief. 'I cannot live without you, my Ravana,' she said. 'I will die with you.'

'No, my queen. Remember that women killed themselves after their men died in war only because they feared that they would be raped and tortured by the enemy. You need fear nothing when my brother Vibhishana rules as king. It is your duty to guide him and ensure the welfare of our people. You are brave and wise and the mother of indomitable Indrajit. Did you not hear the vanaras exclaim that if there had been more Indrajits, many more Ramas would have had to be born?'

Mandodari smiled tremulously in response and he turned his eyes to Vibhishana. 'Give her due respect and follow her advice, Vibhishana,' he said, 'for she is far-sighted and unerring in her judgement.' Vibhishana nodded, his eyes tearing up as he saw again his virtuous brother who had temporarily lost his way.

From the heavens echoed a voice in blessing. 'Ravana, you are now the true grandson of Pulastya. You have been purified by the fire and will soon return to blissful Vaikunta. The gods bless Mandodari, the embodiment of purity and love. She will be revered henceforth as one of the panchakanya, along with Ahalya, Draupadi, Kunti and Tara. Those who evoke these five maidens will be forever redeemed from sin.'

Ravana turned his eyes in adoration at Rama. 'Every child born here will tell your story, noble Rama,' he said. 'Countless will be the boys named Rama, Raghava and Raghuvira, and girls named Sita, Mythili and Janaki. I worship you, great one, whose every step measures the three worlds. I worship you, greatest of yogis, who is the beginning, middle and end of all beings. The one who holds the conch, the chakra and the mace and grants us freedom from fear. The god who embodies divine love with your goddess. Rama, you are righteousness, while Sita is righteous action. You are space and she is the sky. You are the sun and she the sunlight. You are the ocean and she the shore. There is nothing beyond you two. Grant me your blessings, O Narayana!'

So died Ravana, the most powerful of rakshasas and the greatest of bhaktas. Magnificent in life and glorious in death. His story revealed the potent power of love that can save a tortured soul. His spirit emerged as a radiant light and merged with Rama's, for he who thinks of Vishnu when he dies attains the lord's feet.

Mandodari wept for the great love of her life. Then she heard Ravana's voice in her ear. 'My heart is always yours, my queen,' he said. 'Do not weep, for we will be united again in a purer world.'

DAMAYANTI'S RIDDLE

1

The Swan from Heaven

Gagana, king of the swans, flew through the dark clouds, his gold plumes glittering like lightning on a monsoon night. The storm was at its wildest and he was unable to keep to his course though he struggled with all his might. Why, oh why had he not left with his flock before the onset of the rainy season? He would have been safe now in his celestial home in Lake Manasarovar instead of being battered by the gale. But he was the trusted emissary between earth and heaven and had tarried in order to carry a message from Bhima, the ruler of Vidarbha, to Indra, king of the devas.

The divine hamsa scurried for cover in a marble pavilion, shook the water from his sodden feathers, tucked his beak into his body and fell into an exhausted sleep.

Nala, the young ruler of Nishada, whose garden he had landed in, had been sitting alone under a golden canopy, pining for a woman he had not yet seen. Travelling bards had sung praises about a lovely princess when they had passed through his court a few months ago.

'Great Nala, king of kings, tiger among men, more dazzling than Surya!' they had lauded him. 'We bring you tidings of the ravishing Damayanti, daughter of King Bhima of Vidarbha. She is radiant like Ushas, the dawn goddess who rides a golden chariot over snow-clad mountains and fleecy clouds. She is fashioned out of all things lovely by Kama, the love god. Marry her, Nala, and you will be happier than Shiva with Parvati or Vishnu with Shri.'

From that day onward, Nala had been lovelorn and distraught, waiting impatiently to be invited to Damayanti's swayamvara, for it was the practice in those days for a princess to choose her bridegroom from the suitors invited for the occasion. Nala often sat alone in his scented garden, where golden fish darted in lotus pools and dappled does roamed the green lawns. He watched vivid parrots fluttering in the orange trees and peacocks preening atop carved pillars. But all this beauty only served to remind him that the wondrous princess he desired was not by his side to enjoy these blissful sights. An owl hooted in a branch above, the honeybees buzzed around perfumed flowers and the koel banished the silence with its plaintive call. But all he could hear was the echo of a single name: 'Damayanti, Damayanti!'

Nala was startled from his reverie by a glimpse of golden wings flitting through the trees, and hurried to discover the identity of his radiant visitor. Seeing the gorgeous bird in the pavilion, he crept towards him on soft feet and stood gazing at him. Strangely, the swan did not stir or even open his eyes. The king saw that his wings were wet and bedraggled and that he appeared to be severely battered by the storm winds. Nala's heart melted with pity and he caught the bird up gently in his arms and cradled him close to his chest. He then used his soft sash to blot the water gently from his feathers, hoping to warm him up sufficiently so that he came alive again.

The king sighed in relief when the bird finally moved his legs and opened his eyes to gaze at his benefactor. 'Do not fear, beautiful one,' said Nala. 'I am Nala, king of Nishada, and I mean you no harm. Rest awhile in my arms until you feel stronger.'

To his surprise, the swan did not seem afraid but merely drew back his head to gaze into the king's eyes. 'Did you snatch me up thinking that you would become rich with the gold in my plumes?' he joked, speaking in a human voice. The startled king staggered and almost dropped him. The swan laughed and continued to talk in a feeble voice. 'You should know that I am Gagana and that I am blessed by Brahma himself! I have heard wondrous tales about you in heaven, my friend. They say that you are a great warrior and a generous and compassionate king whom his people love. Why, it is even believed that you can speak the language of birds and beasts!'

'All creatures understand the language of love, Gagana,' said Nala, happy to see that the bird was regaining his strength gradually.

'I wish to reciprocate your kindness, Nala, and promise to help you attain your deepest desire.'

'If only you could!' smiled Nala. 'My heart aches to find a way to wed the fair Damayanti, King Bhima's daughter.'

Gagana looked thoughtfully at him, realizing that this gracious and compassionate king was a far finer match for the princess than Indra. 'If that is your wish, I promise that I will help you win the maiden's hand!' he said solemnly.

Nala nodded, not wishing to hurt the swan's feelings by questioning him on how a bird could help him win a princess. Instead, he would try and find out what the swan knew about her, for he seemed to be well-informed about affairs on earth and in heaven. 'Tell me about Damayanti, wise one, for I yearn helplessly for her from dawn to the darkest hour of the night!' he said.

'I was sent by her father to invite Indra to descend to earth and marry her,' said Gagana. Nala looked at him in panic, wondering how he could succeed in his love when her father had chosen the god of thunder as her groom. The swan continued soothingly. 'But I see now that you are more deserving of the princess. You will make her the queen of your heart, unlike Indra who is adored by his wife Indrani and the many apsaras in his court. Permit me to rest awhile in your kingdom and I will then go to Damayanti and tell her about your goodness and your love. As I promised you, I will ensure that she chooses you for her husband and none other.'

Realizing that Nala still looked dazed, the swan said, 'You seem to doubt my powers, O king. Hence I will tell you a story of the ancient bond between the gods and the birds. In earlier ages, swans were not pure white as they are now but had feathers that were both black and white. The devas were attending a yagna in a rishi's ashram when they heard the thundering of the chariot wheels of the dire rakshasa king Ravana. Fearful of his terrifying strength, the gods hid from him by taking the forms of various creatures. Indra became a peacock, Yama a crow, Kubera a chameleon and Varuna a swan. Ravana was taken in by their disguises and went his way, confident that none of his enemies was near. The gods rewarded the birds and the chameleon for their help. They blessed the peacock with stunning beauty and chose the crow to receive the offerings made to ancestors. They endowed the chameleon with the ability to change the colour of his skin and gave the hamsa flawless white feathers and the power of discrimination. And as you know, Brahma and his wife Saraswati have chosen our species to serve as their vehicles. So do not doubt my capabilities, noble king. Trust me when I say that I will help you win Damayanti, though the gods stand in my way!'

Gagana soon arrived at Damayanti's palace in the Vidarbha capital of Kundinapur and attracted her attention with his brilliance and his grace. The princess ran after him, eager to hold him. Her maids followed her, laughing merrily. Realizing that the bird seemed alarmed by their chatter, Damayanti told them to leave her so that she could try and catch the lustrous bird herself. The hamsa pranced before her on its bright yellow feet, luring the princess to a far corner of the garden. She crept nearer and swept the bird up into her arms. The swan surprised her by showing himself to be quite tame. He nestled his head against her chest and allowed her to stroke his golden wings while he pecked gently at her lips that gleamed like ripe cherries.

'So beautiful are you, princess, that I would marry you myself!' he said, to her amazement. 'If only I had not sworn eternal devotion to my wife . . . We swans mate for life, you know. And also, I promised King Nala that I would win your heart for him!'

Damayanti's eyes twinkled. 'We must also remember that you are not of my kind, however talented you may be!' she teased him. 'But tell me more about this King Nala to whom you have so rashly promised my hand!'

'The king of Nishada is dashing and dauntless, perfect in form and nature. He is first among archers, beloved of his people and exalted like the sun. Just as you are a nonpareil in women, so is he in men. And he dies in love for you, peerless princess!' Gagana spoke ardently of Nala's attributes and drew a portrait of the king for her on a lotus leaf. Damayanti felt her heart fluttering in response and she too began to desire a meeting with this dream lover.

'I will have my father arrange a swayamvara and ensure that he sends an invitation to Nala,' she said. 'Ask your noble friend to wait for the news and assure him that I have been won over by your adulation for him.' She dropped a soft kiss on Gagana's head, making him preen.

'I will go at once, princess, to convey your feelings to Nala. Then I must return to my wife who waits impatiently for me on the shores of Manasarovar. I will tell her very little about you, for she will be jealous when she finds out how much you adore me!'

So saying, the bird shot into the air to fly to Nishada again, while Damayanti cradled the leaf with Nala's portrait close to her bosom.

Soon, her handmaidens came looking for her and were startled to find her sitting wan and listless, as if their sparkling mistress had been replaced by a hollow replica. In the days that followed, Damayanti's doleful sighs and her strange silences worried them no end. Her mother deciphered her mood and hurried to the king to tell him that it was time to hold a swayamvara for their daughter.

Why has Indra not come as yet despite the message I sent through Gagana? wondered King Bhima, forced now to agree to his wife's counsel. He sent out fleet horsemen to far-flung kingdoms to deliver the news that his daughter was ready to choose her husband. Many kings and princes, who had heard reports of Damayanti's bewitching beauty, hastened to Kundinapur. The earth trembled to the rhythm of festive drums, the rumbling of chariot wheels and the trampling feet of palanquin bearers bearing their monarchs to the kingdom of the radiant princess. All other affairs of state, including wars, were set aside, as their hearts and minds converged on one cause and one alone.

Devarishi Narada, whose actions often influenced destiny, presented himself before Indra. The god of thunder welcomed him warmly and sought to know everything that was happening in the three realms. 'An unusual peace seems to be reigning on earth,' Indra said. 'I see no kings vying to reach my loka after fighting and dying on the battlefield.'

The sage informed Indra that the kings were all united in their desire to win not kingdoms but the hand of the fair Damayanti. 'If her beauty has such power, then I too will attend her swayamvara!' said Indra. 'There can be no suitor more dazzling than me.'

'We will come with you and hope that she will look on one of us with favour!' said Yama, Varuna and Agni, gods of death, water and fire. Their glorious cavalcades set off soon, lighting up the skyways like a hail of meteors.

Below on earth they saw a resplendent figure in a chariot going to Bhima's capital, followed by decorated elephants and a galaxy of warriors. Indra recognized King Nala and grew afraid that he would eclipse all the celestials with his radiance.

'We must deflect him from his purpose or our mission will be doomed,' he said to the other gods and descended to earth to intercept the king. 'We are the guardians of the realms and have a mission for you, O Nala!' he said. Nala bowed to them and expressed his obedience, dazzled by their luminous forms and commanding presence. 'Be our messenger and tell the lovely Damayanti that she must wed one of us!' said Indra.

Nala was struck speechless by this decree, his heart giving way to despair. How could he woo the mistress of his heart when he had been ordered to promote the devas' cause instead? And how would an earthly maiden, courted by the gods, settle for a mortal? He was lost! His love was destined to fail. He would give up his life rather than eke out his remaining days without the radiant princess by his side. Was there anything he could do, anything he could say to escape his awful dilemma?

2

A Clash with the Gods

King Nala realized that this was a battle beyond all battles, one that would determine his life and his happiness. He could not imagine losing the princess whose vision haunted his every moment, whether he was awake or asleep. He had to find a way to divert these fierce gods so that they would not snatch away his heart's desire. There was nothing he would not do to win his Damayanti, come what may.

The king of Nishada gathered his wits together and politely demurred. 'I am going to the swayamvara myself as a suitor, great Indra,' he said. 'Take pity on this humble mortal and return to the heavens, or at least find another messenger to speak for you.'

However, Indra was adamant on holding Nala to his promise.

'How will I enter her palace when she is surrounded by fierce guards?' Nala asked next, but the god told him that he would render him invisible so that he could sail past all hurdles.

The next instant, Nala found himself standing near Damayanti's crystal palace with its colourful mosaics, set like a jewel amid cool fountains and brilliant flower beds. A bevy of laughing maidens was playing in the arbour and they froze where they stood when the balls they were tossing around rebounded after hitting him. Others bumped into his invisible form and drew back in surprise. They whispered excitedly, pointing to the footprints he left on the flowers scattered on the floor. One came boldly towards him and gasped when she saw her own reflection on his invisible crown and ornaments. Was there magic afoot or were they in danger from an unknown intruder?

Then they glimpsed Nala's divine form reflected in the lotus pond and knew that it was time to alert their mistress. One of them called out to Damayanti in a trembling voice and Nala stood motionless, waiting to set eyes on the entrancing princess.

'What is it?' carolled a koel, or so it seemed to the besotted king. Damayanti pushed aside the silken curtains hanging across the entrance to her palace and emerged, gleaming like a full moon in a midnight sky. In her hands she held a festoon of red roses, for she had been imagining the scene of her swayamvara when she would cast her garland around Nala's neck. She tossed the festoon playfully before her as she danced forward and gasped as it fell around his neck and disappeared from sight. She herself came up against his rock-hard chest and felt his powerful arms gathering her close.

Nala was ecstatic as he clasped this delicate bundle to his heart. He looked down upon her fair face, dewy fresh like a jasmine bud. Her slender body was soft and yielding, draped in a snow-white robe embroidered with glowing rubies. In his mind he heard minstrels singing odes to the beautiful princess of Kundina and her quest for love. He held on feverishly to the maiden, though he knew that he would have to let her go. His mind was swamped by signals sent by his heated senses and he forgot the mantra that Indra had asked him to chant. His form gradually materialized before Damayanti's dazed eyes. She stared at the handsome stranger and wondered if he was god or gandharva. He gazed entranced into her eyes that glittered like clear pools nestled amid snowy Himalayan peaks.

But then Nala's righteousness asserted itself and he dropped his hands from around her body. She staggered and her maids rushed forward to support her in their arms.

'Forgive my trespass into your bower, fair princess,' he said, his voice manly and resonant. 'I am Nala, king of Nishada, here to do the bidding of the gods. Indra, Yama, Varuna and Agni wish you to choose one of them as your husband. Give me your answer at once, I pray, so that I may leave your presence before I give in to my yearning and beg you to consider my claim to your hand instead!'

So this was the gallant warrior that Gagana had described so vividly! Damayanti's heart was filled with rapture. But first she must give him her answer to be conveyed to the gods. 'I fell in love with you the moment Gagana described you and told me of your resolve to wed me!' she said, fixing eloquent eyes on his face. 'I will marry none but you, King Nala, and entreat you not to give up your suit, regardless of all obstacles, human or divine.'

Nala's eyes flashed with joy in response to her bold words, but then despair clouded his mind again. 'How can a mortal ever hope to win against the celestials, divine one?' he asked.

But Damayanti was unwavering in her decision. 'Love is beyond any other considerations,' she declared. 'So let us take a vow together that our union will be sanctified, not sacrificed. Remember that I orchestrated this swayamvara only so that I could marry you. If you love me as you say you do, you will present yourself at the assembly. I will choose you and hence you will bear no blame!'

Nala's heart surged with hope as he watched her speak so bravely. He longed to feel her soft lips under his own. He drank in her beauty for one long moment and then turned reluctantly to carry her reply to the devas.

As he had feared, Indra was incensed by Damayanti's reply and thundered at the messenger: 'You have kept your word only in letter and not in spirit. Now I will do what has to be done!'

Nala quailed, for he knew that there was nothing beyond Indra's powers. But he would go to the swayamvara regardless. He would fight for his love until his last breath.

The sun rose over Kundinapur on the auspicious day, making its temples, palaces and mansions gleam like pink onyx. Bhima's ancestors had built the city with a wonderful granite stone that took on a rich rose-red sheen in the morning light. The huge bronze gates of the city were thrown open to let in the magnificent suitors with their glittering retinues. Princes, kings and gods made their way eagerly to their appointed places within the vast enclosure prepared for the event. Trumpets blared to announce the arrival of King Bhima on an elephant, followed by a column of foot soldiers and richly-robed bearers carrying the princess in a bejewelled palanquin.

The proud father descended from his mount as the bearers set down the palanquin facing the row of suitors. He pulled aside the curtains and helped his daughter step out in front of the impatient audience. The music hushed. The suitors gasped in awe when they caught their first glimpse of the radiant Damayanti, clad in a shimmering silver sari and adorned with fine jewels, her face as charming as the pink lotus blooming in Indra's garden. The heralds began to read out the names and achievements of the various suitors gathered there. But Damayanti's mind was focused on one man alone. Where was he? Where was her Nala?

Damayanti was unable to spot the king of Nishada among those who courted her. For a moment, her heart froze in panic. What could she do if he was not present? She felt faint at the very thought. Once more she scanned the faces before her.

Then she saw him! Her beloved Nala stood mid-way down the line, his eyes fixed on her face. He had come, her noble lover who had enchanted her when he had met her in her perfumed garden!

Then she looked again, rubbing her eyes in disbelief, for there was not just one Nala, but five! Was it her fevered imagination conjuring up false visions to delude her? If there were five Nalas facing her, how would she find the true one?

Her mind raced as she tried to make sense of her strange predicament. The gods knew that she loved Nala and intended to choose him as her groom. They must have taken his form in order to confound her, hoping that she would mistakenly garland one of them. What was she to do now? What if she erred and chose one of the false Nalas? She would be queen of the heavens, no doubt, as consort of one of the gods. But she wanted only her Nala who ruled her heart.

Damayanti felt faint as she wrestled with the dilemma. Her maid softly dabbed at her face and looked worriedly at her. The princess wondered if she should turn back to her palanquin and return to her palace. But no, the visiting kings and gods would consider it a grave insult and turn their wrath on her father. She took a few deep breaths and attempted to calm her mind. This was not the time to panic. She looked closely again at the five identical faces before her. How did one distinguish a mortal from the gods? There were signs that she should look for, she knew. The gods did not blink, while men did. But alas, all her suitors were staring at her wide-eyed, unable to remove their gaze from her face for even a moment. What else? They said that the devas did not sweat and that their garlands were unfading. Was there a nervous sweat beading the face of the Nala who stood in the centre of the line? Yes! And his garland had wilted too in the fierce heat of the sun. Her heart thudded within her as she gazed intently at the suitor she thought was the real Nala.

The princess took a step forward and then another. She homed in on the man who was now smiling triumphantly at her. She raised the garland in her hands.

Then she heard a gasp, quickly suppressed, from the Nala standing to the right of the one she had chosen. She stole a glance at him and realized that this man too was sweating and staring at her with an agonized face. Further, the flowers in his garland also seemed to be fading fast. Was she making a mistake? She saw the gloating look on the face of the man she had chosen first and reeled. This was not the humble, loving face of the suitor who had visited her in her garden and clasped her in his arms! This man appeared to be too proud, too brazen. Should she trust her instincts and back away from this one and choose the other? Her heart pounded as if it would burst.

Then Damayanti saw that the man standing before her cast no shadow, unlike the other one. She had almost forgotten this last aspect—that men cast shadows while the gods do not. No doubt, the devious Indra had tried to fool her by faking some signs. She took a quick step to the side and garlanded the one she thought was the real Nala. For a moment, time stood still. She waited anxiously wondering if he would reveal himself to be one of the gods. But no. It was her beloved king who stood looking at her with his adoration evident in his loving eyes, his charming face. Kama attacked them again with his arrows, filling the air with the fragrance of love. Nala saw before him the apsara whose radiant face had kept him awake through the long nights, her brow adorned with sandal paste, her lips speaking words of passion that only he could hear. It seemed to Damayanti's fevered brain that Nala's splendour had driven the most glorious aspects of nature into hiding. Seeing his radiant face, the sun disappeared behind the clouds. The lion sped into the jungle, frightened by the majesty of his form. And lightning flashed once before it vanished, seeing the brilliance of his smile. They had found each other again against all odds. No one could keep them apart until the end of their days on earth . . .

And then, their reverie was broken by loud voices, raised in protest or in celebration. The gods had resumed their real forms and were angry that their subterfuge had failed. The herald tried to make his voice heard above the tumult to announce that the princess had chosen King Nala of Nishada as her groom. Trumpets and bugles blared, adding to the frenzy of the cheering throngs.

When the noise abated slightly, Nala placed his palm over his chest and made a solemn vow to Damayanti. 'Peerless one!' he said. 'You have chosen me, a mere mortal, setting aside the claims of the mighty gods. You have elected to rule over my heart when you could have reigned over the three realms. How can I ever match your faith, O Damayanti! All that I can promise in return is that I will be eternally true to you. I vow before this august gathering, before the radiant gods, that I will always remain faithful to our love, as long as life and spirit animate this body.'

She bowed her head to honour his promise and moved to stand proudly by his side. The two looked to the gods, ready to face their wrath. Indra's eyes sparked with fury as he saw that all his ploys to win the maiden had failed.

'King Bhima! You have offended us!' he roared. 'You invited us to your daughter's swayamvara knowing well that she planned to spurn us and choose a mortal. You will face our rage and so will your people. I will smite your kingdom with drought and pestilence, turning your fruitful fields and orchards into barren deserts. You will soon rue the day the princess insulted us.'

Hearing his harsh words, the crowds cried out in fear and despair. Their celebration was turning rapidly into a lament. What would they do if the gods scourged them? How would they survive if the elements turned against them?

Damayanti spoke up then, interceding for her people. It was not right that they should pay the price for her choice. She joined her hands in worship. 'Mighty gods!' she said. 'I venerate you for blessing our land with good fortune and abundance. I beseech you to understand that my choosing Nala over you is out of love for him rather than disrespect for you. I have lived for this day, pining for my king from the moment the golden swan spoke to me of his valour and his love. I have been faithful to him in thought and deed and believe that it is our destiny to be together. Exalted gods, let go of your wrath and bless us and our people. Spread your mantle of protection over us, I beg you!'

King Bhima joined her in her appeal as did Nala. The commoners too prostrated themselves before the celestials who finally allowed their reverence to calm their rage. They raised their hands in benediction over them. They gave Nala several boons in order to make him even more worthy of Damayanti's love. Indra blessed him with the speed of a god and said that the couple would have two perfect children. Varuna granted him the power to summon water whenever he wanted and to endow freshness on flowers with a mere touch. Agni gave him the ability to summon fire at will and to be impervious to its fury. Yama endowed him with unrivalled virtue and the skill to cook dishes that would be as delightful as ambrosia.

Tragedy had been averted by Damayanti's piety and honesty, and the gods returned to heaven, well pleased with the outcome, though they had not been successful in claiming her hand. It seemed that love had triumphed and Nala and Damayanti would live happily ever after.

3

Kali and Dwapara

Nala's wedding with Damayanti was celebrated with such pomp and pageantry that all earth appeared to be agog with excitement. Singers, dancers, jugglers and magicians entertained the royal guests. Grand banquets were laid out with an array of delicacies made by the best cooks in the kingdom. Banners, festoons and jasmine garlands decorated all the public places and households. Damayanti was dressed in gorgeous red silk and adorned from head to foot with splendid jewels. Nala was resplendent as he came to the marriage hall on a caparisoned elephant, followed by minstrels and by dancers who were as beautiful as the apsaras in Indra's court.

When the bridal couple looked at each other in the wedding pavilion, their hearts pounded with joy so intense that they felt faint. The priests chanted the marriage mantras, the sacred fire burned bright. The priests sanctified their union amid a shower of rose petals from the devas in heaven and the elders on earth. One by one, the royal women waved lamps before the couple to ward off the evil eye, for no one had seen such a glorious pair before. After a brief stay in Vidarbha, the newlyweds left for Nishada with their retinue, laden with gifts.

Unknown to them though, a storm was brewing in the unseen realm above.

Kali and Dwapara, evil spirits who presided over the dark yugas, exploded in fury when they found out that they were too late to win Damayanti's hand. 'How can the princess choose a human instead of one of us?' ranted Kali. 'We must avenge this grave insult to the celestials! I will strike Nala and his people down with disease and discord, and enmesh them in hatred and anger.'

It seemed that the happy life of the newlyweds would end before it had even started. Damayanti found her happiness disturbed by terrifying visions of impending disaster, of sorrow and separation from her Nala.

Fortunately, Indra took up their cause against Kali as he did not like the demon challenging his decision to bless the king and his bride. 'Bhima's daughter has been honest about her love for Nala and the two have worshipped the gods with all reverence,' said Indra. 'You may not set your will against ours, Kali, or attempt to harm them in any way out of malice. If you do so, your evil actions will rebound on you and you will suffer in the fires of the netherworld.'

Though deterred by the threat, Kali was unwilling to let go of his rancour. He followed Nala to his kingdom, waiting for an opportune moment to harm him. The demon's nature was to oppose truth, mercy and everything that was righteous. He promoted violence, hatred and envy, and drew his power from men who indulged their baser instincts through unbridled sex, gambling and drinking. But Nala was wedded to dharma and ruled wisely and well. His people prospered under his benign eye and were virtuous, keeping Kali at bay with auspicious pujas, yagnas and the chanting of sacred mantras. Unable to enter Nishada, Kali still waited for something inauspicious to happen. And he knew just the right person through whom he could wreak his evil plans.

The newlywed couple had stepped into a charmed world which no one else could enter. In this domain, words held no meaning and all that mattered was a touch, a smile or a languid lowering of the eyes. Nala's kingdom was flourishing, his ministers governed well. He told her that he had no enemies to conquer—except her shyness. 'Oh, where have you hidden the princess who boldly accepted my wooing and flouted the gods?' Nala teased her. 'Where is the dauntless Damayanti who proclaimed her love before the assembled throng, ready to face death or worse?'

She smiled but made no attempt to answer, her body trembling as it travelled a new path to an ecstatic death of another kind. Each day was now a sensual exploration and each night a rhapsody of delight. They played exquisite games that made sense only to them, enhancing their joy when they finally came together. One day, she strolled in the garden speaking to her maid, pretending not to hear his soft call of love. He came up to her and touched her hand but she withdrew it quickly and bent over her parakeet, stroking its soft feathers. Alas, the bird betrayed her, for it echoed the words he had spoken to her the previous night and the moans and sighs she had uttered in reply! 'Oh, hush!' she whispered as she stuffed the bird's mouth with pomegranate seeds, whose pink colour rivalled the blush on her cheeks.

'My king leaves me with no time to recite the scriptures!' Damayanti complained to her maids. 'When do I practise my singing or play the lute when he demands my constant presence?' And then she cast a restless glance at the doorway, the hundredth in the last hour, wondering why Nala had not come to her as yet. What was keeping him away still, her jaunty king? Was there anything more important than making his queen feel cherished and adored?

Nala came to her just then, with impatient stride, leaving the affairs of state half-done. He had seen her sparkling face and her perfumed body in his mind's eye and had grown feverish from want of her. The whole world reeled dizzily around him and nothing was real except his queen. She glanced up again and saw him coming, stumbling in his haste, but pretended to be busy with her maids. He shifted from foot to foot and tried to snare her glance with his adoring look. Finally she deigned to look up at him, but only to fight, argue, question, sulk . . . until their glances mingled and their silly quarrel broke down in smiles and fervent embraces. Her breasts were crushed against his hard body, the robe she wore melted away. Her dark hair grew disordered, the sandal paste on her face was smeared and an emerald earring fell unheeded on the satin bedspread. 'Stop that, you thief!' she whispered as he stole kisses from her swollen lips, while urging him on with her fevered response.

'This is amrit!' he exclaimed, drunk with love. 'Can the nectar churned from the oceans by the foolish gods ever match the sweetness of your lips?' Damayanti melted at his touch, merged with his heart and dissolved into nothing. Was she asleep or dead?

Oh, she hated the morning when her sakhis came to wake them with urgent messages of visiting kings and sages. Nala reluctantly rose and walked away, casting yearning glances at her flushed, sleep-warmed face. Then her friends pounced on her with giggles, asking her where she had lost the ruby anklets she always wore. How could she tell them that her king had thrown them away, complaining that their tinkling revealed to the world that they were sleepless and engaged in love play? 'Where are your bracelets, glittering with gems and pearls?' they asked then. Damayanti dropped her eyes and blushed, unwilling to tell them that she had tossed them aside to don the armlets that Nala had woven for her with tender lotus shoots.

Every moment with him was precious. He hardly allowed her to sleep but she glowed like a pearl regardless. Hadn't the gods said that his touch would keep the flowers fresh? And she was the finest of blossoms, her body gleaming brighter with his every touch. When they spoke, it was not about the gods who had raised their voices at them in anger or about the blessings they had later showered on them. It was Kama, the god of love, who presided over their hearts as the queen invited her Nala closer, ever closer, with a half-smile, a rose-tipped finger run slowly over lush lips, and an extra sway of her slim hips. She revived her beloved king when he came to her, parched and wilting, needing a draught of refreshing wine from her soft mouth.

Gagana returned to earth again from his celestial abode, his golden plumes shimmering in the sunlight. He came to Nala's palace, eager to relish the fruits of his matchmaking. The princess showered kisses on his head and hugged him close in thanksgiving. Soon he was roaming freely in her boudoir and the gardens, telling everyone he saw that he had brought Damayanti and Nala together with his wiles and ploys. Nala too offered him a grand welcome and fed him with choice morsels from his own hands. He gave the swan a royal seat beside him on the dais, lined with soft cushions so that he could watch over the proceedings.

Gagana preened under all this attention and told the radiant couple that he would soon bring his wife and children to visit them. Damayanti designed a charming ruby crown for their winged visitor and he pranced around proudly, never tiring of telling the story of how he had chosen Nala to be her husband in the place of Indra. With every telling, the little rogue's role grew and grew until it became more fanciful than true. Soon Gagana was describing how he had fought off the gods and kings and fled with Nala and his bride, dodging a shower of arrows! The golden-winged bird became the beloved of the court dancers and he in turn gave them lessons on how to walk like he did. 'After all, a hamsa is the most graceful of creations on heaven or earth!' he declared.

It soon became a common sight to see the swan strutting ahead, chattering endlessly, followed by a giggling throng of young girls with ivory skin and hair as black as a raven's feathers.

Such bliss, such joy! The king and Damayanti revelled in their love, and their happiness was complete when in due course they were blessed with two perfect children—Indrasen and Indrasena.

But there was one man whose soul was filled with hatred. Nala's younger brother Pushkara was as malevolent as Nala was kind, as dissolute as his brother was virtuous. Pushkara was idle and extravagant and spent his days in gambling and dissipation. His heart was riven by lust when he saw his brother return with the fair princess. His fierce ambition to inherit the royal mantle if Nala did not marry was destroyed in that moment. His was the wicked heart that the demon Kali hoped to exploit in order to poison Nala's blissful life. But the king remained unaware of the evil that stalked him . . .

4

The Roll of the Dice

Twelve years passed, a period of unalloyed joy. But then, things changed. Nala had grown complacent, puffed up by all the adulation he received from his subjects and from visitors to his kingdom. He grew careless in state affairs and his piety dwindled. One day, when he neglected to wash his feet before his evening prayers, Kali, the source of all that is impure, entered the king's body and took possession of his soul. Nala's downfall seemed to be inevitable now. His ministers, taking their cue from him, grew indifferent to the people's welfare. The rains were scanty that year, and as the ruler did little to help his citizens, famine and hunger began to haunt the land. Even the horses in the royal stables grew dispirited, affected by their king's disregard. The troops in the army were not paid their dues and grew mutinous. The rich oppressed the poor and decadent men preyed on the powerless. Sinners grew in number and offerings to the ancestors and to the deities were no longer made as before.

Soon, the turmoil on earth spread to the heavens and meteors fell blazing to the earth. The sun appeared dim, surrounded by dreadful shadows. Indra's thunderbolt spat out flames, and the weapons of the other gods began to attack one another. The devas' power diminished and their garlands began to fade.

Indra, the god who had performed a thousand yagnas, was troubled and asked his guru Brihaspati, 'What danger threatens us, wise one? I see no enemy at our gates, but all the omens predict disaster.'

Kali appeared before him then, a devilish gleam in his eyes. 'Is it seemly for the gods to be so fearful?' he scoffed. 'Great Indra, you blessed King Nala and allied with him in the war between virtue and sin. Alas, he is now fallen and I will soon destroy him and all that he represents—love, compassion and righteousness. Stop me if you can!' Having uttered the challenge, Kali vanished from Indra's court to return to earth and continue his campaign of evil.

The demon entered the mansion of Pushkara, whose jealousy had grown over the years as he watched his brother prosper, secure in the love of the matchless Damayanti. Now that the two had a son and daughter as heirs, Pushkara knew that he had no chance to inherit the throne.

Kali cleverly played on the greed and ambition of the younger brother. 'You deserve to enjoy all power and pomp as the king,' he said to Pushkara. 'It should be you who rules Nishada and enjoys Damayanti's voluptuous charms in bed! All this can be yours still if you listen to my plan, Pushkara. Invite Nala to a game of dice and I will take care of the rest.'

Was this possible? Could the honey-tongued queen fall into his hands so easily? Pushkara leered, his jaded appetite reviving at the thought of having the queen in his bed. He hurried to Nala's palace and professed the deepest affection and regard for him. 'You are so skilled, dear brother, in everything you attempt,' he said. 'No man or god can match your expertise with horses, women or even at the game of dice. Let us play together, you and I, and spend a pleasant evening trying our luck!'

Nala knew in his heart that gambling was a vice and that a king should set an example by shunning these games. But he was secretly tempted to play, convinced by his brother's fulsome praise that he could not be beaten in anything, including the game of dice. After all, there was no harm in playing when he was certain of winning. Thoughts of how Damayanti would react crossed his mind, but then he told himself that he was the king, not she. What did a woman know about the pastimes of kings? Seeing him weakening, Pushkara coaxed his brother, telling him that it was only a friendly game after all. Nala nodded and the gaming table was set out and they began casting the dice. The first few throws favoured Nala, encouraging him to make bigger wagers, confident that he would win. His brother plied him with drink and waited for Kali to make good his promise.

Seeing that Nala was fully caught up in the game, Kali signalled to Dwapara, his wicked companion, to enter the dice and control the way it rolled. The lamps flickered. Nala's loyal steeds in the stable whinnied and stirred restlessly. An owl hooted plaintively somewhere inside the palace. A shadow passed over Nala's face as he felt a deep unease stir in his heart. But he continued playing, his ego refusing to let him accept defeat.

Now Nala began to lose at every throw. He staked piles of gold and silver and lost them. He wagered precious jewels, then his horses and his elephants. He lost them all, one after the other. His ministers whispered in his ear, begging him to stop. But Nala's intellect was clouded by the influence of Kali and he continued to play, foolishly hoping that the next roll would reverse his fortune. Hearing of their king's rash gambling, his people gathered worriedly at the gates, fearful of where it would all end. A maid hurried to convey the news to Damayanti who was playing with her children in her chamber. She rushed at once to her husband's side and advised him with wise words to leave the gaming table.

Realizing the danger of Nala abandoning the game, Dwapara allowed fortune to turn in his favour. And the king returned with increased fervour to his gambling, believing that he could win everything back. Alas, that was not to happen, as the odds turned again and his losses mounted.

Now, Nala would listen to no one, not even his loving wife. Distraught and discouraged, Damayanti returned to her chambers, summoned their charioteer Varshneya and asked him to take her children to Kundinapur along with a letter to her father, King Bhima. In this she spoke of Nala's gambling and her fears for her children's safety if the game were to end in disaster. Varshneya did as he was bid, taking Indrasen and Indrasena to their grandfather's court. He then went his way mournfully, finally seeking employment with King Rituparna of Ayodhya.

Held in thrall by Kali, Nala rashly put his country at stake, his eyes glazed with the gambling fever. Nothing mattered to him now, not his position, not his wife and children, not his countrymen. He soon lost his kingdom and everything he owned—all but his radiant queen. Pushkara, his heart burning with lust, stopped Nala when he was about to leave the gaming table, aghast at the extent of his defeat. 'Where are you going, brother?' mocked Pushkara. 'You still have a beautiful wife to stake. Let us play for Damayanti. If you win, you can take back everything you have lost so far!'

Kali exerted all his influence on Nala in an attempt to force him to accept this final humiliation. Would the unlucky king succumb to the lure? The courtiers watched in despair and the ministers in terror. Damayanti, who had rushed back to witness the final stages of the game, stood petrified in fear, wondering if destiny would make her a slave to the beastly king. 'I will die sooner than be forced into his bed!' she resolved, watching with tears rolling down her cheeks.

Nala glared at his brother, his pride touched to the quick. His heart smote him with remorse. He had fallen so low that his vile brother imagined that he would sacrifice the princess he had sworn to protect! Torn between rage and anguish, Nala stripped off his glittering bracelets, necklaces and rings and flung them on the gaming board. He shed his rich robes and turned from his court, his courtiers and the splendours of royal life.

Angered by his disdain, thwarted in his desire to lay hands on Damayanti, Pushkara shouted abuses at him. 'Pauper, beggar, fool!' he called after his brother. 'Leave my kingdom and flee to the forest! I warn you that if my men should find you anywhere, they will kill you and throw your flesh to the vultures.' Pushkara turned fierce eyes to the assembled throng and threatened them as well. 'Anyone who provides shelter or food to Nala and his wife will face my wrath. I will have you mercilessly flogged and hanged at the city gates.'

Humiliated and heartsick, Nala left his domain, his head hanging low, his eyes red with grief. Behind him walked Damayanti, clad now in a simple sari, resolved to share in her husband's sorrow as she had in his joy. Plodding on wearily, they travelled to the limits of the city, shunned by their people who were not only afraid of Pushkara's warning but were also scornful of a king who had so foolishly gambled his kingdom away. Even Nala's old friends were afraid to offer shelter, fearing the malice of the cruel Pushkara.

The exiled king and queen entered the forest outside the city and wandered without direction or purpose, trying to survive

on fruits, berries and water from ponds. Tortured by pangs of
hunger, Nala attempted to capture a bird pecking at the ground
by throwing his loin cloth over it. But the bird flew into the air
carrying away his single garment. 'I am Dwapara, who controlled
the dice and made you lose your kingdom,' he said. 'It irked Kali
and me that you should be left with even this one piece of cloth!'

Can I sink any lower? thought Nala in anguish. Standing
alone and naked in the wilderness, Nala turned to his wife and
said, 'Alas, precious queen, your husband has been reduced to
penury due to his folly and must pay the price for his sins. But
you do not deserve to suffer when you are without fault, except
for choosing me as your husband. I beg you, therefore, to take
this path leading to Vidarbha and return to the life that you are
accustomed to. Forgive me if you can and pray that I should meet
an early death, for a life such as this is demeaning to any honest
man.'

Damayanti reached out to grip his shaking shoulders. 'O
king—for you will be king and husband to me, whatever your
condition, however poor you may be—there is little comfort I
can offer you except to reiterate my love and loyalty. My heart
bleeds for you but my eyes remain dry as I have no more tears to
shed, parched as we are, travelling under the harsh sun. However,
I must contest your words and what they imply. How could you
think that I would leave you alone in the jungle, forlorn and
friendless, fatigued and faint from hunger? If you think it wise
that I should seek shelter in my father's kingdom, I beg you to
accompany me. Let us go to him together and seek his support to
win back your lost fame and fortune.'

Nala sank down on the rocky ground and buried his face in
his hands. Then he looked up at her with such anguish that her
tears began to flow again.

'What is it, my king? Did I wound you in some way with my words?' Damayanti asked, sitting beside her husband and cradling him in her arms.

'How could I, who swore to protect you with my powerful arms, go now before your father as a supplicant?' he asked. 'Look at me now as I sit here without even a cloth to cover my nakedness. Do you not think that your father and your people will scoff to see me thus? Will they not chastise you for choosing me over the lords of thunder and fire? Leave me, dear one. Leave me to my fate—whether to live or die in the wilderness.'

They sat together awhile, united in misery, and then rose to continue their wandering again. Nala repeated his arguments over and over but Damayanti shook her head each time, telling him that she would never leave him as long as there was breath in her body. Finally, when night fell, the two lay down to rest under a spreading banyan tree, with its root for their pillow and the hard earth for their bed. Damayanti fell into an exhausted sleep. But Nala, tormented by guilt and by Kali's presence within his body, was unable to rest. He sat up and looked down at Damayanti's tear-stained face, her body shrouded in dust and torn by brambles. *Should I leave her now while she sleeps?* he wondered. She would not leave him of her own will, but if she woke up alone, she would have no choice but to make her way to Vidarbha, seeking solace with the family that awaited her there. Her virtue would protect her from danger and her grace and demeanour would proclaim to the world that she was high-born.

Nala carefully tore off a piece of her sari to wrap around himself and rose from her side. He stepped away from her, propelled by Kali's evil influence. Then his love forced him back to her again and he gazed piteously down upon her innocent face. What a monster he had been to reduce her to this sorry plight!

She would suffer terribly when she realized that her heartless husband had abandoned her in the perilous forest.

Soon, however, Kali pulled him away from Damayanti, for the demon was jealous still that Nala should possess the princess whom he coveted himself. Nala left, only to return again, his love reminding him that he had sworn never to leave her.

Finally, Nala became convinced that she would have a chance at happiness only if he left her. He was cursed, and if she stayed with him she too would be destroyed. The gods themselves had courted her and perhaps they would come to her help when he removed himself. He fell to his knees and kissed her on her forehead and on her cheek. He whispered a silent farewell. 'I must part from you, my love. You are faultless, unswerving in your loyalty, readily giving up the comforts of the palace in order to follow me into exile. The harsh wind and sun assault your soft skin and yet you struggle bravely on, disregarding hunger and thirst. I release you now from our vows so that you may go in peace to your father. May the forest spirits safeguard you. May Indra, Agni and Varuna protect you.' He rose to his feet and walked away, not looking back lest his heart should prove to be his undoing.

The light of dawn turned the skies grey as the king left his Damayanti behind, his senses bereft of reason. Kali laughed at him, his vile spirit rejoicing that Nala would no longer enjoy the love of his queen. In the tree above, the koel buried its face in its chest, unable to sing as it listened to the plaintive mourning of the heartbroken king

5

In the Heart of the Fire

Damayanti stirred from her sleep, stretched drowsily and sought her husband's warmth, forgetting for a moment that they were no longer lying on a satin bed under a silken canopy. Not finding him, she sat up languidly and opened her eyes. She recoiled in horror as she saw the looming shadows of the forest and heard the cries of wild birds and beasts. She had forgotten the harsh reality of their exile during the long night, but now their plight hit her with greater force. Where was her husband? She called out to him, softly at first and then louder, her voice rising in panic. When he did not answer, she stumbled to her feet and crashed through the bushes looking for him.

'Where are you, Nala? Are you perhaps playing a foolish jest? Or have you gone looking for wild berries to soothe our hunger? Answer me now, my king, before I lose my reason! My body shudders, fearing that you have abandoned me, forgetting the vows you took to protect me. Come before me, my love. Tell me that you have not deserted your faithful wife who knows nothing but her love for you. Answer me, Nala! Answer!'

Then she ran, falling, then rising again, seeing Nala in every shadow and in every stirring of the leaves. Her body was soon bleeding, torn by the harsh brambles, but no trace could she find of her beloved king. 'I curse you, evil spirit, who has taken over my husband's heart,' she ranted, 'for nothing else could have persuaded him to forsake me!'

Panicked, anguished, blinded by tears, Damayanti roamed through the dense jungle, finally stepping unawares on a python lying across her path. She felt her leg caught in a bind and assumed that it was a creeper, until the snake wrapped its coils around her, tighter and tighter. Soon, she could not move, she could not breathe. The serpent opened its jaws wide before her terrified face. She screamed then, an anguished wail that sent the birds screeching into the skies. Her cry of horror startled a hunter nearby and brought him running towards her, his arrow already flying through the air to pierce the snake's head. He ran closer and used his axe to slash off the snake's head. Then he began to tear away at the coils that caged her still.

Damayanti had fainted in his arms and the hunter carried her away from the carcass of the python and laid her down gently on the ground. His eyes roamed unhindered over her fair face and her curved limbs. He bent over her and began to tear away her clothes so that he could indulge his lust. She woke with a start, feeling his rough hands on her body, horrified to see the beast that now sought to devour her. She tore herself free and backed away, calling out a warning to him. But, inflamed by desire, the hunter rushed towards her, intent on making her his prey.

'I saved you and you owe me your life and your body, fair one!' he leered.

'Keep your distance, beast, or brave Nala will tear you to pieces!' she shouted as she ran from him.

'Where is he? There is none here to come to your aid!' he replied, advancing still. She was a gentle maiden alone in the fierce jungle. Who would she turn to for help? 'Come to me, my beauty,' he said, eyes burning with desire.

Nala floundered through the forest, sheltering behind thick trees whenever he spotted trumpeting elephants or stampeding herds of bison. His mind went back again and again to the dice game, when he had fallen prey to his brother's plot to destroy him. He was struck with fierce remorse that he had left his gentle wife alone in these dangerous woods. How could he be certain that she would find her way to her father's kingdom? Perhaps she had already fallen victim to a lion or a tiger. How could he have done what he did? What darkness had seized his soul that he committed one sin after another? There was nothing left for him in the world of men that had so cruelly separated him from his beloved. He would renounce its temptations and torments and spend his remaining days in the arms of nature. He would survive on nuts and berries, sleep on smooth, sun-baked rocks, listen to the birds sing and drink the clear waters of jungle brooks. He would accept life as it unfolded, free from the lure of ambition and desire.

Even as he reached this momentary state of clarity, the world shocked him rudely out of his reverie. Nala saw panic-stricken deer and bears running helter-skelter and heard chattering monkeys and parrots overhead as they fled from the fury of a forest fire. Thick trunks blazed like torches and black smoke eddied towards him, making him choke and gasp. His instinct for survival prompted him to flee from the advancing flames. But his newfound spirit of renunciation advised him to stay where he was and allow the fire to consume him. Was it not better to suffer a few moments of pain than to endure the anguish of a life without Damayanti?

He closed his eyes and girded himself to stay where he was.

The hunter now stood just a few feet from Damayanti, gloating as his eyes took in his luscious prey. She raised a hand before her and uttered a final warning. 'Indra's boon protects me,' she said. 'Take one more step forward and you will be struck dead!' But her stalker laughed and rushed forward.

Immediately, a flash of lightning stabbed fiercely down at him from a clear sky. He crumpled in mid-stride, his body reduced to a smoking ruin.

'Thank you, great Indra!' she sobbed as she ran away from the spot, through the forest filled with wild animals. Her ordeal was far from over. Wild buffalos came charging at her, trampling everything in their way, forcing her to run and hide. Creepers hanging from trees revealed themselves to be hissing serpents that sent her screaming and tumbling over tree roots. She came upon a band of brigands plotting an attack on a passing caravan and fled deeper into the shrubs, fearful of attracting their attention. When she was ready to collapse, she finally emerged from the oppressive forest and threw herself down on a rock near a lagoon. She looked longingly at the azure waters, desperate to soak her tired limbs in their coolness. Then she noticed the bubbles rising to the surface, followed by the snouts of lurking crocodiles, waiting to attack the deer that had come to the water's edge.

Everywhere she looked there was only danger and death.

She heard a chilling snarl and turned her head to see a tiger crouching low, staring at her with golden eyes. Desperate and careworn, Damayanti called out in despair. 'O Nala, tiger among men! Can you not see me cowering before this dreadful creature? Do you not recall your vow to protect me with the strength of your arms? If you will not honour your vows, what hope remains for me to live any longer on this earth? Watch if you will and see your queen torn to pieces by this tawny beast. And remember that she never stopped loving you even for a moment.' She joined her hands in prayer and closed her eyes, waiting for the tiger to end her life with one fierce blow.

A tense moment passed and then another. She waited still, bracing her mind for death. When she opened her eyes, however, the tiger had turned away and was gliding to the lagoon to stalk the tender deer. Was fate playing games with her? Damayanti lifted her eyes to the lofty mountain range that raised its hundred peaks to the sky, and pleaded with the mountain god to tell her if he had seen her Nala. But the hills were silent, the mist on their summits dissolving as the sun rose higher, scorching her with intense heat. So passed an endless day of misery and when night fell she huddled against a tree trunk, listening to the strange cries of the creatures of the night. Another day passed in torment and another, until she came upon an ashram from which rose the smoke of sacred fires.

The sages saw the frail form of the woman, her beauty radiant still in her careworn face, and asked her if she were a jungle spirit or a mountain goddess. 'I am just an unfortunate woman whose husband deserted her in the forest!' she said, telling them her sad story and stirring even their ascetic hearts to pity. 'Will I meet my Nala again? Will we come through our trials to be united once more?' she asked.

'You proved at your swayamvara that love is mightier than Indra's lightning or Agni's fire, purer than Varuna's waters or

Yama's dharma,' they said. 'Now you must fight a fiercer battle, to free your husband's soul from the vices that caused his downfall. If you win this battle, your love will be invincible, my child!' She stood with bowed head listening to them, but when she looked up again, they had vanished without a trace. Was all this just a cruel trick played by her deranged mind?

'Alone again!' she lamented, sinking to her knees under a soaring Ashoka tree. 'Majestic Ashoka, whose very name signifies one who destroys grief . . . Free me from pain and unite me once more with my Nala!'

Alas, the tree made no answer and all she could hear was the wind rustling among the leaves. She rose again to search for her king and came upon a group of merchants resting with their horses and elephants by the side of a river. She rushed into their midst, seeking news of Nala, only to see them shrinking in horror on seeing her crazy manner and her dishevelled form. Their leader took pity on her and told her that he had seen no stranger resembling Nala on their path. He had his women bring her some food and also allowed her to rest at the edge of their camp.

Damayanti sank into a deep sleep, glad to be in human company and hoping that the morrow would bring better tidings. But it seemed that destiny had another plan in mind. She woke up startled, hearing terrified voices and the mad whinnying of horses. She saw wild elephants attacking their camp, trampling over the men and upending the fires they had built to keep themselves warm during the night. Fanned by a brisk wind, the flames spread across their tents, feeding on the piles of goods, giving them little time to escape. Damayanti ran from the fire until she reached a curving brook that held the flames at bay. When morning dawned, she saw that only a few men had survived, and they were picking desperately through the smouldering embers to salvage at least a part of their belongings. She heard them wailing loudly and cursing the woman who they thought had brought down this blight upon their heads.

'We must find her and stone her to death!' they shouted, their eyes burning with hatred. She ran away again, far from these vengeful men, fearing that they would throw her into the fires that still burned. What more did fate have in store for her?

Steeling himself against certain death, Nala stood before the advancing flames. Then he heard a desperate voice calling to him, addressing him by name. Who could it be—a spirit or a man dwelling in this wilderness who knew that he was near? The voice wailed louder. 'Nala, come to me. Come save me!' it called out.

He had to answer the desperate plea. Even if he were to die, it would be better if he did so while helping another. Nala ran towards the fire and felt its hot breath on his face. The voice appeared to be coming from the very heart of the roaring flames. He plunged in, not pausing to think, feeling the heat burn away the piece of cloth he wore around his waist. But wonder of wonders! His body was not burned but glowed like burnished gold, protected by a many-coloured cloak that fluttered around him and kept the fire away. He remembered then that Agni had blessed him with his protection when he had won Damayanti's hand, and dived further into the flames. He saw a mighty Naga writhing in pain on a rock as the flames surrounded him. His body was human till his waist, his face was that of a wise old man, and above it rose a snake's hood. The giant serpent reduced himself to the size of a thumb and begged Nala to carry him out to safety. 'I will reward you richly, O king! Have pity on me and save me,' he cried.

A final leap, a scattering of sparks and the snake was in his hand. Nala raced through the fire and carried him out of harm's way. But when he tried to place him on the ground, the Naga begged him to walk ten steps further, counting out the steps aloud. Nala did so, but when he said 'Dasha' or ten, which also means 'Bite!' the snake bit him, making him scream and drop him to the ground. To Nala's shock, his own body grew bent and misshapen and his skin became dark and mottled. He saw too that he was now clothed in the coarse garb of a servant. What was happening to him? Why was he being punished for performing a good deed?

Terrified and weeping, Damayanti scrambled away from the angry merchants who blamed her for their calamity, and travelled further on the forest path that finally took her to the capital city of the Chedis.

Looking at her bedraggled form and her haunted gaze, the street urchins teased her and threw stones at her. When she staggered past the palace, ready to drop, the queen mother spotted her from the terrace and glimpsed the nobility that lay hidden beneath her wretched appearance. She had her maids bring her in, give her food and clean clothes. Damayanti told the queen mother that she was merely a serving woman who had been separated from her husband. Listening to her genteel words and captivated by her charming face, the queen employed her as her daughter's companion. It appeared that Nala's queen had finally found relief from her travails. But could she be happy when she still had no news of her husband?

After biting Nala, the snake reverted to its giant form and spoke to him, explaining that he was Karkotaka, ruler of the Nagas, cursed by Sage Narada to stay rooted in one spot until rescued by the valiant king. 'The poison that has transformed your body will gradually over time drive out the evil Kali who possesses your soul, Nala,' he said. 'Further, your changed appearance will protect you from the men sent by your brother to kill you. They will not recognize Nala in the hunchbacked, squint-eyed Bahuka who will find work in Ayodhya as King Rituparna's charioteer. Bide your time and use your wits to win back what you have lost, Nala. I must go now, but I will leave you with something priceless that you must guard with your life.' Karkotaka handed him a gift and vanished from the spot.

Nala went his way, pondering over the fantastic turn of events. Perhaps the worst was now over. After a few more days of travel he found himself at the gates of Ayodhya where he was fortunate to capture the king's attention by calming the frenzied horses that had overturned the royal chariot. He advised the king's charioteer on how he could charm the steeds with ease. 'Feed them well. Control them with affection, not the whip,' he said. 'The secret to winning them over is love and nothing more!'

The grateful king placed him in charge of his stables and later made him his cook as well, for Nala's skill with food was without equal, thanks to Yama's boon.

Hearing that his precious daughter had been exiled to the forest along with Nala, King Bhima sent out men to roam far and wide looking for the two. One of his emissaries, Sudeva, spotted Damayanti among the royal maids in Chedi and verified her identity by the mole on her forehead that was shaped like a lotus bud. Damayanti knew Sudeva well and agreed to his entreaties to come back with him to Vidarbha to be reunited with her parents and her children. When she went with Sudeva to reveal the truth to the king of Chedi, he graciously allowed her to leave, happy that she would be returning to her life as a princess. This was what Nala had wanted—to see Damayanti safe in the bosom of her family. But where was the king himself? Was he alive or dead?

Damayanti was sleepless, unable to enjoy a life of luxury when she knew he was suffering somewhere in hunger and fear. She had to do something to rescue her Nala, for her heart told her that he was alive still. Oh, why was fate so cruel? And why had her husband not come to Vidarbha to look for her? He had professed ceaseless love, enduring loyalty. Had it all been just a sham? Had he taken another wife, perhaps, and forgotten the princess who had chosen him over the gods in heaven?

6

The Riddle of Love

Damayanti did not know what to think or what more to do. But then she had a visitor—one whom she trusted more than anyone else, for he had been loyal to her, never abandoning her, unlike Nala. In fact, it was she who had gone to the forest, leaving him clueless as to where she could be. But here he had come to Vidarbha again, looking for her. She gathered Gagana into her arms and rained kisses on his soft head. She stroked his feathers with a loving hand and offered him his favourite foods and drinks.

'You must be careful that I do not fall in love with you, for my wife will not like that!' he joked, his eyes gleaming softly with delight on being reunited with her. In her moment of dark despair, her winged visitor brought new hope to the woeful Damayanti. Gagana had visited Nala's palace after a long stay in Manasarovar, only to hear the dire news of their exile into the forest. Finding no trace of him or Damayanti in Nishada, the golden swan had flown to Vidarbha to look for her.

She shed a flood of tears as she told her old friend all that had transpired since the fateful dice game had torn her life apart. The hamsa, stricken with sorrow, was reduced to a pale shadow of his usual merry self. He comforted Damayanti, and together they considered and discarded various plans to find the missing Nala.

'What if he does not want me anymore?' she wept. 'That would be a greater blow to me than even death!'

'How can that be? Do you think your love is so feeble that it can be blown apart by just a strong gust of wind?' asked Gagana. 'Perhaps Nala stays away from you because he blames himself for his gambling that reduced you to such straits. He must be weeping just as bitterly to be separated from his queen as you weep for him. Do not give up hope, Damayanti, but bend your mind towards bringing him back to you.'

The two spent many hours together until they came up with an ingenious plan. But first, Damayanti had to convince her father not to give up on Nala who he strongly believed had died in the forest fire. She spoke to him movingly, and finally Bhima agreed to send out his men to search one last time for his missing son-in-law. Before these agents left, however, Damayanti spoke to them and gave them several specific directions.

King Bhima's men fanned out far and wide, looking for Nala. At every gathering, big or small, they read out a riddle that Damayanti had written out for them. 'If anyone should reply to these words, note down his answer carefully, find out everything you can about him and return at once to me,' she said. 'But do not reveal to anyone that the riddle comes from Damayanti.' The men were puzzled by what she said, but carried out her orders faithfully.

Would anyone answer? Would she find happiness again? Damayanti stood at her window overlooking the palace gates with Gagana by her side, waiting endlessly for news of Nala.

Long distances did Bhima's men travel, visiting far-flung kingdoms. Everywhere they read out Damayanti's words, but no one paid heed to them or attempted to answer. Many days and then months passed and even Gagana began to lose hope.

Finally, in Ayodhya's court, the messenger from Vidarbha received a reply to his verse. The man had read out the riddle as always:

> 'You cut our cloth in half
> And left me in the woods alone
> Tell me, Gambler,
> Where did you go?'

And a dwarf with a twisted body had answered,

> 'He lost everything he had
> Then a bird stole his clothes and took flight
> A wife should not get angry
> When she knows her husband's plight.'

The question and the answer made no sense to the emissary, but he gathered information about the dwarf and returned home. Damayanti was greatly excited to hear his report, as was Gagana.

'The dwarf Bahuka seems to be a great charioteer and cook like my husband,' she said. 'But clearly, he cannot be Nala whose regal splendour dazzles men and gods alike.'

'However, Bahuka seems to have some information on Nala,' said Gagana. 'How else would he know that the king left you after the bird had flown away with his garment?'

Damayanti resolved to send Sudeva to Ayodhya, for he had a keen eye that had helped him discover her identity when she had been living in hiding in Chedi. 'Inform King Rituparna that my father is holding a second swayamvara for me and that they have but a day to reach Vidarbha,' she said to Sudeva. 'Only my Nala will be able to bring the king here within that short time and by this means I will be able to discover him.'

Rituparna was excited at the thought of marrying Damayanti whose beauty was renowned far and wide and summoned Bahuka to make ready for the journey. The dwarf listened to the news with a stoic face that hid the tumult that rose within his heart. He had abandoned Damayanti, no doubt, but that had been due to his concern for her. He had never stopped loving her even for a moment. However, his wife seemed to have given up on him. She had decided to wed another, forgetting the bliss they had shared for twelve long years. *How could she choose another?* he lamented. *Am I nothing to her now? Has she given me up for dead?* His innate fairness told him however that he could not blame her when he had abandoned her so cruelly in the forest. She would be justified if she hated him for that.

He could not bear that thought. Was she not the mother of his children? Would she give up their bond so easily? Maybe, just maybe, all this was a ruse devised by his intelligent and resourceful queen. Perhaps she had come up with this riddle in order to bring him out of hiding. How could he suspect her of being disloyal to his love? Not his Damayanti, not unless she had received conclusive proof of his death . . .

Nala no longer knew what to believe, whom to trust. The tormenting force of Kali that raged within him urged him to forget Damayanti and to give up all hope. As matters stood, he had to obey his master's orders and take him to Kundinapur. Perhaps he would be able to discover the answer to his questions there.

Bahuka harnessed the finest horses in the king's stable, and the chariot soon left for Vidarbha, with Varshneya attending on them. Nala's ageing charioteer had still not realized that the dwarf was his old master Nala.

The chariot sped through the countryside, easily spanning the distance between Ayodhya and Vidarbha. The king marvelled at Bahuka's skill with the horses and spoke of his own talent with numbers. He was able to calculate the odds so accurately that he never lost a game of chance. Nala listened with keen interest, knowing that he had to master the art of dice if he wanted to win back his kingdom from Pushkara.

Rituparna demonstrated his prowess by predicting the exact number of leaves and fruits on a low-hanging branch of a tree ahead of them. Nala snapped the branch off as they flew past and verified the king's count. Truly, Rituparna was gifted! Looking at his admiring face, the king said, 'Teach me the magic of handling horses like you do and I will help you master numbers.' Bahuka agreed readily. They made camp for the night on the way so that they could enter Vidarbha at sunrise. And through the night, they stayed awake, learning all the nuances of the skills they desired. The king taught him the mantra known as Akshahrudaya and Bahuka taught him the Ashwahrudaya, the secrets of numbers and horses.

The chariot wheels thundered as the visitors entered Bhima's rose-pink city. Damayanti stood watching from her palace window. She had spent a restless night, dreaming that she was wrapped in Nala's powerful arms once again. He had shown her with words and caresses how much he loved her and how he had pined for her every moment when they had been apart. He had sworn that he had been faithful to her in thought and deed. But then, she had woken up to the realization that it had all been just a dream.

Now the very sound of the horses' hooves seemed to tell her that Nala was near. However, when the visitors alighted from the chariot, she could see only Rituparna, Varshneya and the dwarf she had heard about. Looking closely at Bahuka's long nose, his bent back and his coal-black beard, she knew that this could not be her handsome Nala. Had her elaborate plan failed? Was fate toying with her, raising her hopes only to shatter them again? Gagana saw the tears spilling down her cheeks. 'Do not lose hope, my queen,' he said. 'We will discover the truth, never fear.'

Damayanti calmed herself. She would trust her instincts that told her Nala was close by and that he yearned for her just as she did for him. She sent her maid Kesini to find out all she could about the dwarf, for she knew that he held the key to the puzzle. Kesini took some food and drink to Bahuka who was attending to the horses in the stable. While he ate, she posed again the riddle devised by her mistress. 'Why did the king leave his devoted wife as she slept in the forest?' she asked.

'Does she not know that her anger is of no avail against a husband who lost all he owned in a single night?' he asked in return.

He plied her with questions in his turn, seeking to know why Damayanti had decided to remarry. 'Does she no longer love Nala?' he asked. 'Has she forgotten the Nishada king who she chose as her husband in the presence of the gods?' Kesini studied his face and saw the anger and anguish that he was unable to conceal. But it was still difficult to see King Nala within this dwarf's body.

Kesini returned to her mistress to report what she had heard and seen. Damayanti was torn. Here was a man who seemed to know everything about her and Nala, but was physically so different from her king. Had he perhaps killed Nala after learning everything about him? No. She would not let such dark thoughts enter her mind. She must find some way to resolve the riddle of her life. She would find out if Bahuka possessed the powers that had been granted to Nala by the gods.

But before she could execute her plan, her father came to see her. And what he had to say seemed to spell the end of her hopes.

Rituparna had been puzzled to see that no preparations had been made for a swayamvara in Kundinapur. There were no banners or festivities, and more important, no other king or prince had arrived for the event. He could see that Bhima too was baffled by his unexpected arrival and that he did not believe his explanation that he had made the long journey merely to pay his respects. When the king persisted in his queries, Rituparna told him the truth: 'A messenger came to Ayodhya to invite me to Damayanti's second swayamvara. He said that she had abandoned her search for Nala and had resolved to wed again.'

'That would indeed be the wise course for her to follow!' nodded Bhima, struck by a sudden thought. He would use this opportunity to get Damayanti married to Rituparna without delay, thereby ensuring her happiness. He had already been cursing himself for allowing her to choose Nala when she could have been Indra's queen instead. The man she had chosen had gambled away his kingdom and abandoned her in the wilderness. His precious daughter had waited long enough for Nala to return to her. Now it was time she wedded Rituparna and enjoyed a life of luxury as his queen.

Bhima told his daughter that this was his decision, rather his command, not only as her father but also as her king. 'We have done all we can to trace the unworthy Nala,' he said. 'I agreed to all your requests and sent out men repeatedly to trace him, but to no avail. I am convinced now that he has been killed by his foes or by the forest fire. The arrival of King Rituparna at our court provides me with an opportunity to correct the mistake I made in allowing you to marry Nala. You will wed the king of Ayodhya tomorrow and live the life to which you were born!'

Damayanti cried out in anguish when she heard this. She begged her father, seeking to change his mind. But Bhima was adamant and refused to hear even a word of protest. The die had been cast. Her marriage would take place the next day and her vows to Nala would become as the dust under her feet.

She had but one evening to unravel the truth. Was it even possible to do anything to change the course of events? Gagana came to her and the two planned their next move in desperate haste.

Damayanti sent Kesini again to watch Bahuka from hiding as he cooked his evening meal. She had told her maid to provide him with all the necessary ingredients, but not allow him access to fire or water. The faithful maid watched in wonder as the dwarf conjured up fire and water from thin air. Soon, the delicious aroma of his cooking filled the air. Then she saw how the dwarf revived the faded flowers decorating Rituparna's chariot with just a touch of his hand. She reported all this to Damayanti who realized that Bahuka was imbued with all the boons given by the gods to Nala. There was one last test that she wanted Kesini to carry out.

Damayanti sent her son and daughter to play in the garden under her balcony and asked Kesini to bring Bahuka before them.

The charioteer gasped when he saw his children, grown so much taller during the period that they had been separated from him. He recognized their sweet faces and ran forward, eager to embrace them, but stopped himself at the last moment. 'Remember that you are Bahuka!' he told himself and stood gazing at them, his love overflowing from his eyes.

'O Gagana, is this Nala?' Damayanti whispered when she saw how Bahuka reacted on seeing Indrasen and Indrasena. 'This must be him! Why else would he be so affected on seeing them? Help me discern the truth, golden one.'

'Enough of this game of hide and seek!' exclaimed Gagana, hopping excitedly from foot to foot. 'Remember that your father plans to wed you to Rituparna when the new day dawns. Have Bahuka brought before you and all will be made clear.'

Damayanti nodded. She would speak to Bahuka directly. Hopefully, that would reveal the truth. If not . . . the alternative was too horrible to contemplate.

'Bring Bahuka to me at once!' Damayanti ordered Kesini. As the maid went away to carry out her command, Damayanti paced up and down—hope and fear warring within her.

When Bahuka entered her chamber, wondering why he had been summoned into the palace, he heard a voice addressing him from behind a screen. The voice was low and its cadence reminded him of his queen, but he could not be sure.

'It seems that you are the only one who could answer the riddle posed by King Bhima's men,' said Damayanti, waiting to hear Bahuka's voice. 'So tell me, stranger, why does an honourable king who had vowed eternal love send his loving wife back to her father?'

'It was because he knew that he could no longer support her in the manner she was accustomed to. He wept as he left her, praying to the gods to protect her. He hoped that her shining virtue would guard her from all enemies,' he replied, his voice anguished and low. 'The poor wretch was not in his right mind then, having lost so much and being under the influence of a wicked spirit.'

'Does he know how she suffered, beset by jungle creatures and beastly men, alone and lost in the wilderness?' she shot back, refusing to accept his explanation. 'Does he even care that her heart broke within her when she realized that the man she had trusted with her life had so cruelly abandoned her? Tell me, Bahuka, tell me this answer too if you will!'

The dwarf was silent, unable to justify his actions in any way.

'Why did he gamble away his wealth, his kingdom, his people, when he knew well that gambling was a vice forbidden by the gods?' she asked then. 'Why did he not listen to his wife, his ministers or his people when they begged him not to continue playing?'

'It was desire and temptation that clouded his senses, my lady,' he confessed. 'His ego made him believe that he was invincible, and he fell further into sin, finally losing everything he owned.'

'And then he left her to suffer, not knowing if he was alive or dead, when he could have easily come to her at Vidarbha and owned up to his mistakes. He could have allowed her to choose whether to follow him or live in her father's palace.' Her voice broke and she fell silent.

'It was pride that held him back, O queen, for he knew that he had erred gravely. He could not show his face to her father when he had betrayed all the vows he had made when he married her.'

The dwarf now knew that it was his Damayanti who stood hidden behind the screen. The jealousy that still troubled his heart provoked him to ask her a few questions in his turn. 'If the queen loves her Nala so much, why then did she abandon him?' he asked. 'She swore to love him forever but then decided to marry again. Is her father not preparing for her marriage with Rituparna when the morrow dawns?'

'So, you now blame his faultless queen?' Damayanti's voice rose. 'Can you not see that there is no one else invited to the so-called swayamvara? What can she do when her father forces her hand?'

Bahuka stayed silent, angering Damayanti.

'Why do you question me when I have suffered for so long when it was in no way my fault?' she asked. 'Did I ask my king to gamble? Did I force him to desert me when I followed him into the forest? Love is not just about passion and beautiful appearances. It is about perseverance in the face of trials, and Nala failed in this test.'

As she spoke, the angry Damayanti advanced step by step and now stood revealed before Bahuka. He gazed at the radiant face of his queen from whom he had fled in the dark of the night, leaving her alone in the haunted forest. She was dewy-eyed, as lovely as ever, standing with her eyes fixed on his face.

Damayanti knew now that it was Nala who stood before her, though he had somehow concealed himself within this strange form. She had to stake everything now on the power of her love to bring them together again. 'What purpose does it serve to revisit the past, to throw accusations at each other? Has our love not been tested enough through so many tribulations?' she asked. 'I chose Nala earlier knowing well that he was mortal and that my other suitors were divine. I choose him still, whatever his form or his position in life. I recognized him when the gods took his form. Can I not identify him when he himself has taken another form? What more must I do to prove my love? How much longer must I wait for this agony to end? Tell me now!'

Gagana emerged from behind the screen, unable to stay silent any longer. 'Well, what more do you need, Nala?' he asked. 'If I had been around when you started gambling with Pushkara, I would have dragged you away by force! And if I had been the messenger to Rituparna's court, I would have recognized you at once. You are more fortunate that any god or mortal that Damayanti is so loyal to you. How could you doubt her, knowing that this second swayamvara is only a ploy to bring you out of hiding?'

Damayanti stood waiting anxiously, knowing that this was the most formidable riddle of all. In Bahuka's answer lay her future happiness.

7

The Nectar of Her Lips

Bahuka seemed frozen, unable to say or do anything, as the two souls who loved him stared at him in fierce hope. And then, he reached within his vest and pulled out a shimmering cloth that he fastened around himself. This had been Karkotaka's parting gift to him—a magic cloak that would reverse the spell that had changed his form. He was transformed before their astonished eyes into the glorious Nala they knew from their days when he had been the king of Nishada.

Nala's eyes gazed into hers, revealing all the torment that he had undergone without her by his side. Their love soared like a golden flame and vanquished the dark demon within him. Kali emerged trembling and stood before the couple with his head bowed. Nala had been able to vanquish the power of Kali over him by shedding his weaknesses, one by one.

'I have suffered for a long time and a great deal due to the viper's poison and your queen's curse, Nala,' said Kali. 'Spare me now and I will grant you a boon. Henceforth, all those who listen to your story and resolve to fight against their sinful impulses will be freed from my influence. They will understand that love is the only force that can redeem the soul. I beg you, great king! Show your compassion to one who seeks refuge at your feet.'

The gracious Nala nodded his forgiveness and Kali at once vanished into a Vibhitaka tree. At once, the tree lost its beauty and its fruits became inedible. Nala, however, was finally himself, free from the poisonous spirit that had pervaded his mind for so long.

He took one step forward and then another and dimly heard Gagana's voice talking still. 'Perhaps I should give up my home in Manasarovar and come live with you both so that I can watch over you,' he said. 'I wonder though if my wife will agree to my plan. What sacrifices I have to make in order to help you helpless mortals!'

The mortals smiled at each other over the hamsa's head, feeling as if they were parents to a noisy child who rarely stopped talking. Then, without knowing how, they were in each other's arms. Damayanti buried herself in Nala's embrace, sobbing. He lifted up her face between his tender hands and showered kisses on her brow, her eyes and then on her soft lips.

They heard some strange sounds then and realized that Gagana was singing: 'His thirst grew greater as he drank the nectar of her lips!'

Nala renewed his vows of love, telling his queen that he would never leave her side again, whatever destiny might throw at him. And this time, he knew that he would keep his promise. Soon, King Bhima was informed of the happy reunion. Rituparna felt a pang of loss, but knowing that there was little he could do, he wished them well and left for his own land.

The devas rejoiced as the godlessness that had prevailed on earth now vanished with the defeat of Kali. Men offered worship to them again and the gods in turn restored the balance of nature. Indra blessed the earth with timely rains, and flowers and fruits sprang forth in lush abundance. Men and women were faithful to their vows, the weak and the voiceless were protected and the rulers enforced the law of the land.

But Nala had one more battle to fight—the final battle to reclaim his kingdom and his life.

Pushkara was angry and dismissive when Nala presented himself before him, seeking to play another game of dice to try and win back all that he had lost.

'What is it you can stake when you have lost everything?' he scoffed. 'Unless you are ready to stake Damayanti this time!'

Nala bit his lip to control his anger and said calmly, 'A single throw of the dice—that is all I seek, Pushkara. I stake my life this time and will gladly bare my neck to your sword if you should win again. Or perhaps you would prefer that we resolve our conflict by facing each other in single combat.'

Pushkara knew that his debauched life had made him far too weak to even give his brother a good fight. Instead, he would roll the dice one last time and put an end to him. He would then take Nala's wife to his harem, forcing her to make love at his command. His eyes glinted as he accepted Nala's challenge.

The gaming table was set up again, this time in the court. The brothers sat opposite each other. Pushkara cast the dice for Nala's life and sat back, happy with the result. Nala took the dice in his hands and closed his eyes for a moment to invoke the gods. The dice rolled. The courtiers watched in rapt silence.

Pushkara's smirk died on his lips as he saw that he had been defeated. He gasped and looked again. 'Last time, Kali and Dwapara controlled the dice, but not this time!' said Nala. 'You will never utter Damayanti's name again, nor will you look upon her face. I hereby reclaim my kingdom, but will treat you well, despite your sins. I grant you a share of the lands so that you may live the rest of your life in comfort and peace, far from here.'

His brother had no choice but to accept with a bowed head.

Nala took back the reins of his kingdom and brought Damayanti home from Vidarbha to rule by his side, like Vishnu with Shri, the goddess of good fortune. His people rejoiced under Nala's noble rule and the loving tyranny of the swan with the golden plumes.